RESOLUTION BURNING

Recent Titles from Peter Tonkin

The Mariners Series

THE FIRE SHIP
THE COFFIN SHIP
POWERDOWN
THUNDER BAY *
TITAN 10 *
WOLF ROCK *
RESOLUTION BURNING *

The Master of Defence Series

THE POINT OF DEATH *
ONE HEAD TOO MANY *
THE HOUND OF THE BORDERS *
THE SILENT WOMAN *

ACTION *
THE ZERO OPTION *

* *available from Severn House*

RESOLUTION BURNING

Peter Tonkin

This first world edition published in Great Britain 2006 by
SEVERN HOUSE PUBLISHERS LTD of
9–15 High Street, Sutton, Surrey SM1 1DF.
This first world edition published in the USA 2006 by
SEVERN HOUSE PUBLISHERS INC of
595 Madison Avenue, New York, N.Y. 10022.

British Library Cataloguing in Publication Data

Tonkin, Peter
    Resolution burning
    1. Mariner, Richard (Fictitious character) - Fiction
    2. Tankers - Antarctic Ocean - Fiction
    3. Ships - Fires and fire prevention - Fiction
    4. Suspense fiction
    I. Title
    823.9'14 [F]

        ISBN-10: 0-7278-6346-0

*For Cham, Guy and Mark,
as always.*

Except where actual histori
described for the storyline
publication are fictitious an
is purely coincidental.

Typeset by Palimpsest Boo
Polmont, Stirlingshire, Sco
Printed and bound in Great
MPG Books Ltd., Bodmin,

One

Chopper

The Westland Lynx AH Mk7 chopper seemed to hesitate, hanging uncertainly in the stormy air. 'We should be there, Captain Mariner,' called the pilot, looking out into the whirling, smoke-grey clouds all around them. 'And something that size should stand out like a sore thumb, even in this. But I'm damned if I can see a thing.'

'We can't go on much further,' added the young navigator uncertainly. He was seated in the observer's seat, looking at instruments which showed, side by side, the north-easterly heading and the fuel gauge trembling just under the sixty per cent reading, which was the point of no return. Or it was down here in this God-forsaken place. In these God-awful conditions it certainly was. He swung round to look anxiously into the ill-shaven face belonging to the huge man wedged in the left-hand rear troop seat away behind him, beyond the mountainous box of equipment he had hefted aboard, single-handed, all those exhausting hours and stormy kliks ago. The navigator had been much struck by how tired but how determined the mysterious passenger had seemed. Now all he saw of the grey, dark-stubbled face was the indomitable sparkle of the ice-blue eyes.

'We go down,' grated the huge passenger, Captain Richard Mariner. 'I haven't come all this way to give up now. They need me by all accounts and I'll be damned if I'll desert them without a fight.'

'And they've wounded aboard,' said another voice – that of a doctor, like the Westland chopper and the rest, lent to

1

Richard by the British Antarctic Survey, and seated at his shoulder now. 'We can't just leave them.'

'So we go down as low as we dare – and quickly!' ordered Richard.

'But carefully, for God's sake,' pleaded the young doctor. 'We'll be no good to anyone if we end up swimming in this lot . . .'

At Richard's command the little helicopter tilted forward and began to descend with all the grace and care of a dragonfly seeking a lily pad on the foggiest of stormy mornings. Richard pressed his face to the icy perspex beside him, looking past the grey ghost of his reflection, with the bristle of its unshaven cheeks and chin, and the dazzle of the eyes, focussing all of his fearsome concentration downwards.

Richard's cheekbone, pressed against the burning chill of the aft window, transmitted the conditions outside directly into his head. Rain poured through the hearts of the huge clouds in whose blinding grip they were. The thunder of the relentless drops against the shuddering fuselage compounded with the throbbing of motor and rotors and all seemed to drum into his skull as though his brains were in a spin dryer. The immediacy of the sensation seemed to revitalize his tiring thought processes.

Where was she? Richard silently raged. The pilot commented that something that size should stick out like a sore thumb. Frustration welled still further. He clenched his teeth – perhaps to stop himself grinding them. In London, when the emergency call came in and he had agreed to answer it, finding her had seemed to be the easiest part. Getting down to Antarctica within the forty-eight hour time-limit Crewfinders usually advertised seemed like the hard bit. Begging or borrowing some transport from Antarctica up into the heart of the Southern Ocean – even with the willing assistance of the British Antarctic Survey – had seemed a truly tricky proposition. But finding a supertanker whose precise coordinates they had had up until twelve hours ago had seemed like the easiest thing of all. Especially finding a blazing supertanker that was sitting in the middle of an oil slick on an otherwise deserted ocean. That had seemed a

2

piece of cake compared with all the rest. Or it had until now.

The battering power of the icy gusts seeking to hurl the helicopter away to destruction every five seconds or so pulled him back to the present. The pilot observed, 'I have to be flying almost due west at the better part of fifty knots just to sit still in this lot . . .'

Gusts of wind sent claws of chill draught through the helicopter's door seals like the fingers of burglars come to steal them all away. And to purloin the priceless equipment tightly packed in the open area immediately in front of Richard's juddering seat. Equipment he had managed to collect along his whirling way from London to here, some of it in New York, some in Houston, some in Mexico City; still more of it in Buenos Aires and the last of it in the BAS base itself. Perhaps Crewfinders' motto should have been, 'The impossible we perform at once – miracles take a little longer.'

Suddenly, those icy fingers of Southern Ocean storm wind smelt strongly of poisonous fumes. Richard's fine nostrils flared. His bright eyes narrowed. His drifting mind focussed on the here and now. There was a chemical, throat-burning stench, terribly out of place in this timeless wilderness. Richard knew it all too well: it was the odour of burning oil. His ill-shaven cheeks twitched into a ghost of a smile. The foul stench of the burning oil was the sweet smell of success to him. It was probably only the downpour, he thought grimly, that was keeping the poisonous gasses at bay. The foul weather, he realized, was probably the only thing stopping the helicopter's exhausts from setting the fume-filled sky alight. And that, in all sorts of ways, was very good indeed. For at the least it meant that he was nearing his goal. At last.

The greatest buffet of wind so far came roaring out of the south-west, strong enough to make the helicopter jump and judder. Powerful enough to rip away the lower swathes of the teeming cloud and reveal the surface of the ocean all too close below. Large grey battlements of water marched in series eastward, as though a range of mountains was on the move. From the crests of the waves the wind-clawed sheets of spume flew seemingly horizontally, the only pallid shades

3

in the graphite and granite, a charcoal-sketch of a scene. Richard's eyes narrowed further, seeking for white horses amongst the wilderness of water, which was threatening to wash the helicopter's landing-gear. There were none. The waves were wind-torn, but none of them were breaking. And he was certainly close enough to them to be absolutely certain. Any closer, he thought darkly, and they would all be swimming. Moreover, if he looked back over his shoulder, he could see that, for a swathe far wider than his field of vision, the sullen waves refused to yield to the wind – and they gave no bright foam at all.

As though entranced by the realization, Richard strained round to look ahead into the mysterious, oily dark calm. And he knew all too clearly the potentially fatal miscalculation that his near-exhaustion had tricked him into. For there was something moving in the smoke-grey fog: something huge. And it seemed to be approaching at an incredible speed.

'Up!' he yelled hoarsely. 'Bring her up a hundred feet. *Now!*'

The helicopter leaped up into the air at once, instantly obedient to his call. The Rolls Royce Gem 42-1 standard motors screamed at the top of their specification as the full-pitched rotors grasped the air. And, in the heartbeats before the clouds closed over Richard's vision once again, he saw what he had come here looking for.

The stern of a supertanker swept under the helicopter's soaring wheels, spitting up spray and streaming with water, seemingly as close as the waves had been only an instant earlier; the closing speed of the near collision dictated by the combination of wind and wind-shadow. The force pushing the tanker eastwards as the chopper effectively flew westwards through the unexpected calm behind it, seeking to hover on the spot. A closing speed in excess of fifty knots.

The helicopter's fuselage tilted as the nose began to rise, the rotors clawing desperately at the stormy air, pulling her higher and higher above the complex of companionways and massive metal boxes which comprised the rear of the bridge house. Hangar-sized boxes, piled atop one another like a giant baby's toy bricks, rising in stepped series to the upper

4

reaches of the navigation bridge itself. From this angle, thought Richard dreamily, the companionways looked weirdly like a print by Escher. A wild impression lent disorientating strength by the circumstances. For, as the chopper's fuselage tilted and turned, powering up into the stormy wind, the racing figures aboard the tanker seemed to be scurrying inwards upside down.

Then the physics of the Westland Lynx's desperate manoeuvre threw Richard further back in his seat so that his narrow eyes saw just how close the great white-painted after walls of the bridge house came to taking off her tail as they rose up step by step beneath her. The red-painted decks swept by, level stepping up on top of level, until the uppermost, seemingly the size of a couple of tennis courts, arrived, apparently close enough for him to touch. Spitting up sinister, claret-tinted spray, high enough to wash the streaming fuselage, adding to the hissing rumble of the downpour, it slid beneath them like the red rim of the Grand Canyon.

The pilot seemed to relax a little then and the navigator glanced over his shoulder with a pallid grin. 'Didn't need the full hundred feet after all.'

'*No!*' bellowed Richard. 'Don't stop! Up! *Up!*'

The Westland whirled and began to climb again, its fuselage upwards, its tail hanging a little lower. And almost immediately, over the thunderous buffeting of the wind came a sinister grating squeal from behind them and a little way below. The chopper shuddered; swung round as though held by some huge fist. It hesitated for a heart-stopping moment, then shuddered free. Richard looked back, stricken, to see the uppermost ten feet of the vessel's communications mast topple forward like a chain-sawed tree-top. But at least the helicopter seemed unscathed by the encounter.

And when the twenty-foot blade of the funnel came, blessedly clear, on the left, he could look directly over to the ship's house sign painted on its side: the letters 'TAAF', for Les Terres Australes et Antarctique Français, in a blue circle decorated with Adelie penguins, leopard seals and whales. And beneath the circle, her name: *La Dame Marie*.

There was no smoke coming from the funnel, Richard

noted, his senses super-sharpened by the shock of near disaster. Of course there wasn't, he thought with febrile rapidity. That was the reason he was here. That, amongst other things. Then he was thumped on the shoulder and he jerked round to look at his companion.

It was at this point that Richard realized that the young doctor was shouting, wordlessly, in shock. 'It's all right,' Richard reassured him. 'I think we're going to make it . . .'

Then the right wheel of the landing gear hit the railing at the front edge of the decking. The whole fuselage swung wildly sideways; further even than it had when they hit the communications mast. Something – someone, perhaps – screamed. The cabin of the game little chopper shuddered and leaped wildly. There was a slow groan and a whip-like crack. The fuselage swung in contra-motion and Richard found himself looking right down the sheer precipice of the white deck-house front, as though peering over the edge of a cliff at Dover. A line of white rope whipped across the cliff-face: the top deck safety rail. Thank God it was only rope, thought Richard. If that rail had been teak, they would all be dead on the deck by now. And the deck was where they wanted to be, in fact.

'Down!' he yelled, his throat raw and rasping.

The nose of the helicopter dropped obediently and Richard was thrown forward in his seat, to look directly ahead under the lowest rags of streaming grey mist, at the receding cliff of the bridge's sheer forward wall. Like the aft wall, it was white painted – but the widening angle revealed that it wasn't so pristine after all: it was stained with blood-bright rust and bruised with flare-marks and smoke damage, like the face of a prizefighter after a terrible boxing match. At its foot, the deck was painted with red lead, running with pulses of blood-red water bright enough to bring nightmare impressions that if the bridge was a battered face then the throat beneath it had been cut. The windows – from the wide bridge windows to those on the lower decks – were all staring blankly; dark and dead, as though this were a deserted ghost ship.

The impression was short-lived. Men came boiling out of

the port-side bulkhead door on to the red weather deck. Men who moved upright – unlike their dream-like companions from the Escher inspired companionways aft of the great white-painted structure. Men who ran, staggered and stumbled in the deluge. Some coming under their own steam, others on stretchers.

'This is it,' yelled Richard to the doctor. It was time for action, not observation or reflection. The wheels kissed down, lifted, then kissed down on the receding deck again. The chopper settled for an instant. They would have to be fast. And for all sorts of reasons – not least of which was the fact that this was not the ship's helipad. The Lynx was dancing wildly between sheaves of massive pipes, between tank-tops and Sampson posts.

'Something doesn't feel right,' bellowed the pilot, adding to the urgency. 'Her undercarriage may be damaged. Better get a move on . . .'

Richard hit the release of his groaning seat harness and heaved the sliding door back wide. Then he kicked out the sturdy little steps with enough force to make their hinges groan. Almost out of control, he tumbled down on to the red-painted metal. Here he crouched in the overwhelming batter and bluster of down-draught and Southern Ocean gale, disregarding everything except what his bare hand pressed to the wet red metal beneath his feet was telling him. The metal was hot but not burning. As though the sun had shone on it for an hour or two quite recently. Had the air been still, the water would have been lifting off it in delicate veils of steam. He glanced under the belly of the helicopter. The right wheel looked wonky to him, though the long tail of the fuselage looked OK, unlike the communications mast it had just beheaded.

'You're right!' he bellowed to the pilot. 'Your wheel's damaged. Try and hold still as you are. Let's go, Doc!'

The young medic loomed briefly in the doorway above Richard as he rose, stooping. The solid box of equipment screamed across into the opening between the men. Richard reached up and grasped it, pulling the great weight out and down. There were straps that allowed him to heft it up over the bright orange shoulder of his wet-weather gear. 'Clear!' he shouted.

Then the wave of wounded men arrived. There seemed to be no one in charge of them, but they presented themselves in clearly pre-arranged order. Richard swung his precious equipment clear of the rush, then slid out of the straps again, returning to lend a hand. This was not officious interference on his part: he knew the lay out of the chopper's cabin and could fit in stretchers and seated casualties almost as effectively as the doctor. The doctor and he had planned for this eventuality and had a routine of their own in mind. And he, of course, was all too vividly aware of the undercarriage's damaged wheel.

Richard ended up half in, half out of the chopper, right knee on the door frame, left foot on the fold-out step behind the strong left wheel which persisted in skidding sideways along the slick deck as the brutally persistent wind tried to blow them into the front of the bridge house.

The first few stretchers slid in easily enough, the doctor swinging them into position, caught between the brutal need for speed and the absolute requirement for gentle care. The first couple of casualties were faceless – features seared almost to anonymity then bandaged like Egyptian mummies. The next few were slightly less graphically hurt, but all of them lay as still as death. Six stretchers in. He turned to assist the walking wounded.

He had helped half a dozen up and in when the pilot began to call his warnings. 'How much more room?' Richard shouted to the doctor.

'Maybe one more, but . . .'

'Who's next?' yelled Richard over his shoulder. Then he switched into his execrable French. '*Encore un fois! Seulement un.*'

But even as he called, the wind slammed into a squall and the helicopter lifted off and thundered up into the roiling overcast. Richard flew out sideways. He had an instantaneous vision of himself reaching out and catching the undamaged wheel or the sturdy step, hanging on until he could fall safely on to his feet. But even as he tumbled backwards, the sight and sound of the little Lynx were gone, hopping back up over the bridge house as nimbly as she had come, snatched away by the gale. Blowing both it and him, like the tanker, helplessly and powerlessly, easterly across the storm-riven waste of the Southern Ocean.

But it was decking, not water, that welcomed Richard when he landed. It was only an instant – though it had seemed longer to him – between the time he was flipped free of the fuselage and the time that he landed on the deck. He landed flat on his back, hitting it first with his heels and then with his head, crashing on to the *Lady Mary* like a falling tree; like the top-sliced communications mast. Falling on to red metal decking hard enough to switch out even the vastness of an Antarctic morning when it hit the back of his head – a cosh the size of a football field.

The pilot pushed the throttle up but held the helicopter in straight and level flight due east as the young navigator helped the doctor wrestle the half-dozen new passengers safely and securely into place before he collapsed back into his own position. It took some time for the young man to complete the process. Then it was as though pilot and navigator were alone again as the doctor fell to tending the terribly damaged bodies the ship had given him, through the good offices of their ex-passenger, Richard Mariner.

The wind continued to pound relentlessly behind the chopper, driving her along the same eastward track as the tanker was following, infinitely more slowly, far below. Away from the smoky effluent of the stricken vessel, the clouds seemed to lift, and the day to brighten slightly. The rain eased and the air cleared. So that when the navigator at last looked up, having strapped himself safely and securely into his seat and checked his instruments – double-checked indeed against the old-fashioned map, folded and secured to the right thigh of his flying suit – it was possible to see ahead for the better part of a hundred miles.

'Jesus Christ!' said the youngster, stricken by the view. 'What in God's name is that?'

That was a wall of black cliffs, which seemed to stretch

right across the eastern horizon. The cliffs rose from a perpetual wilderness of white foam directly into the stormy grey sky. And, as the wind continued to tear the clouds ever more destructively, it was clear that the mountainous cliff-tops reached far up into the highest whirling hearts of the scudding overcast. The upper slopes were only lost at last to view where the glaciers and snowfields broke the utter blackness of the rock and began to match the wildly writhing mists that perpetually veiled the lower sky.

The vertical corrugations of the cliff-faces overlapped and pushed together so that it was impossible for the navigator to tell if what he and the pilot were looking at was one time-scarred island or a whole mass of craggy black fangs. But there was no doubting that – solid and single or spread like shark's teeth – there was a sheer wall hundreds of feet high and maybe a hundred miles wide. And that wall was standing straight across the stricken tanker's course.

The young navigator had never seen anything to match the rugged wilderness of the scene. It seemed so inevitable that nothing could possibly live in such a place that he hardly even noticed that there was nothing moving there at all. Nothing living at any rate. No specks of animals; no clouds of birds. Nothing, of course, that told of human habitation.

But there was movement – unlike any he had ever seen before. Along the black sheernesses of the cliffs there bounded numberless white waterfalls – too steep by far to be called rivers or streams. They simply tumbled out of the pouring overcast and exploded in wild white waterfalls tumbling from level to level, serving to define the depth and precipitateness of the valleys that time and the elements had simply chopped into the vertical black rock. And the tumbling water did not come down gently to the beaches or lowland slopes where it could meander towards the surf. The falls simply leaped suicidally into the welter of foam at the cliff-feet. Or threw themselves like high divers into the still black waters of inland fjords, the arcs of their last cascades pulled away like smoke by the ruthless power of the winds. It was as though the whole vast spectacle had simply heaved itself up out of the Southern Ocean like the back of some unimaginable monster a moment or two ago.

As the helicopter began to swing back to reverse its course and go home, the navigator craned round in his seat entranced. Even at this distance the place still exuded a sullen, overwhelming threat.

'What is that?' the navigator repeated to the pilot.

'That's Kerguelen,' answered the pilot. 'The remotest place on earth. And just about the most dangerous. And it's just where that tanker the *Lady Mary* is going to end up in a terribly short space of time . . .'

'Unless the guy we just dropped off aboard her is as good as they say. Or as lucky . . .'

Two

Luck

Two of the strongest of *Lady Mary*'s stretcher bearers held Richard's unconscious body and two others picked up the equipment he had been planning to carry on his own. Then the whole group began to stagger back towards the bridge house. Richard swung massively between his two slight rescuers, arms across their shoulders and feet dragging over the deck, almost on his knees. After a few testing moments they reached the outer door to the A-Deck corridor and the leaders put the pack down so that they could open it and let the others lift Richard in out of the storm.

The A-Deck door was a big steel door with a high sill stepping in from the outer weather deck into the confines of the bridge house itself. The sill was needed because the outer deck was always running with water even though this section of it was under the shelter of the big bridge wings which extended the navigation bridge itself, three decks above. That fact was a mixed blessing however, for while the wings offered the distant promise of protection from the downpour, they also served to funnel the steady gale into a near hurricane through the constricted tunnel. It took even the most experienced crewmen several staggering minutes to release the big door catch. Then the heavy metal portal swung with a vicious force as though some kind of life were in it.

Once the door was safely and steadily open, they swung the big pack of equipment in and stepped after it, carrying Richard carefully. His feet caught on the sill and held them up for a moment or two longer as the storm sent a Niagara of rain and spray into the corridor around them. It was this activity, however, that began to bring Richard back to consciousness. They were working quickly rather than carefully – all too well aware of the wind and rain thundering past them into the bridge itself, making the floor in here like ice.

As Richard swung in at last, his knees hit the floor and he very nearly pitched forward on to his face together with the two exhausted men who were carrying him. The jolt brought Richard the next step towards a painful half consciousness. He realized where he was and what was going on around him. As he did so he registered that it was not just the floor that was like ice. So was the atmosphere.

Richard shook his head. All at once, as he had been in the helicopter less than fifteen minutes ago, he was far more concerned by the piercing smells of burning oil and chemical fire retardant. Groggy but intrepid, Richard tried to pull himself upright and turned his head to look about – just in time to see a figure finally swinging the door closed against the cold and the wet. And in so doing, plunging them all into darkness. Indeed, apart from the raving of the storm outside, into absolute stillness.

Only then did the desperate nature of *Lady Mary*'s predicament truly come home to Richard. She had no way on her – and so was drifting backwards with her bridge house acting like a huge square sail, dragging the great length of her red-decked hull slowly across the Southern Ocean. Drifting inevitability eastwards at the dictates of the prevailing westerly wind towards the forbidding black cliffs of Kerguelen Island. She had no power to her motors as he had observed already – no fumes coming out of her tall blue-painted funnel. There was no throbbing engine, the signs of activity that would usually make the still frame of her hull tremble with vital life. It all remained dull and dead, lacking even the faintest pulse. He had been warned of this situation, of course. The destruction of the motors, the fire aboard and the leakage of the oil were what had brought him here after all. These, amongst other things.

Now the atmosphere warned him that the situation aboard

13

was worse even than he had suspected – had become worse since he had set out; and much worse since his last – indirect – contact with the stricken vessel. She had no power for her heating and air-conditioning systems.

And the terrible, stinking, still and silent darkness told of the greatest danger of all. She had no power to her emergency lighting and communications circuits and no auxiliary power left in back-up either. Her alternators must be dead – even their faint familiar flutter in the fabric of the ship around him stilled. The crucial supply of everything needed to let her call for help and to begin to help herself was gone. *Lady Mary* was not only crippled but heart-attacked and brain dead into the bargain. Even her massive emergency batteries must be drained.

None of the equipment Richard had carried with him at such cost and with such strain out to the vessel would be any use at all without power. All the rest of it had been heavy enough; batteries had been out of the question.

'OK,' he began, in the universal slang that has slid into all European languages. He pulled himself up and looked around, trying to orientate himself in the narrow, night-black corridor, among the suddenly hesitant crowd of freezing men.

But then a noise behind him made him turn again. A beam of light glimmered out of the throat of the companionway that stepped down beside the central shaft of the dead lift. Someone else was coming down from the navigation bridge. A voice came before it, a kind of sound-companion to the beam of light. 'My God,' it called in French. 'The Captain is spitting with rage. Communications are *really* down now. Down and out. Three metres of the mast gone! It's no wonder the *rosbifs* call those things choppers! Guillotine would be a better name for this one, the Captain says . . .'

Impulsively, Richard stepped forwards towards the dull golden shaft of brightness, gathering his breath to explain, perhaps to apologize. But his boots slipped on the wet linoleum once again and this time there were no shoulders to hold on to. His feet skidded out from under him and he measured his length on the floor. He landed flat on his back, like an acrobatic comedian. But the result of his fall was not in the slightest bit funny. His head landed last of all, hitting the deck with a crack like a rifle shot, the second time in ten minutes; but this time less heroically.

Richard had the faintest, fleeting impression of brightness on his face. Cold brightness that faded into icy darkness. And of a cool female voice saying, this time in English but with a strong French accent, as it too faded away into immeasurable distance, 'Now that's what I call bad luck . . .'

Richard woke up in the disorientatingly familiar surroundings of the Captain's cabin. For a mind-bending moment he thought it must be one of the numberless cabins that had filled the later years of his career at sea; that he had somehow flown back in time and would rise to find himself in command of this dead and desperately dangerous vessel.

He sat up, and his head began to pound and spin. He sat still, breathing deeply until things began to settle down again. With calm and control, his memory returned; and so did a sense of desperate urgency. He swung his legs out of the big bed. At once the black hair that forested his thighs stirred into goose-bumps in the clammy chill of the air. He looked down. At least he was still wearing his underwear. Vest and shorts would hardly do, however. He'd need to scare up some thermal long johns as soon as possible. If he could find any in the ship's slop chest that would come near to fitting his massive body.

With that thought uppermost in his mind, trivial though it was in the circumstances, Richard began to search around for his missing clothes. They weren't far away. He found them lying neatly folded on a chair, close to the bed. As he moved towards them, he caught sight of himself in the mirror above the little sink beside the bed. He froze, frowning. He looked terrible – white-skinned, black-eyed, roughly bearded. A white bandage sat high on his forehead, rakishly askew, making him look more like Blackbeard the Pirate than anyone who could be looked to for help, advice and leadership in a desperate fix like this. He felt the rough bandage and realized it had been put there to protect the bump on his skull. Put there with some care but less expertise.

15

He pulled it off, and he thought, so the ship's doctor is on the butcher's bill of hurt and wounded too – if they had had one aboard at all. Along with the senior officers and half the crew, by all accounts. There was more needed to resolve this situation than turning up with a bundle of useless equipment and trying to look helpful. He needed to start with the very basics of leadership – even if he had been called for in person and his reputation was likely to have preceded him. What little was left of *that* after two comic pratfalls.

There was no power – so no running water, therefore. There was half a kettle-full left from some long-forgotten coffee time. There was no electricity to heat it up however. He sloshed that into the sink, cold as it was, and borrowed the Captain's shaving tackle in the grim assumption that the owner was in no condition to object. A cold shave restored some lean authority to his face. Then the Captain's hairbrush gave order to his shock of black hair – except for the bit covering the tender bump at the back. Once his face was right, he swiftly slipped the neatly folded clothing on to his powerful frame.

By the time Richard stepped out into the corridor and began to walk towards the navigation bridge he at least looked the part he was here to play. On this deck, there were enough windows to allow some daylight in. But to be fair he could have found his way in the dark quite easily. The corridors and companionways were as familiar as the cabin to him. The layout and design were the same as the vessels he had commanded throughout the later part of his career. For this, indeed, was an early member of the *Prometheus* series of tankers, an old Heritage Mariner supertanker sold on and renamed; put under the flag of the TAAF, the French Antarctic Protectorate.

Only the decoration was different – like the practical red lead of the decking. And little touches here and there – in Heritage Mariner vessels there were teak handrails in the corridors. Had there been one on the A-Deck corridor it would have saved him a compounded headache and a second brief sleep, he thought ruefully. But then, had there been one on the top deck he would be dead – and the *Lady Mary* ablaze

16

and sinking with the burning wreck of the chopper on her main deck.

The walls were light blue above waist level and dark blue below – the line showing where the handrail should have been. The cheerful paint was blistering and beginning to crack now. The thin, slippery linoleum was marbled with sapphire and terracotta – looking much richer than it was. It was bulging along the outer edges and wearing thin beneath the choke points.

This observation was enough to take Richard into the corridor behind the navigation bridge. Aware that first impressions might well be crucial, he paused for a moment to straighten his gear before stepping purposefully into the main command centre of the stricken vessel. Richard immediately found himself in an environment that was, once again, entirely familiar to him. A broad navigation bridge stretched from side to side of the bridge house – and was extended beyond watertight bulkhead doors out on to the bridge wings. The main feature of the place was the wide clearview window with its tilting panes that overlooked the red length of the deck, and the restless wilderness beyond. The panes were spotted and smeared with rain and spume. Like everything else, the wipers of the clearview system had died with the last of the power.

Beneath this all lay the command and navigation instrumentation. The helm, control levers and displays that showed speed, heading and all the rest. Or would have done so had they been alive. The radar displays, collision alarms and weather predictors were all black and blank. The helm, which seemed to be reading hard a' port, was stuck and solid. Behind and slightly to either side of it, stood comfortable chairs fixed to the deck for the Captain and his navigating officer. They should have been occupied by the watch officer at least. He glanced around the outer reaches of the place. On one far side, stood the empty Pilot's chair; on the other the little doorway leading back into the radio room. The equipment was all dead. And the bridge was utterly deserted.

With his mind racing, Richard stood at the helm, between the Captain's chair and the Navigator's, with his hands resting on the tiny steering wheel. There was a kind of ghostly vibration there – the closest thing to life in the whole place – except for the wind, which battered against the walls of metal and glass, thudding like fists; almost powerful enough to make the great structure tremble out of its deathly stillness. The only sensation of movement was the movement of the oceans around the seemingly dead-still vessel. And the faint trembling in the immovably frozen helm.

Richard remained for a moment, his eyes narrowed, looking along the massive length of the main weather deck at the restless corrugations of the grey seas following her. He stared at the tell-tale breadth of the oily black water in the centre of which the *Lady Mary* sat – and the way the westerly wind was tearing the tops of the waves, hurling them eastwards towards Kerguelen.

But there was really nothing to see back there except the Southern Ocean and the oil slick dragging behind them. There was nothing there at all – unless he could pierce more than 800 miles of stormy seas and make out the tiny black hump of Île de l'Est, easternmost of the Crozet Islands, also part of the TAAF, and *Lady Mary*'s last port of call as far as he knew.

And then it struck him. Although he was gazing along the deck towards the bow, he was actually looking backwards along the vessel's oily wake. Anyone wishing to look ahead and have some idea of the vessel's actual course and heading – not to mention what she might expect to encounter next – must be standing on the after deck and looking ahead over the stern. Where, in fact, the crew on that first strange sighting had been standing, like inverted figures in an Escher print.

No sooner did the realization strike him than a thumping noise came echoing down from the deckhead above him, making him glance up in lively recognition that he was by no means as alone as he felt aboard this eerie vessel. He was in motion once again, turning decisively away from the helm and the Captain's chair. Half a dozen purposeful strides took him back to the door out on to the command bridge's lateral corridor. Half a dozen more took him to the door at the end of the corridor. He swung this open against the pressure of the wind and stepped out on to the top of the outer companionway he had seen from the chopper on his arrival. At least it had stopped raining, he thought. More, he realized, looking up at the scudding overcast; the clouds were breaking up. He could just about make out the white disc of the useless Antarctic summer sun. With a wry smile, he launched himself downwards.

The steps ran down the outer side of the bridge house for one deck level and back across its depth. So that when Richard came to the foot of this first flight, he had a choice – he could go on down another level or he could step sideways on to the highest of the after decks. This red-floored deck reached across the width of the bridge house and was almost as deep as the command bridge had been. But it was utterly open, bound only by white-painted posts topped with thick safety rails of rope. It looked back across another deck, identical but one deck lower and the same width further back. Then across the almost semi-circular poop deck, chopped flat at its very end, past the jack-staff with its ragged duster of a flag and away over the high square stern.

Right at the mid-point of the upper deck's after safety rail stood a little group of figures intent on looking away eastwards, dead ahead – as though if they looked hard enough they could make out Kerguelen's huge black basalt fangs already. With no further thought or hesitation he hurried over to them.

As Richard neared them he could see that there were three. All were slight, in spite of the fact that they were well wrapped up in bulky wet-weather gear. As he neared them he realized what was going on. They were using an old-fashioned sextant to shoot the fleetingly-visible sun. He stopped short, struck by the apparent incongruity. Here they were, on a modern vessel helplessly trapped in the middle of a terrible crisis, calmly and quietly going about an exercise that sailors had been doing for centuries. Luckily – later, he would think by the grace of God – he made no comment. He simply walked on over to them, simply calling, 'Hello.'

The central figure, with the sextant to his eye, simply raised one hand in a faintly imperious gesture. Then returned to adjusting a knob on the ancient instrument's side. The slight figure nearest turned and came towards him, pulling back a bright orange hood to reveal a tumble of golden curls. ''Allo,' she answered in clear English only slightly accented with French. 'How is your head?' Her wide blue eyes looked enquiringly at him, unclouded by any real concern.

Richard recognized the ghostly voice that had faded with the torchlight following his unlucky accident in the A-Deck corridor. 'Fine, thanks,' he grinned ruefully and rubbed the lumps on the back of his head. There were two, overlapping. Each felt about the size and shape of a hen's egg. He remembered what else the voice had said as it approached down the companionway and he glanced up to see the work team trying to salvage what they could from the wreck of the mast one deck up. He grimaced.

'I am Sophie Bois, Navigating Cadet,' continued the familiar voice. When he looked back courteously at the speaker, her eyes also were up on the work team high above. 'This is Antoine, Engineering Cadet.'

Antoine slouched coolly around, one hand on the railing. He was as stylishly chilled as Richard's own teenage son. He had that long, Gallic face seemingly designed to set off a Gitane cigarette in the corner of his lips. And indeed, there was a toothpick there instead.

'You know the Captain . . .' continued Sophie brightly.

'I thought the Captain was dead,' Richard interrupted, shocked out of his normal good manners. If they had got something as vital as that incorrect, then the people who had called him here may have got other things dangerously wrong.

'Captain Giscard is dead,' Sophie confirmed, almost brightly. 'And so is the First Officer . . .'

'And the Chief and the First Engineering Officer,' supplied Antoine, coolly subdued, nodding his head in independent rhythm to the twitching of the toothpick. 'All dead.'

'So I am the Captain now,' added a third voice brusquely. Richard looked up into the face of the officer who had been using the sextant. He looked up and caught his breath.

A riot of chestnut hair with russet highlights, even in this dull light. A pale face, saved from being oval by the strength

20

of the cheekbones, the breadth of the huge almond-shaped eyes above them. The resolute square of the chin below. A long, straight nose, flaring into perfectly patrician nostrils. A wide, generous mouth. And those huge eyes, coloured somewhere between hazel and chocolate, disturbingly flecked with gold. Every inch her mother's daughter.

Stepsister to Richard's wife, Robin, who was also speeding here to offer help. Stepdaughter to his father-in-law, close friend and partner, Sir William Heritage. So close a family member, even though she was an utter stranger to him. Seemingly so close, despite the fact that she had remained with the French side of her maritime family when her mother, Helen DuFour, came north over the Channel into the board-room of Heritage Marincr and, eventually, into the bedroom of Sir William Heritage himself.

Richard had never met Julie DuFour, nor even seen her photograph in this millennium; but he would have known her anywhere. And he had come more than halfway round the world at a moment's notice to help her if he could. But he had come near to worsening her desperate situation instead.

'Permission to come aboard, Captain DuFour,' he said, formally, and put out his hand to shake hers.

She glanced up at the ruin of the radio mast, then down at him again. In the silence before the formal reply, he saw that Sophie had not been exaggerating when she had said, 'The Captain is spitting with rage . . .'

'Permission granted, Captain Mariner,' answered Julie DuFour coldly. She did not return his gesture and waited until his hand fell to his side once again. 'Not that I have any choice in the matter.'

Three

Heading

Although Richard had not noticed it during his first, brief visit to the navigation bridge, the equipment he had brought with him was all up here. It had been stowed in the chart room aft of the main bridge itself. Acting Captain Julie DuFour glanced down at it five minutes later as she unrolled the chart and placed the sextant upon it. 'We could really have used this stuff yesterday,' she said icily, with no hint of gratitude for what he had paid, risked or achieved. 'Before the Captain got killed, the power went down and things got really tricky.'

'That will be our first priority, surely,' said Richard equably, stoically refusing to feel aggrieved at her lack of courtesy. 'Getting power back.'

Julie nodded. 'We're working on it and your help will be valuable. Getting the Captain back as well,' she added obscurely. Then she continued, her tone speaking volumes as to the strain it was taking to be even this civil to him, 'But we have one priority even more important still.' She gestured to the map and the sextant. 'One of the last things Captain Giscard did was to plot our position at noon yesterday. He was busy so he used the ship's Global Positioning System. GPS is not accurate down here. The charts of the local waters all say not to rely upon it – certainly not for anchoring or close-shore work. But it gives us a baseline to work from.'

As she talked, Julie was tapping figures into the only functioning electrical equipment Richard had seen aboard so far – a solar-powered calculator. They all stood in silence as she completed her calculations and leaned down over the map. Richard forbade himself to mention that an old-fashioned sextant was hardly likely to be more accurate than the GPS at these latitudes – unless very skilfully used indeed.

When Julie straightened, her face was folded in a frown and her cheeks were, if anything, a little paler. 'You know how to use a sextant?' she demanded, as though she had been able to read Richard's mind.

'I do,' confirmed Richard.

She heard something of his reservations in his voice, perhaps, because her frown deepened. She snapped, 'It's too late for another noon sight. But my observations were absolutely accurate, I assure you. Please check my calculations.'

'Spot on,' he confirmed after a few moments.

'Then check my chart work if you please.'

'Absolutely accurate,' he said again after a few more moments.

'I feared as much. You see what it means, of course?' She gestured to the lines and crosses on the chart.

'The wind and current are pushing you along this course which is running a little north of due east at almost a mean knot,' Richard answered slowly. 'As you move eastwards under the wind, so you seem to be swinging northwards a little. Just a degree or two. That's not really important now, but it might be later, because it's pulling you further up towards the centre of the Kerguelen archipelago – straight for Kerguelen Island itself.' He straightened to his full height and continued, 'You've certainly come more than 20 nautical miles since yesterday's noon sight, even allowing for GPS error. Perhaps 24 or 25.' He paused while he did the mental arithmetic. 'That's quite some distance. Say 30 statute miles. 40 kilometres or so. That's one hell of a speed for a drifting hulk . . .'

Richard's deep rumbling voice stilled like the motors. The dazzle of his eyes narrowed, looking at the lines on the chart and calculating further – along the lines that Julie already had, he suspected. 'Four days to Kerguelen, at that speed. Five at the outside.' He paused, looking around the small group of worried faces. 'We're in the Roaring Forties, after all – well, just in the Roaring Fifties by a minute or two of a degree. But stuck in the winds that moved *Cutty Sark* and God knows how many clippers like her through these waters at speeds of up to 360 miles in a day.'

All three of them nodded in dumb agreement – but he suspected only Julie really saw the full import of what he was saying. He had last spoken to his wife Robin when she had arrived in Durban and he had arrived in Rothera nearly eighteen hours ago. She had been at the harbour, just about to go aboard the ocean-going tug *Sissy*, one of the most powerful vessels in the world. *Sissy* had a bollard pull in excess of 250 tonnes and was capable of 25 knots. More importantly, she had huge fuel tanks allowing her to sustain a cruising speed of 17 knots for the better part of a week if need be.

But Durban was 2,000 miles north-north-west of here. Seventeen knots was roughly equivalent to 20 mph. A hundred hours' sailing, then. He looked at his watch. If Robin had left in *Sissy* at the same time he had climbed aboard the final plane flight for his rendezvous with the BAS Westland chopper, then she would still be three days away. With only a day or so in hand to find them in this wilderness, then somehow get some lines aboard and tug them off their collision course towards one hundred miles of cliffs, half of which were the slopes of a huge volcano, it was cutting things far too close for comfort. In all sorts of unpleasant ways.

'Right,' he said decisively. 'Where do you want me to pitch in?'

'I am tempted to send you aloft to put right some of the damage you have done,' she answered tartly. 'But there is more urgent work to be done. Upon you, rather than by you, just for the moment.'

'What do you mean?' he demanded, uncertain whether this was some new kind of Gallic insult. He drew himself up to full height again, in spite of the pounding of his head and a slight feeling of giddiness.

'The back of your head,' explained Cadet Sophie. 'It is bleeding again.'

'That's not bleeding,' said Julie. 'That is the Trevi fountain. We should be throwing money at you, Captain, and hoping for luck.'

'This is going to hurt,' said Julie DuFour matter-of-factly, ten minutes later. Her brusque tone just failing to mask grim satisfaction. At least that's what Richard thought he heard beneath her gruff voice. She applied what felt like a red-hot poker to the wound at the back of his cranium and he flinched. But he held steady and remained silent – just. This time he was grinding his teeth. He could hear the sound in his ears, like thunder beneath her icy tones.

They were in the ship's infirmary. Only now it was simply a morgue, full of the crew members it would have been a waste of time to load into the chopper. They lay on the half-dozen or so beds, covered with sheets – though the once-white cotton simply served to give unnerving impressions of the twisted, scorched and roasted horrors that lay beneath. Ideas compounded disgustingly with every breath through the nose.

'I allowed Sophie to see to you in the first instance,' Julie continued coldly. 'She found you and it seemed best to be quick. But I see now it was a mistake. This is quite a wound. When I have finished cauterizing, I will shave, stitch and bandage. Then I will run a test or two for concussion. I do not want you becoming giddy at inappropriate moments or in unfortunate places. As you see, all the beds in here are taken. And unfortunately we have more guests waiting to check in.'

'You don't want me added to the waiting list.'

'Indeed. For the moment I want you to be a bellboy, not a guest. Or, more precisely, perhaps, a *concierge*.'

'And what in heaven's name do you mean by that, Captain DuFour?'

Richard had suspected the answer before he asked the question, of course. At least that was what he thought to himself as he slowly, laboriously and very, very carefully negotiated the vertiginous ladder down into the engineering section. It would have been hard enough under full light with a clear head – but he was doing it in the near dark alleviated only by the fading glimmer of the dying torch beam that Sophie was pointing down at him from high above. And his head was full of all too active trip-hammers.

At the bottom of the ladder two men waited with what looked for all the world like a dirty white deep-sea diving suit, thick glass face mask, oxygen tanks and all. At least they had better torches. And they would need them, where they were going.

As with the upper works, the engineering sections were of standard *Prometheus* design and thoroughly familiar to Richard in spite of the fact that he was a navigator and not an engineer. Right down in their depths lay the great motors; fire-damaged, still, and dead for the moment. In the higher levels – where Richard and the others were bound – stood the ancillary equipment. Equipment in many ways more important to the ship's safe existence than even the motors.

There were a dozen or more rooms down here with big airtight safety doors like the dungeons beneath some tyrant's castle. Rooms full of pumping equipment designed to keep the oil in the bunkerage and the huge cargo tanks safely and precisely stowed and balanced. Rooms full of computer equipment designed to monitor and, where necessary, to move the cargo from tank to tank maintaining balance and sheer. If allowed to slip beyond control, sheer would simply tear the massive hull apart. There were rooms full of heating and refrigeration equipment in order to maintain a constant temperature in the cargo areas so that the volume of the oil they were carrying would not expand – or contract – catastrophically as the voyage proceeded through waters and climates with widely varying temperatures.

Most important to their immediate plans, was the great cathedral space that housed the ship's great generators, amid a maze of pipes and lines, wires, cables, transformers and so forth. Julie had been flattering him a little, saying she wanted him to be *concierge*. She had meant *handyman* of course. Without further thought, he began to hum James Taylor's tune of the same name, setting the tempo to the throbbing of his head.

Like the pump room, the main engine room and so many other vital areas down here, the generator room was protected by the most powerful and deadly fire-fighting equipment aboard – the Inert Gas System. It was this IG System that necessitated so many airtight doors, for it worked with deceptively simple efficiency. Once triggered, it flooded the immediate area, deck to deckhead with CO_2 gas designed to snuff out the slightest spark of fire within seconds.

It was, unfortunately, equally efficient at snuffing out the slightest spark of life in anyone trapped within the room. Or, should the airtight doors not be closed properly, the lives of anyone in the next room – or the next – and so forth until the CO_2 tanks ran out of gas.

These thoughts and James Taylor's tune were more than enough to take Richard down the ladder on to the metal of the deck at its foot. The two men waiting there were already suited up but their headsets were thrown back, and they chatted tersely – tensely – in much less fluent English than their Captain spoke, as they helped Richard suit up. 'We go in. We see what is matter with generator and we try fix. OK?'

'Sounds good,' answered Richard affably enough.

'We engineers. You engineer?'

'No. I'm more a kind of handyman. But I know my way around.'

They exchanged Gallic looks that said, What bloody use is this big *Rosbif*? And, Why did we waste time and light on him?

When he was suited up, all three of them pulled their headsets into place, tightened them safely and tested their compressed air. Richard's smelt and tasted of rancid rubber and he found himself hoping that theirs did too. Particularly when he saw that they had torches while there was none for him. Then, side by side, they shambled off.

As they moved the French engineers called to each other – and, Richard supposed, to him. But their thick accents became utterly impenetrable through the face masks and under the surging hiss of the breathing regulator.

Richard's opinion of the French engineers began to grow more positive as they neared the generator room, however. He saw they had built a solid and impressive-looking little airlock on the outside of it. The area they were crossing now was massive, but sections of the floor were of heavy-duty mesh, covering darker depths below. Simply opening the door would let the CO_2 come flooding silently and invisibly out in a huge deadly river – to settle who knew where – and with who knew what fatal effect. Using the airlock, however, they could control the amount of the lethal gas released into the sections down below. They had overcome this terrible danger by fashioning an airtight little room of metal with a solid-looking, snug-fitting wooden door. They had welded it together and then welded it in place – judging by the oxyacetylene equipment still standing ready on its little trolley beside their work.

The downside to the solid, metal-sided airlock was its size, of course. The three men crowded in together like the pieces of a 3D jigsaw. Richard was able to close the door behind him but only just – and had the generator room's door not opened inwards, they would all have had to get back out again. But it did open inwards – though with obvious diffi-culty – and the three men stepped over the sill into an echoing cavern one after the other.

Richard turned immediately as the last one in, preparing to close the door behind him once again, and came face to face with Captain Giscard. At least, amid the disorientating shock of the encounter, he assumed it was Captain Giscard, next guest destined for the morgue three decks above: the ghastly little *hôtel* of which Richard had been appointed *concierge* by another of Miss Julie's grim little jokes. The corpse was wearing a Captain's uniform, at least, though overalls would have been more practical down here, what-ever he had been doing when he died.

The corpse was hanging on the back of the door, his hands frozen on a hook high above the main handle, as though he was pretending to be an old coat. He was looking back into the room with such fierce fixity – seemingly directing his glassy gaze straight over Richard's shoulder – that the Englishman swung round and found the two engineers crouched over a twisted pile comprised of several other bodies.

'Leave them,' called Richard. 'We don't have time.' His voice was gruff; desperate. Given an extra edge at the very least by the shock he still was feeling. The dead men were the engineers' friends no doubt. But they had vital work to do here; priorities other than grieving, farewells and closure. Or indeed, of getting them up to the overcrowded infirmary, in spite of what Julie had said.

'*Ecoutez!*' he snarled, slipping into his ugly but serviceable patois, and repeating his brutal order. He might not be an engineer, but he knew what he was doing here. That at least was part of the reason he himself had been called out to the stricken ship. There had been a time when the whole of his professional life had been to come into corpse-strewn disasters such as this. To come out to them, take command of them and to bring them safely home.

He left Captain Giscard hanging on the door and stepped past the pile of corpses on the floor as he herded the stricken engineers towards their primary objective. The basics of the situation were immediately clear to him. Not least because the system was standard *Prometheus* design and he had been dealing with it for more years than he cared to count.

The ship's generators were of the same basic design as any others, with the added complication that they could be driven either by the motors or by their own smaller oil-fuelled power source. The system was logical enough – they had to run when the ship's great motors were idle – at anchor for instance. But by the same token they could function like the battery of an automobile, gaining power from the movement of the major propulsion system and saving bunkerage into the bargain.

No doubt the generators had died when the fire in the engine room killed the turbines themselves, then some malfunction in the equipment had caused the automatic switch-back over to independent power to fail. And when the Captain and his team had come down here to put things right, some stroke of incredibly bad luck had tricked off the IG System and killed them all – and the generators into the bargain.

As an explanation it begged an awful lot of questions,

29

thought Richard, his mind ticking over rapidly – for he was used to situations such as this and still well-trained to handle them. But it would have to do for the time being. They could maybe look a little closer later – after the job was done. When his head was clearer, perhaps; and when it was throbbing less fiercely.

The generators were controlled from a main control panel that had a red ignition button designed simply to release an electrical spark which would set light to the oil jets and start a series of massive magnets spinning in a coil the size of a chimney. The coil was secured against the after wall, reaching up through the deckhead above. Beneath it sat the big squat oil-fired power source. Richard crossed to this behind one of the engineers as the other stood by the console, waiting to push the ignition button, as though igniting the pilot light of a gas-powered central heating system.

As soon as they were in position, Richard's companion called, '*Tirez!*'

In answer, a distinct *click* echoed across the silence of the room. But there was no answering cough and *whoof* of power. No reassuring grumble of the magnets beginning to spin within the massive coil.

'*Encore!*'

Click!

'*Encore un fois . . .*'

Click!

'*Merde . . .*'

Richard was in motion before the idea in his head was even properly formed. It seemed clear enough to him that the CO_2 had got into the ignition mechanism itself. The oil would not fire unless they could get a steady, reliable flame that could overcome the inert gas's malign influence. He walked around the pile of corpses with hardly a second glance. He approached the hanging Captain Giscard and lifted the handle at his hip. He saw at once why the door was hard to open, for the dead Captain's toes dragged reluctantly across the non-slip treatment on the metal of the floor. Even so, he swung it wide and stepped out. He closed the door carefully behind himself and passed on through the airlock into the

30

massive darkness of the deck. It was only as he moved out into stygian blackness that he realized he should have brought one of the torches with him. But he knew where to find what he was looking for whether he could see it or not.

When Richard came back into the generator room, the engineers were still stuck in their unimaginative routine. He listened to the dull routine as he closed the doors safely once again.

'*Encore* . . .'

Click!

'*Merde, merde, merde! Enfin. Encore!*'

Click!

Richard pulled the trolley across to the distant glimmer of torchlight, coming to rest beside the lugubrious engineer as he called, '*Merde* . . .' again.

Richard's French was not only ugly; it was also unusual. It was, for instance, fully packed with technical words that would be gibberish in the average conversation. He could hardly manage, 'Where is the nearest taxi rank?' But he was confident and fluent with, 'Please prepare the suction lines to discharge the slop from the Number 11 Wing Tank.'

But this was by no means an average conversation.

'Listen. Is there an opening into the oil jets down here?'

'But yes . . .'

'Where is it?'

'Naturally, it is here. But why . . .'

'Here? Does this open into the oil jets directly?'

'Certainly. Directly. But why . . .'

'Open it. I will insert the lance. Call to your colleague to press ignition when I say so.'

'Are you certain this will work, Captain?'

'Of course not, Engineer. But at least we can be certain there will be no explosion, is that not so?'

'Truly, my Captain.'

The engineer opened a small door in the side. Richard lifted the lance of the oxyacetylene welding equipment. With a practised hand he adjusted the taps on the gas bottles. For an instant he allowed the oxygen to flow across the point of the lance. Then he pushed the button for the electric ignition. Even in the inert gas conditions of the generator room, the pure oxygen allowed the flame to come alive. Richard paused for an instant, making certain that the flame was steady.

'*En avant . . .*' he said.

The engineer opened the little door even wider and Richard pushed the lance through it.

'*Encore,*' grated Richard, and the engineer echoed his command, shouting across the generator room, though his tone was flat and hopeless.

Click!

'*Encore un fois . . .*' He did not let any desperation into his voice. He held the flame of the lance still, in the heart of the thing, and gritted his teeth. There were probably a thousand reasons why something as simple as this should not work – and only one or two chances that it would.

How lucky did he feel? What did the song say? Abruptly it replaced *Handyman* in his throbbing cranium: 'Luck, be a Lady tonight . . .'

Click!

Whoof . . .

The oil burners puffed into flame. Richard pulled the lance out and the engineer slammed the door. They stood there, side by side, as the flame on the lance guttered and died. But as they did so, the *whumph, whumph, whumph* of the generators told of the power system beginning to come to life.

The three of them stood back, looking up at the stirring giant. Carried away on a tide of euphoria, Richard buffeted the hopeless, lugubrious one on the shoulder. 'Well done!' he said. 'Well done . . . What is your name?'

'Honore, Captain.'

'Well done, Honore. And well done . . .'

'Raoul, Captain.'

The engineers fell to securing the door more tightly still, isolating the gathering flames against any further action with the fire-fighting equipment.

Richard felt the instant of wild exultation linger, and he savoured it. This was better. This was the beginning of a way back. They were heading towards safe haven now.

'Let there be light!' he bellowed.

And there was light.

Four

Power

The steady grumbling of the generators was all but lost beneath a range of other sounds by the time Richard had returned to the navigation bridge. As he came bounding up the companionways and striding along the bright blue corridors, he was at first startled by the sudden stirring of the lifts within their shafts beside him as the cars returned automatically to proper deck-level, opening and closing their doors as though giving a ride to ghosts.

Next, he became aware of the bubbling of the water in the pipes as it was heated up and circulated. Then of the creaking of the heating system; the susurrating whisper of the warming air-conditioning fans. And, as he stepped into the navigating bridge itself, of the whirring, clicking and pinging of the instruments as they too began to come to life. He paused amongst all this vital activity that he had brought about and listened, narrow-eyed.

There were no emergency alarms sounding. That was something. A pleasant surprise at the very least.

But then an alarm did sound with deafening force and he nearly jumped out of his skin. It was the 'Now hear this!' announcement: someone had an important message to make.

It was Julie DuFour. Her familiar, decisive Provençal accent boomed through every cavern and corner of the stirring ship. She must be down in the Captain's cabin, Richard realized at once – there was a loud-hailer down there in the little office beside the Captain's lounge, of course; twin to the one up here on the bridge. One corner of his mouth raised in the

33

ghost of a wry smile: it was just as well he hadn't made himself too comfortable in poor old Captain Giscard's quarters – he'd a feeling he'd be out of there by dinnertime and Julie would be in. The privileges of power.

'The navigating watch officer is Cadet Bois,' began the brusque announcement. 'Cadet Bois, report to the bridge and assume the afternoon watch. Everyone else aboard report to their normal duty stations and do their best to prepare for Captain's inspection in two hours' time. The current time is 1300 hours local time, and ship's time will be set to that. Cold buffet luncheon will be served from 1400 in the officers' dining area and all crew will report there at that time except for the watch officers whose food will be brought to their watch stations. Please do not linger over your food. We have much to do and little time.

'Navigating officers and Captain Mariner report to the bridge immediately please. Engineering officers also, as soon as they have checked for major damage below. But take care all of you and be alert for signs of CO_2 poisoning. I will be on the bridge should anyone wish to report anything important to me. I will give a full update of our position and plans at 1800, as per normal ship routine. Pour out and dinner will proceed from 1830 hours. That is all.'

Richard looked around the empty bridge as the echoes of the brusque announcement died. He thought of Julie's first words to him: So I am the Captain now. She was certainly taking the reins of command firmly enough.

Time would tell whether she could ride the whirlwind too.

Sophie Bois appeared moments later, puffed out and almost aglow with excitement. Gold curls glinting and blue eyes shining. As they waited for the Captain to arrive with her surviving navigating officers, Richard observed the cadet go through a basic watch-keeper's routine. She checked the logs. Richard watched with something akin to revelation, thinking how impressive it was that the records of the ship's most recent – disastrous – movements had been kept up to date. That would be down to Captain Julie no doubt.

Then Sophie checked the position on the ship's GPS and cross-checked it against the Captain's noon sighting with apparent satisfaction. Richard felt a great deal of satisfaction too that the GPS was still working. He had no idea what equipment had been housed in the top of the mast – and he prayed it was only the radio aerials. His prayer seemed to be answered during the next few minutes – for as Sophie checked, so the automatic equipment began to respond.

Next she checked the heading – remembering to reverse the course described by the automatic equipment by 180 degrees. Everything aboard was set on the assumption that the ship was actually heading the way she was pointing – rather than drifting backwards. Then she began to check the radars – starting with the vital collision-alarm radar. Her busy fingers at the setting buttons made Richard suspect that the practical young trainee was resetting the focus to point astern rather than ahead. Intrigued, he went across for a closer look.

So that when Julie DuFour ran on to the bridge a few moments later, she found them almost cheek by jowl above the readout. 'Captain Mariner,' she said in English, in her icily disapproving tone and with some asperity. 'I need you in the chart room now please.' She might as well have said, Leave my officers to get on with their jobs, *s'il vous plaît*. Have you not done enough damage already?

Richard obeyed with cheerful equanimity, but as he moved, his eyes remained on Sophie for an instant. Logic dictated that once she was satisfied as to the position, situation and heading of the vessel – and, of course, that the ship was in no immediate danger – she should check for incoming communications. But all she did along those lines was to glance across to the door of the radio room. And Richard, following her gaze, noticed that its blue-painted edges were etched in black, and, above the lintel, a tell-tale sooty mark reached right up to the deckhead above. So it really didn't matter at all that he had wrecked the aerials, he thought. It seemed like the equipment they were attached to should have been down in the infirmary. With its operator, judging by the fire-damage round the radio-room door.

'Radio burned out like the motors?' he asked as he entered the chart room.

'Radio and both radio operators. Poor Marcel dead – Jean-

35

Luc lucky to be alive. And you should have been alerted that our radio was failing even before the final catastrophe. You will have to tell me exactly what it is you have brought out to us now that we have the power to employ it.'

'Communications equipment because, yes, I got the message about your radio. It's better than anything you'd have had aboard in any case. State of the art,' he said. 'I'll give you more details whenever you want. I can get it out at once, if you want. It's been aboard for – what? – four hours now. Like me. Time's a'wasting, and as you said in your announcement just now we don't have much to play with.'

'After the first briefing we will set up your equipment if you have time. But I have other priorities; and so do you if you are fully under my command. I want you to come on my Captain's inspection with me. That is a higher priority still – for me at any rate.'

'Of course.' Richard's eyes narrowed speculatively and she saw it. 'It's your command. I'm here to help.'

'*D'accord.* If we are lucky then Jean-Luc, the Assistant Radio Operator, will be well enough to help you too, in due course; but he was injured fighting the blaze, as I said. He must remain in the infirmary the time being. The new infirmary, of course – not the morgue, you understand. *However*, we only need to be able to communicate with the rest of the world when we are certain it is safe to do so. And when we have something of use to tell them.'

Richard opened his mouth to ask just what it was she meant by these unsettlingly cryptic remarks, but he was forestalled by the arrival of the navigating officers. They were young, plump and vaguely mutinous. The senior of them, the Third Officer, was dark-haired, ill-shaven, sloppily dressed and clearly carrying a sizeable chip on his shoulder. The other was blond, neat and boyishly young, a male counterpart of Sophie Bois – unsettlingly like a twin. Julie brusquely called them Three and Four. But Richard soon got to know their names. The unhappy Third Officer's name was Lucien. The eager young Fourth Officer's name was Emil. In due time he would learn more about the engineering officers Honore and Raoul, though Julie insisted on calling them Three and Four as well, which brought confusion – confusion which she used quite calculatingly.

Julie DuFour's command technique – to begin with at least – seemed to Richard to be 'Divide and Rule'. Only later did he begin to understand why this was so. And how wise the apparently arrogant and divisive young captain actually was.

'Three, Four . . .' she snapped as the deck officers arrived. 'Have you secured the communications mast?'

Both of them nodded. Clearly they had been the men stuck up aloft while the Captain had been shooting the sun at noon, he thought. And neither of them looked very happy about it.

'It is waterproof? Wind proof? Weather proof? Safe and secure?'

Again they nodded. 'It's not much use as it stands, Captain,' expanded Emil. 'But at least it's not going to deteriorate much before we get a chance to try a proper repair.'

'Very well. Three; you will prepare reports for the log detailing damage and what has been done to correct it. In the meantime, you all heard my orders just now. We will be returning to standard watches on the bridge. There will be day watches for the engineers certainly. I will decide whether we can afford to leave the engineering areas unmanned at night in due course. But I don't want anyone keeping watch alone, day or night. When I talk to the whole crew at 1800, I will break them into work teams and assign a team to each watch-keeper. I will make that decision after Captain Mariner and I have completed the full inspection.'

'But . . .' Sulky Lucien didn't like the sound of this.

'No buts, Three. I do not expect all your areas to be perfect and all your records up to date except for the report about my mast – far from it. Any more, in fact, than I expect you to look like a proper officer for the moment. But I do want you shaved and dressed smartly by pour out. And I do want to know what is working properly within your area and what is not. What – perhaps who – we can rely on and what not? There is too much I do not know. I cannot make sound decisions until I have certain situations clear in my mind. It is always so after such a crisis I should imagine.'

'But Julie,' Lucien wheedled, clearly relying on more charm than Julie actually credited him with. Until he saw the glint in her eye.

'Captain, surely we must simply call for help and abandon ship if help is not likely to come immediately?' interposed the youthful, blond Emil.

'No, Four. We cannot do that so easily. Think! We are at the heart of a great lake of highly volatile oil in deteriorating weather conditions upon the remotest sea on earth. If we could get off without poisoning ourselves or setting the ocean on fire, we would certainly freeze, starve or drown.

'As things stand, *La Dame Marie* is by far our safest refuge, even in her current condition and situation, and we should consider abandoning only if the water begins to close over the top of her. Besides, we have a responsibility to try and save her. To save her at the very least. What would happen if we just abandoned her? She would drift on to Kerguelen! She is moving at only a knot, perhaps, but her bulk is so massive that the impact would be colossal. Consider what a catastrophe that would be! So much destruction, in such a place. Like Crozet, like Adelie Land, Kerguelen is a part of France! What hope would there ever be of convincing the Americans of our title to Antarctic territories if a French vessel did such a thing down here! Even if the hull ruptured and sank with no further explosions, there would be a quarter of a million tonnes of oil spewed over the place; all over a unique environment protected by all the laws of international conservation! I am surprised that it is Captain Mariner standing here amongst us and not some outraged representative from Greenpeace or Friends of the Earth!'

'You might like to consider also,' said Richard, now that Julie had less than wisely included him in her tirade, 'that Kerguelen is a volcano. Imagine what might happen if *Lady Mary* hit it hard enough. If she exploded with sufficient force Kerguelen could go up like Krakatoa. Krakatoa right beside the Antarctic ice shelf. The destruction would be incalculable . . .'

'Precisely!' snapped Julie, less than grateful for his support. 'Consider also, young Emil, that if we do not fight this to the very end then we will never work at sea again. Our employers would be destroyed. Our friends and families would be shamed. *La France* herself would be damaged! It is inconceivable that we should abandon ship and run away. We are a French crew upon a French vessel drifting through an area of French influence towards a French island. We must fight to save the situation as hard as if we were drifting down the River Seine on to Île de La Cité, putting Notre Dame and the heart of Paris at risk!'

'To the barricades, *mes braves*!' whispered Lucien, the scruffy Third Officer, with more than a hint of a sneer.

'Thank you, Three,' snapped Captain Julie. 'You have just drawn the middle watch.'

'That's the First Officer's!' Lucien looked around, huffing with indignation. 'Midnight to four is the First Officer's watch . . .'

'Think,' said Richard easily. 'If the Second Officer is now Captain, then the Third Officer must take the First Officer's duties.'

'Ha!' said the youthful Fourth Officer. 'He's got you there, Lucien.'

'And you will take over my old watches, Four,' continued Julie. 'Though neither of you will actually be performing the First and Second Officers' duties in full. I will decide what you will need to do beyond your usual duties as Third and Fourth Officers when I have seen what there is to see at the inspection. I do not plan to hold any drills today but you will remain at lifeboat stations as Third and Fourth Officer. Cadet Bois will take my emergency post. I will take the Captain's. And Captain Mariner will take the First Officer's.'

'That means I'm on watch now then, Captain,' said Lucien, obviously reckoning that a simple watch under these circumstances would be much less stressful or work-laden than preparing for the Captain's inspection.

'Cadet Bois will take the afternoon watch through until four. You have your other duties.'

'But she should take the forenoon watch from eight a.m. to midday. If we are being *logical*, Captain . . .' persisted Lucien with sulky arrogance.

'May I take that, Captain DuFour?' asked Richard. 'It's a while since I kept watch, but I think I can cope, under the circumstances. If a London city gent like me can drag himself out of bed by eight a.m., of course . . .'

'Thank you. We will see. That would allow me some freedom, at least. In the meantime, I will take the first night watch from eight p.m. to midnight tonight. It is during the night watches that things have gone most terribly wrong, so far.'

It was upon this darkly thoughtful observation that the engineers arrived. Out of their deep-sea diving rigs they looked strangely subterranean, thought Richard, more like moles than morays. They were as easy to tell apart as the deck officers. One was older, thin and grey-haired. His face was deeply wrinkled, as though the skin was too big for his skull. He looked like a bloodhound and Richard was not at all surprised to recognize the lugubrious tones of Honore, who always looked on the dark side of things, certainly when it came to re-igniting oil-burners, at any rate. The other was younger, fresh-faced and bald as an egg. That must be Raoul, therefore. And so it proved: the old one answered to Three and, eventually, Honore. The bald one answered to Four and Raoul.

The captain transferred her attention from one pair of numbers to the other like the most heartless coquette. 'Well? What have you to report from the engineering areas?'

'We have restored the power, of course.' Honore's dark-ringed, baggy eyes slid away from Richard as he spoke, clearly unwilling to share the glory of his success with the man who had engineered it.

'Yes, Three. Thank you for that,' said Julie brusquely. 'But you have been down in engineering for a good long time now. What else have you done or discovered?'

'We have not pumped out any of the rooms yet but there is a schematic on the engineering central computer which shows what has been flooded by the IG System and what has not.'

'Good, Three. I do not want anything pumped out yet. I do not want to rush into replacing the oxygen in some of

40

the areas. Patch your schematic through to my bridge computer and I will make some decisions when I have inspected matters in more detail for myself. What else have you to report?'

'Clearly the engine control room has not been flooded with inert gas . . .' began Raoul, not to be outdone by his more elderly colleague.

'Yes, Four. I worked that out. I could not imagine the pair of you staying in those suits while you checked the central computers. What else have you *done*?'

'Well . . .' Honore's face seemed to grow, if anything, even longer.

'Oh come on, Three. You've been down there for the better part of an hour. You must have done something other than look around like a couple of tourists at Les Invalides. What have you actually *done*?'

'Well, Captain,' said Three, his voice shaking with something more than advancing age, his watery eyes ablaze with indignation.

Richard saw what was coming and closed his eyes. As the lids fell he saw Julie's face blench with realization too.

But there was no stopping Third Engineer Honore's self-righteous whining now. 'We enlisted the aid of Cadet Antoine who is still on watch below. We three have detached Captain Giscard from the door where he died holding himself upright, then carried his body out into the main area and laid him there as best we could, for he is set solid. Like a statue in the Louvre, in fact. This took some time as we were careful with our airlock and, as you say, you did not wish the generator room pumped out as yet. Then we carried out Chef and placed him there also.'

Fourth Engineer Raoul took up the sorry story, echoing the aggrieved tone of his colleague, though the face of the bald man could hardly have been more different. 'Then we untangled First Engineering Officer Le Blanc from General Purpose Seaman Li and General Purpose Seaman Fuuk and carried them all out with us. This all took some time as well for they are all stiff. As Honore said, "like statues in the Louvre". Or Maison Rodin.'

She's going to regret that crack about tourists at Les Invalides, thought Richard.

Julie's voice was husky but her tone held no weakness in it – nor even the faintest hint of apology. The closest she came was to allow them their names beside their titles. 'You have done your duty, Three, Honore – though I would not have shared your priorities. It is preserving the living, not honouring the dead, that must take precedence with all of us now. I will arrange for crewmen with less important concerns to bring the dead up to the infirmary as soon as it is safe to do so. And now that the power is back on we can move some of the dead into the meat lockers. In the meantime, what can you tell me about the ship's motors?'

'Why, nothing.' Honore seemed faintly surprised that such knowledge should even be demanded of him.

'Four, Raoul?'

'Nothing, Captain. They are as they were left after the fire. The main engine area is one of those still flooded with inert gas. And as you know, the initial damage was to the monitoring systems as well as to the propulsion units themselves. There is nothing further even on the computers.'

'Then we must consider pumping out the engine area first of all so that we can get down there, make some kind of assessment and try to make repairs. I want the ship under power within the next twenty-four hours if that is possible.'

The engineers exchanged looks. Looks and shrugs. The shrugs looked dangerously hopeless to Richard. The French for no chance, from Emil. She's mad to even think it, from Honore.

'In the meantime,' persisted the Captain as though she had seen none of this. 'I would like the pair of you to check the spares manifest, then look in the stores themselves. So that you are completely up to date with what we have aboard to help with the repairs when we complete our assessment and the real work can get under way.'

'Yes, Captain.'

'Three – Lucien; not you, Honore. Third Officer Lucien, now I think of it, I would like you to check the lading manifests while these two are checking the spares. The computers

42

in the First Officer's office should be up now that the power is on. First Officer Le Blanc may have had his faults but he kept good records. Everything will be clear and up to date.'

'Until yesterday's emergency, at any rate,' allowed Lucien grudgingly. 'But why, Captain?'

Julie looked out of the clearview at the dark slick smoothing the grey sea. 'That oil we are surrounded with looks awfully light to me. Suspiciously refined. I want to know how much of it is cargo and how much of it is bunkerage. There's no point in having Honore and Raoul fix the motors if all our fuel has gone over the side and we run out of gas the instant the propellers start to turn.'

Lucien opened his mouth to continue the discussion. But just as he did so, a gong sounded. 'That's lunch,' said Julie decisively. 'Grab a bite before you get to work, all of you. Food, Lucien, but no wine, remember. And take it with you to the lading computer. I'll be round in an hour. You can report to me then.'

And, so dismissed, the officers trooped out of their Captain's presence. But they did not go happily or silently. And it was only half in jest that Richard said to Julie, 'Well, now I know what it must have felt like to have sailed aboard the *Bounty.*'

'What?' she spat, swinging round on him.

And, all too late, he realized that there were two ways to take that remark, depending on whether one supposed he was likening the officers to Fletcher Christian and his mutineers – or comparing Julie herself with Captain Bligh.

One glance was enough to tell him that she had taken it in the wrong way, for it had not really occurred to him that, abrupt, angry and stressed though she was, he really thought of her as a sadistic martinet. But catching her eye he was abruptly glad that, after what she had done to the back of his head in the way of nursing and healing, she didn't have a cat-o'-nine-tails handy after all.

Five

Report

No sooner were the mutinously-muttering officers all gone than Julie, continuing to treat Richard's remark with more disdain than it actually deserved, walked past him as though he didn't exist and picked up the internal phone. Looking out along the deck at the worrying slick, she pressed the button marked C – for *cuisine* as it turned out.

'*Oui?*' Richard heard the monosyllable distantly.

'Mr Song? It's Miss Julie here. Whatever you are sending to the bridge watch, send three portions . . .'

'*Oui!*'

'*Merci.*'

That at least was wise enough, thought Richard. Fluster your officers and flatter your crew. Especially your *Chef de Cuisine* – and, he suspected, the Chief Steward too.

'So . . .'

Suddenly, and a little disturbingly, those wide hazel eyes were focussed hard on Richard himself, green and gold flecks glittering, as her outrage over his imprudent remark faded under more important business. And he discovered that he didn't know whether to be flustered or flattered himself.

'What is it that you have brought to me that is so much better than the equipment we originally had aboard? And which is now destroyed at both ends courtesy of my fire and your chopper. What have you brought? Precisely?'

'Precisely? Precisely, I have brought you a state of the art portable communications centre – *just* portable. It is a Hagenuk Marinekommunikation 4000 Series, one kilowatt,

44

HF radio transceiver – covering the ranges from 10kHz to 30MHz. It is fully programmable – and indeed it already has some basic programming in beyond the standard. It will automatically communicate with Heritage Mariner Headquarters and the Crewfinders' offices in London, with Durban and with a seagoing tug called *Sissy,* as well as with the British Antarctic Survey HQ and their ship *Erebus.* I believe it will also communicate with both Crozet Island and the scientific station at Port aux Français on Kerguelen, if it is manned.'

Warming to his subject, Richard continued enthusiastically, 'It works on the detachable front panel, which is an LCD digital display unit because I couldn't carry the PC control terminal that also came with it. It is stand-alone, of course, but will integrate with anything that is left in the Radio Operator's larger system . . .'

She shook her head. 'Nothing left in the shack. No aerial either, come to that, of course.'

'Fine,' Richard continued, 'if there's nothing left of that then it is stand-alone. It is fully compatible with DSC and the Global Maritime Distress and Safety System and OK for the R&TTE Directive, of course. It is SOLAS approved and has its own unique recognition code registered and ready to go. All I have to do is plug it in and we can get started.'

'Get started with what?'

'With calling in some help. You'll need to be quick on your feet. You're between two and three thousand miles from anywhere – except Crozet and Antarctica. And Kerguelen, of course – but we don't want to go there. That's four days hard sailing by any reckoning, and you don't have much more than four days to play with before you run aground on the island and likely as not explode.'

'But perhaps I don't want any help.' Julie's voice was quietly calculating. Just for a moment Richard seemed to see something half hidden beneath her icy Gallic reserve – and the constantly updated anger that he seemed to be generating in her. Something that might make him reassess everything, if he could get some kind of a handle on it. But then it was gone and she was looking at him, wide-eyed and challenging.

It took all his strength to hold his tongue. And once again, he was glad that he did. Whatever retort he might have made would have been derogatory in oh so many ways.

He met her eyes and she saw what he was thinking. And she sat and waited for him. Was she waiting for him to start shouting her down – like Lucien and the others clearly wanted to? Like Giscard and Le Blanc may have done? Or was she waiting for him to catch up? See things through her wide eyes? Work it out for himself?

'You're scared, aren't you?' he said, a little hoarsely, at last. 'No. Not scared. Worried. You think there's something incredibly dangerous going on here and you're hesitant to pull anyone else into it with you.'

Had this been a question rather than a calculating speculation it nevertheless received no reply – beyond the slow lowering of her eyelids. Her lashes were long and chestnut, he noted with disorientating vividness. And they matched the most distracting sprinkling of freckles dusted across her cheekbones and the bridge of her nose.

A shadow fell across them then and Richard looked up to see a tall oriental man looking down upon them both. His face was still, expressionless, almost featureless. An ageless ivory oval cut by a dead-straight, lipless mouth. Short black hair, large black eyes.

A plate was placed soundlessly between them. Spring rolls presented on salad with a bowl of soy between.

'Thank you, Mr Song,' said Julie.

Mr Song vanished, leaving the fragrant food and a slightly disturbing atmosphere. A sensation almost of threat.

'You were saying? I'm *scared*?' She reached for the food, her tone conversational, as though they were socializing at a restaurant in Paris rather than facing the terrible dangers in the Southern Ocean.

That was a phrase he would live to regret, Richard could see. Like Julie's crack about Les Invalides to the engineers Honore and Raoul. He echoed her movement, took a spring roll and continued thoughtfully, 'You are uncertain precisely what is going on aboard but you are worried that it is not accidental. You are hesitant about pumping the inert gas out

46

of certain areas. Why could that be? Because you are worried about putting the oxygen back, perhaps. Which means you think there is something in there that might re-ignite. Re-ignite after thirty-six hours down and cold in some areas – and after twenty-four in all the others. Down and very cold in this atmosphere – especially since you lost your internal power and all that went with it.'

Richard took a speculative bite of the spring roll and was pleasantly surprised. It was packed with meat, not vegetables. What were these called? *Nems*? Yes. *Nems*. Which meant some of the crew at least were not Chinese but Vietnamese or Thai. He thrust the distraction aside and continued speaking.

'And the only thing I can think of that might re-ignite under such conditions is some kind of incendiary device. So, the first thing worrying you is the possibility that you have some kind of sabotage going on here. Sabotage and murder, in fact. OK, let's say you have. Let's say you have sabotage at least. The first question then is this: was the work done some time ago? At your last port of call, perhaps? Or is the saboteur still aboard?'

Richard dipped his *nem*, bit into it and chewed leisurely. Then he continued to speculate feverishly. 'You would prefer to believe that the work was done some time since, because that would mean the deaths of the men killed so far are all almost accidental. Certainly nothing personal or calculated. People being in the wrong place at the wrong time.' He chewed on his *nem* and swallowed. Then dipped it in soy and bit again as he thought carefully.

'If you have a saboteur aboard, however, then the speculation gets far darker far quicker,' he continued. 'Because he may not just be destroying your ship, he may be slaughtering your crew as well. On purpose; *with malice aforethought*, as English law has it. And there is some temptation towards that view, isn't there? It could hardly be just random chance that has killed every experienced officer aboard. The navigating officers with their navigating equipment. The engineers with the motors. Even your Radio Officer burned out alongside his radio equipment.' Another bite, a little more rumination. She sat silently. Her eyes shut; giving nothing away. Abruptly – almost irrelevantly – Richard was struck by how incredibly defensive she actually was. She really was giving nothing away here.

So, once again, he continued. 'The next question, then, is this. Is the sabotage finished? Is the damage sufficient? Are enough people dead? If the devices you suspect are all over the place were put aboard with timers, then have they all gone off? Maybe not, you think – hence your worry about pumping out the inert gas and pumping the oxygen back. Or worse. Is the saboteur still aboard with his work half done, waiting for a chance to finish the job? Whatever that job might be?

'And that brings us to the third question, doesn't it? What was the saboteur's secret job in the first place? You've lost your motors, your communications equipment, your power, light and heat. You're losing oil into the bargain but you've no idea as yet whether it's cargo or fuel; and the difference is likely to be crucial – if you ever get far enough on top of the situation to get your motors started. You've lost your senior officers. You've been left adrift in one of the most dangerous places on earth, coming down upon one of the most formidable rock formations upon the planet. And a volcanic one at that. You have seemingly no real chance of stopping your ship before she collides with Kerguelen and goes up like an atom bomb. Or *Lady Mary* goes up like an atom bomb; and maybe Kerguelen goes up in sympathy like Krakatoa, as I said . . .' He popped the last of the food into his mouth and licked his fingers. She did the same. And still she did not speak.

'But why?' he concluded. 'For what conceivable reason? What in God's name is going on? Logic dictates that if there is a good reason for whatever has been happening then the men most likely to know about it are the senior officers – and they're all dead now. So you're on your own and you don't know who to trust – with the possible exception of yours truly because I've just been dropped into the middle of this as an innocent bystander. So you're going to choose work teams to sit with your watch-keepers and watch the watchers like the Latin proverb says. That will be a start – as long as someone's watching out for you. But you're stuck until you sort it out, aren't you?' He leaned forward, fixing her with his most intent stare.

'And then, even if nothing else major happens – even if you aren't hurt or killed – is four days long enough to find out whatever is actually going on and stop it? Can you possibly discover what is being plotted and who aboard is involved – and end it at the same time as you fix the ship and get her to safety? Or will each step you take towards getting everything back to normal just force the hand of your saboteur if he is still aboard? Which I guess you think he is – because as I said, you've got watchers watching your watchers and you're still wrestling with the sixty-four thousand dollar question: What in God's name will he do if you start calling in the cavalry? Who else will he kill – and what more damage will he do – when he hears they're on their way? Who else will he kill and what more damage will he do if they arrive and start trying to bring you to safety? You have, what, twenty lives left at risk here now? How can you possibly risk gambling with the lives of anyone trying to help rescue you?'

Julie looked up. Her face was so white that her freckles seemed almost shocking. Like speckles of heart's blood. Her eyes were huge. Not just their size – nor the luminosity brought by unshed tears – but the way the pupils had expanded. As though she had just woken, or had taken some powerful drug. Or had fallen utterly in love. And at last, they seemed to be opening her mind to him a little – her mind if not her heart. 'How do you know all this?' she demanded.

'Because I've been there and lived to tell the tale,' answered Richard, with a calculated lightness he was far from feeling. 'What do they say? Been there, done that, got the T-shirt . . . That's why I'm here. This is what I do!'

'Very well, then. If we agree that you have explained my thoughts with some accuracy, what does your T-shirt advise that we do next?'

'You don't need to ask me that,' he answered easily, trusting the continued lightness of his tone to keep pompous paternalism at bay. 'You do your duty as you see fit. Take it one step at a time and keep your eyes open at all times.'

'Even when I'm asleep?'

'Especially when you're asleep.'

'I think I will need to trust your eyes then, will I not?' Her huge eyes fixed on him with the most disturbing intensity.

'You can if you need to,' he answered. The lightness in his tone gave way to an earnestness that made the *basso profundo* rumble of the words hoarse and almost painful.

'*Bon!* Then let us proceed.' Julie sat up suddenly, sparking with almost frenetic energy. 'My first duty is to inspect the ship. And yours is to make sure I survive the experience.'

They began on the navigation bridge with Navigating Cadet Sophie Bois. And, all things considered, it was she who fared best of all. Probably because she was the one who was doing the best job. 'I have brought the log up to date, Captain,' she reported. 'Everything relevant to conditions, course and so forth is recorded here. We have, as you and Captain Mariner estimated, moved about one nautical mile. And see, the anemometer readings persist in showing the wind due west. But our course, according to the GPS update, persists in running north of east – allowing for the inaccuracies, taking relative readings and moving certain measurements 180 degrees from their original setting. It is as though we are turning slowly left.'

Julie grunted and started to check the enthusiastic cadet's observations and calculations.

'Can you say why that is?' asked Richard, intrigued.

'I believe I can, Captain. It is because the rudder has swung hard-over. You see the reading on the helm? We proceed in reverse, therefore the blade of the rudder, hard over as it is, pushes us round across the wind, no matter how persistently it blows . . .'

'Well observed,' said Julie thoughtfully. 'Now that we have some power back, perhaps we should consider trying to reverse the rudder's setting. If we can swing southwards rather than northwards across the wind, then we may, with luck, drift into Resolution Passage rather than on to Kerguelen itself.'

'We will want to bring the helm to midships in any case before we start the motors,' Julie continued as Richard followed her off Sophie's bridge and down towards the cargo-handling areas currently under Lucien's command. 'We wouldn't want to start the propellers and chew the rudder to pieces.'

'That would really screw things up,' punned Richard.

Julie gave a dry bark of laughter – which surprised him. He was used to getting groans rather than guffaws when he exercised his wit.

There was no funny side to Lucien's report, however. 'I understand the lading programmes very well indeed,' he persisted sulkily as the three of them crowded into the First Officer's lading control room. 'It is the First Officer's fault. His records are neither as up to date nor as accurate as you said they would be, Captain . . .'

Richard joined Julie and stood at her shoulder as she frowned into the flickering screen of the lading computer monitor. He saw at a glance that there were ten tanks; all except the first were divided into a centre tank and two wing tanks. The first was simply port and starboard. There were two tanks in permanent ballast, filled with cold water to protect the bridge and the forecastle head – but there were bunkerage tanks aft of the rearmost. Forward of the foremost there was nothing marked, so he assumed that the empty spaces in the forecastle head were storage areas or workshops of some kind.

The other tanks were filled with a standard mixture of dirty oil – mostly refined to some degree and varying between bunker fuel oil, diesel, medium and light fuel oils – with some more volatile gas oil thrown in. Enough to keep a good many simple vehicles and facilities running for some time. More than enough to blow the side off Kerguelen's central volcano if things went from bad to worse.

And, to be fair – which went against the grain – he could see Lucien's problem. One set of figures showed where the parcels of cargo had been assigned and gave the tonnage of each in every tank. Others gave specific gravities, volumes and ullages – measuring the distances between the tops of the cargoes and the decks above. It was these that did not add up. And, abruptly, he realized why.

'The heating coils went down with your power,' he said to Julie. 'Look, the bunker fuel oil in tank three should be at 48 degrees Celsius. Look at it now – not much above body heat. Of course the ullages are way off. And your diesel should be at 16, not 6 – so should most of the rest of it. Boy! Does it need heating up with a vengeance! I think we got the power on just in time to stop the whole lot setting like tarmac.'

Richard never actually finished saying 'tarmac', because there was a sudden, powerful thump of sound. It was more like being punched in the ears than actually hearing anything. Like the report of a large gun being fired nearby.

The bridge phone rang at once and Julie snatched it from its cradle. 'Captain,' she spat.

Sophie's voice answered at once, calmly, still in control of her watch. 'The main deck is on fire, Captain,' she reported.

Six

Heat

Richard and Julie ran fast to the lading office window and stared down the main weather deck. Richard's mind went into overdrive and it was all he could do to keep from yelling orders. The whole deck was awash with heavy dark fumes. Crinkling like curly hair, in little grey waves reflecting the big waves of the Southern Ocean, they swept back from the forecastle head to the foot of the bridge house, threatening to wash up over the window like surf against a cliff. The waves of smoke sat up, as though contained by the safety rails at the edges of the invisible deck, but a second glance made it clear that they were cascading overboard right along the great ship's length. They had to be issuing from the furthest point of the bow, therefore. And pouring out at a disturbingly rapid rate. The question was – were they coming from anywhere else?

'Engine Room?' As she spoke, Julie was clicking icons on the First Officer's slave to the central command computer.

'Yes?' answered Honore's unmistakable depressed drawl from the engine room.

'Can you monitor the temperature schematic for the cargo holds there or can it only be done through the lading records?'

'Through lading.'

'*Merde*. OK. You and Four get to Emergency Station One – the A-Deck corridor, portside door,' she added, glancing over to Richard. 'With your suits and as many more as you can carry, though I know they're really heavy,' she continued. 'And check the air in the tanks. Lucien?' She swung round decisively to face the Third Officer.

'Yes?' he answered uneasily.

'Lucien, I want you to stay here and monitor the temperature schematic on the cargo holds until I send Sophie down to relieve you. Then I want you out with the fire teams. What file is the schematic in? I want to view it from the bridge.'

She clicked out of the engineering icon subset as she spoke and clicked on to cargo. 'If there was any appreciable rise in cargo temperature, all the alarms would be ringing,' she said, almost to herself.

'Well, if it's not a tank fire then it's the chain lockers or the paint store,' observed Richard, assuming with some authority that these too would be in the bow sections, forward of the forward permanent ballast tank, just as they were in the *Prometheus* tankers he had commanded. 'No; wait a minute. There's the carpenter's store down there too, isn't there? You don't have any wood aboard – no handrails in the corridors or teak safety rails on the decks. I've only seen rope so far. So what do you keep down there? Engine spares? A metalwork shop?'

'A metalwork shop. Just the sort of facility we would use to help fix the motors . . . Yes.'

'I'll meet Honore and Raoul at the A-Deck portside door, Emergency Station One, if you agree,' he said. 'You'd better put out a hail for the best fire team you have aboard.'

'Oh, *Grace Dieu!*' she gasped. 'Thank heaven you were here. I would never have thought of that.'

Richard took the ironic response for a 'Yes'.

As he ran down the corridor to the muster station he heard her calling, 'Lucien, get Mr Chow and his team to Emergency Station One, please. I'm going up on to the bridge. Mr Chow and his team . . .'

As Richard reached the A-Deck muster point he saw Sophie hurrying out of the lift and turning towards the lading office door. It looked as though Lucien would be lucky to find the time for a wash and a brush-up before pour out after all, he thought grimly.

Honore and Raoul were at the door almost as soon as Richard was and he stepped into the suit he had worn earlier down in the generator room. This time he was struck by the

54

weight of the thing – possibly because Honore was volubly preoccupied with it too. As Richard's mind half-consciously registered the Third Engineer's complaints to the slightly more cheerful Raoul, he looked anew at the suit he was putting on himself. The fabric – gas-proof and probably flame retardant – was multi-layered, thick and heavy. The boots, straps and belt were by no means light. And there was a pair of big compressed-air tanks on the back, with the regulator and everything else that entailed. And the helmet – strengthened across the skull like a hard hat – had a thick glass plate on the front sealed to the material with metal edging riveted into place.

Raoul checked the air pressure in the tanks and they were ready to go. A square, athletic oriental man arrived, with three intense bantamweight colleagues in tow. It was easy enough to guess who this was.

'Good day, Mr Chow,' said Richard in his rough but fluent Cantonese.

Mr Chow nodded, a perfunctory gesture – but courteous. '*Bonjour*, Captain Mariner,' he answered gently. His voice was surprisingly deep and resonant.

Lucien also arrived and hesitated, glaring at Richard, clearly on the point of telling him to mind his own business – when Julie reappeared. She was clearly having second thoughts about just going immediately to the bridge. Her management instincts were sound, Richard thought. She had the makings of a gifted commander. There was after all a pecking order to establish here. To send them out without an established command structure would simply be bad leadership. And, as she wouldn't be in charge herself, she wanted to wish them luck in person, as likely as not.

'Lucien. You are here. Good. Well done. Get suited up please. You are in charge, naturally.' As if to emphasize Lucien's responsibility she passed him a walkie-talkie as she spoke.

'Of course, Captain. As you wish,' he grated, stuffing the little instrument into a pocket, almost, but not quite, speaking between clenched teeth.

'Excellent. Mr Chow, your team will be under the Third

Officer's command, of course. Captain Mariner and Fourth Engineer Raoul will help. Honore, I need you back in the engine control room and I will be sending Emil down to the lading section of cargo control in engineering. You said the control areas were clear of CO_2?'

Honore grunted an affirmative. She pretended not to notice the pantomime of huffy resignation with which he was pulling off his suit again. She turned to the bald young engineer instead. 'Raoul, I want you particularly to assess any damage to the machine shop and the extra engine parts we stow down there. Report what you find to Lucien at once – or to me upon your return. I will be on the bridge. I will keep a close eye on the cargo temperature from there. And Emil will double-check on the spot.

'Also, I have the First Officer's schematic for conditions in the ancillary sections, so I can warn you of any hot spots in the chain lockers or the paint store. I have checked it already and it looks as though the main seat of the fire is in the machine shop. That is where the temperature is most elevated according to the sensors. So that's where you'll have to start, Lucien. And you'll have to work fast, I'd guess, to stop the paint store going up. As you know, there is no Inert Gas System in the forecastle head – but the smoke is likely to be toxic. If the paint catches fire it certainly will be. Thank God there is a tank full of cold water between it and the first of the cargo tanks.'

'And, *quel horreur*, the flames may burn us, too . . .' said Lucien ironically. 'For we are not protected by cold water.' Then he pulled on his helmet and shouldered through the scrum towards the door. He wrenched it open and stepped out into the waist-high river of smoke that was flowing past.

The rest of them followed suit. A hand on Richard's arm held him back till last.

'Please check,' said Julie, her voice wheezing in the fume-filled corridor, 'for other . . . devices . . . in the lockers and the paint store . . .' As she spoke, she pressed a second walkie-talkie into his hand.

'Especially in the paint store,' said Richard, slipping the little radio into a pocket as he stepped out on to the deck.

The smoke came up to Richard's waist; only occasionally did it puff up as high as his chest. And this was important in the end. Like those ahead of him, he walked with exaggerated care to begin with. His faltering steps were slowed by a combination of things: the weight of the suit, the carpet of fumes, a range of invisible, unexpected deck furniture. The heavy glass faceplate thick enough to bend light, like water could, seemed to put his feet in different places to where he expected them to be.

At last, characteristically running out of patience, Richard switched off his air supply – saving it for later. He pulled his helmet back and allowed it to hang from his shoulders; things improved immediately. The westerly wind brought clear, clean air to his face and only very occasionally did he cough or wheeze. The fumes he was wading through were still thick and oily, but he was able to see through them more clearly now. He took less care, but stumbled less often. He began to catch up with his more careful colleagues. Soon he was in the lead and they too pulled their helmets off and trotted at his heels. Except for Lucien who remained childishly grumpy about the situation and everyone else caught up in it.

The central section of the ship, lying between the two tanks in permanent seawater ballast, was effectively made up of box-shaped tank sections. The forwardmost of these had a rough 'A' shape attached to the front of it, with the point aiming forward, so that there might be a sharp bow instead of a flat wall to push through the water when the ship was in its usual forward motion. This shape, point forward, was the forecastle head. Deck-width at weather-deck level, it sloped inwards and backwards as it fell, to form the cut-water of the bows. Then, below the water-line it ballooned into a bulbous bow section designed to make progress through the water steadier and also to house the forward thrusters. And within the hollow section of the forecastle head there was a deck-deep space divided into two large areas even before the lower – narrower – chain-locker space which held the chains for the great anchors hanging on each side of the prow itself.

These upper spaces were accessed directly from the fore-castle deck by heavy metal trapdoors. The traps were long and sectioned – no mere inspection hatches, but designed to open far enough to allow sizeable pieces of engine and wood-work to be taken in and out. And the steps beneath them were equally wide. On the one side, the trapdoor opened on to one of these steep, broad companionways leading down into the machine room and the triangular machine-part store beyond. On the other, there stood the paint store and the workroom associated with it. In each area, the simple layout was cramped and complicated by the requirements of the anchor winches, though the anchor chains themselves were stored in lockers immediately below, also accessible by smaller trapdoors in the lower decks, which formed the floors of both the machine room and the paint store.

The last piece of deck furniture before the almost trian-gular spade of the forecastle head – both on port and star-board – was the forward fire control point. Here a weatherproof, metal-sided unit stood almost shoulder high – tall enough to be showing above the smoke. These housed a pair of lengthy hoses and the pump mechanism needed to fill them full of cold seawater. Beneath the hose connections stood a range of variously coloured tanks, some designed to mix foam with the water as it was pumped through; others designed to be pulled free and used independently, to pour anything from inert gas to metal powder on burning equip-ment – or into blazing areas.

The fire control points also contained a range of safety equipment as well as phones connected to the forecastle head safety system. These were old-fashioned handsets designed to allow easy communication in emergencies at strategic points in all the areas below. And beside them, fire alarms, extra suits, spare gloves and helmets, torches and so on. It was part of the First Officer's duties to oversee the mainte-nance and upkeep of these – though the actual day-to-day responsibility often got passed down to the junior officers.

As Mr Chow opened the fire point and his team began pulling out the hoses, Richard, Lucien and Raoul continued on; Richard and Raoul pulling their headgear back into place and starting up their compressed air again. The hatchway to the machine room was open. Not open wide, but improperly secured. It should have been waterproof – damn near airtight, thought Richard. It was clearly neither, especially at the extremity closest to the main deck, from which the unrelenting smoke was billowing.

Lucien caught at the half-fastened handles and lifted the heavy metal slab with dangerous anger, slamming it wide almost spitefully. You never knew with fires, thought Richard. Slam that door-section open too quickly like that and you could cause an eruption as you started an oxygen-rich draught that fed the fire. Number Three had been lucky to get away with that.

Lucien looked over the edge with careless irritation. Richard and Raoul craned more gingerly to see inside. The square section of hatchway belched black smoke but remained utterly dark. No flames immediately obvious, thought Richard; but then on the other hand, there was no smoke without fire.

'Are these suits flameproof?' Richard asked.

'Yes,' answered Raoul.

'You want me to take a look down there before we start hosing everything with water?' offered Richard.

Lucien's face resembled something in a fish tank as he looked up, weighing the odds. 'No,' he decided at last. 'It's my responsibility. I'd better go or I'll never hear the last of it.' His voice was gruff; he was clearly adding to his list of grievances the fact that the Captain had found a way of shaming him into doing his job properly in spite of himself.

Richard stooped and began carefully sliding the second and third hatch-sections back, turning a square into an oblong that looked disturbingly like a grave. He glanced across at the trapdoor into the paint locker but that was sealed tight. He'd look in there later as he'd promised Julie. If he got the chance.

'You want a torch, Lucien?' asked Raoul, gesturing to the fire point.

'No. There's one at the foot of the companionway. Or there was the last time I did the First Officer's job for him!'

Lucien gave a twisted grin that looked more like an irritated frown gone wrong as he stepped over the lip of the hole. 'For *La France!*' he said, mockingly. '*La France* and the Little Captain!' And then he was gone.

'He has started calling Captain DuFour the Little Captain,' explained Raoul disapprovingly. 'He calls her that after . . .'

'The Little Corporal, no doubt. That's what they called Napoleon Bonaparte in the days of the Republic – *Le Petit Corporal*. Yes I know.'

'How do you know these things? You are *Rosbif*!' said Raoul, caught between amusement and outrage.

'I may be *Rosbif*,' answered Richard equably. 'But my mother-in-law is *Provençal*.'

'Ah.' Raoul nodded, as though that explained everything. Perhaps even the barbaric but fluent French.

'Not only that,' persisted Richard, feeling it was time to disseminate a little more information, 'but my mother-in-law is also the Little Captain's mother. Truly. Mother and daughter. *Madame* Helen DuFour. *Captaine* Julie DuFour. Consider that, *mon brave*. You may answer to the Little Corporal, but I answer to Madame Bonaparte.'

'*Zut alors!*' Raoul's tone was theatrically awed. Richard was really beginning to warm to the engineer's dry sense of humour.

'*Captaine*,' said Chow's deep voice at Richard's shoulder. 'Is it time to check on the Third Officer? Ship's procedure dictates that he should have called in his first report to the fire point by now. It has been one minute since he went down.' He glanced across at the still, silent black handset hanging in the big metal case. 'It may be that he is still angry enough to continue with his carelessness, but however this might be I cannot deploy my hoses until we know more about the situation *la bas*.'

'You're right, Mr Chow. I'll go down,' decided Richard. 'Hand me one of those torches, would you? The big one with the lanyard. That's the job. And it seems to be working too. Excellent. Now, if Number Three or I haven't called up within three minutes, you had better start hosing.'

'Certainly, *Captaine*.'

Richard stepped carefully over the lip of the hatchway, exercising all the caution that Lucien had disdained in his tantrum. He stared downward for a moment. There was a steep stairway at his feet almost broad enough to grace a modest chateau, except that it had yet more rope for rails instead of banisters. Beyond that, nothing but darkness and smoke. What did the Germans call it? Night and Fog?

He sucked in a lungful of rancid rubber air, switched on the torch and started down. The smoke closed around him with disorientating suddenness, for it was still pouring relentlessly upwards. And it struck him then – as it should have struck him earlier, he knew – that while the lights were on in the rest of the ship, there were no lights at all down here. He took the rope of the railing in his left hand and eased the torch in to his right, flicking its beam on to full.

Shining the powerful golden blade down into the dense smoke below, he went on downward, step after step. Weirdly, the smoke seemed to thin a little then, as though sitting waist-high on the weather deck above meant that it left the air pure to waist-height down here. For the hot, light fumes gathered upwards to the deckhead, leaving the lower air relatively clear, like low cloud obscuring a hilltop.

After twelve steps – his unconscious mind was counting carefully – Richard stepped down on to the deck and flashed the torch around again, trying to orientate himself. Trying to remember where Lucien had said the phone point was. It was shoulder high – he was certain of that – and therefore still invisible, lost within the up-welling fumes. But, with any luck, there would be a light switch just beside it. He let go of the rope railing and reached up with his left hand, trying to feel for a wall where the phone might be hung.

And as Richard stood there, with his arm extended outwards and his torch beam shining straight ahead, Lucien appeared. Like some kind of underground animal following the light, he pounded up, the torch beam pointed towards Richard.

Richard really only saw his legs with any clarity – but as the Third Officer came charging past him, running up the steep companionway, Richard got the overpowering impression that the Frenchman was carrying something – something like a

61

large dustbin. And the bin was belching smoke and flames.

The bin – or whatever it was – was clutched to Lucien's chest in an ungainly bear hug. And it was big. The Third Officer had to tilt his head to see round the top of it and its base kept catching on the pumping knees. It was easily a metre in diameter and the better part of one and a half metres high. It looked like galvanized metal – or it seemed to in the glimpse of it that he actually got.

Richard was simply charged aside, forced back as the desperate man blundered past, but then he swung round and followed him up, already shouting with desperate urgency, 'Chow! Hose him down! *Hose him down at once!*'

Richard's head and shoulders burst up out of the thinning smoke in the hatch, just in time to see Lucien reach the fire control point, still running for all he was worth. Mr Chow had either not heard Richard or had not had time to react to his orders. The hoses hung idly as the men who held them stared, riven with increasing horror.

'Chow!' yelled Richard once again, but his words were lost in another almost silent concussion of sound. What had been a bin belching smoke became a geyser of foaming fire as the oxygen-laden westerly wind got into it at last.

Lucien staggered on forward while Richard, still bellowing, leaped on to the deck behind him and went into a flat run, desperately trying to catch him. Richard was used to crises and his mind was icily calculating the best point to rugby-tackle the running man, so as to bring him down on one side – and let the blazing bin slide free of them – as he ran. He would have made it, too, even weighed down by his suit, had not Raoul pulled a hose across his path and tripped him accidentally just a metre short of his goal. And so Lucien ran on unchecked as Richard stumbled, keeping himself erect only by a tremendous effort of will.

They would never know what was going through Lucien's mind then. Chow was certain that his helmet and faceplate were still in position and the fire was foaming off them – but he was by no means certain and he could certainly see nothing of the face inside. Or so he would report to the Captain's inquiry later.

Raoul was equally certain that the detonation had blown the faceplate open and the flames were burning inside the suit itself. It was even possible – and this was what Richard helped Julie enter into the log and record for Lucien's family at home in Clichy – that the Third Officer realized the danger and did what he did through heroism, not through panic or pain.

But the fact was that Lucien didn't hesitate or deviate; he never even slowed. He charged straight past the fire control point and the crew standing helplessly beside it and he threw himself bodily overboard, still clutching his blazing burden. And Richard, just a whisper more than an arm's length behind him, was lucky not to follow him.

Lucien tumbled once, head-over-heels, spraying whatever was in the bin out into the air – where it flamed with such intensity that not only was his burden burning when he reached the surface of the water, but the man himself was fearsomely ablaze.

Just before he hit the water Lucien's compressed-air tanks exploded as though he had been struck between the shoulders by a mortar bomb.

Burning officer, blazing debris and still-flaming receptacle all splashed down into the water at once, making a great ring of fire on the surface. The waves closed together over Lucien at once. They rose in a great foaming mound above him. And that was the last any of them saw of him as the simple weight of the suit and equipment dragged him immediately down.

But then, beneath the horrified gaze of Richard and all those standing with him, in stead of guttering and dying in the icy Southern Ocean water, the unquenchable flames from the incendiary caught hold of the fumes from the oil slick and began to spread over the sea like wild fire.

Seven

Squall

It was the rain squall that saved them – for the time being,
at least. That's what Richard maintained but there were
others aboard who believed that it was his quick thinking.
And still others who asked 'saved them from what?' – the
cargo was cold, thick and moribund – it needed heating in
any case. The only real danger posed by the burning ocean,
they maintained, was the outside chance that its flames might
ignite the leak at its source – wherever that was.

And, to be fair, it was this fear that was the first to occur
to Richard himself in the instant after the waves ignited
below him and before the heavens opened above. He had to
find some way of containing the floating inferno before it
spread up into whatever tank had been leaking and ignited
the oil inside it like a gargantuan Molotov cocktail.

The first reaction from the fire-fighting team was to turn
their hoses on the rapidly spreading fire. Heavy arcs of water
soared out over the blazing water into the heart of the inferno,
but all they seemed to do was to drive the fire in ever-
widening circles away from the foaming centre. Not only
outward, across the stormy water but inwards towards the
crippled vessel's side.

'Stop!' bellowed Richard in his huge quarterdeck voice.
And mercifully they obeyed.

But then, as though disdaining the order of a mere human,
the Rain God started. Without warning – without even a
rumble of thunder or a more powerful gust in the steady pressure of the westerly, thousands of gallons of precipitation

64

came bludgeoning down on to *Lady Mary*'s deck. In an instant there was water up to Richard's ankles and it seemed that, like the smoke that started this, the roaring downpour would be miraculously contained by the railings along the side of the deck. But no, even as Richard blinked the spray from his eyes he saw the water was cascading down into the sea.

But the simple laws of physics dictated that much of the swirling runoff slid directly down the vessel's black-painted hull. And where the streaming metal vertical of her side met the heaving, blazing horizontal of the ocean, the rushing rainwater pushed the seething flames away. In hardly more than a second, a moat of black water opened up all along *Lady Mary*'s side. 'Hose the scuppers,' bellowed Richard. 'Hose the scuppers all along the side.'

There were no real scuppers, of course. The skin of the deck simply followed a tight curve through 90 degrees to become the skin of the side. The uprights of the rope-topped safety rails marked the point of transition. Those and a steady, rule-straight line where red deck paint became black hull paint.

Chow and the fire crew obeyed at once and added the weight of their hosed water to the deluge – but the fire remained doggedly alight and it soon became clear to Richard that water was never going to be enough. He looked around the streaming deck, his teeth clenched so tightly that his jaws ached, seeking inspiration. And then he saw it. Without a further word he ran to the fire control point and turned the handles of the foam canisters with brutal force. The long snakes of the hoses in the hands of Chow's men and Raoul's team writhed in seeming agony as the combination started coming through. But then the great jets of thin water cascading over the side were replaced by creamy, milk-white foam. And, within a few more moments, the rain-created moat was filling with a low but stable wall of foam, which clung to the metal – even under the force of the rain – and kept the flames at bay.

But Richard did not stay to see his plan work any longer. He was running up the deck as fast as he could, just clear of the safety rail himself, one eye ahead for obstacles, one eye to the side, keeping watch over the spreading fire. There were two breakwaters on the deck, low metal walls shaped like arrow heads pointing towards the bow, designed to control the power of any really big seas that came aboard. The first of these nearly sent him over the side, such was the force of the water streaming out from its length. He actually had to wade through the torrent as though crossing a flooding stream in spate. But even this fell into the old proverb, 'What doesn't kill you makes you stronger', for the lateral power of the flood was slowing down the wind-driven spread of the fire as though some gigantic fire hose was spraying water at a superhuman rate down upon it.

Once Richard got past the obstacle, he found that he was running further and further ahead of the flames. Then, at the second breakwater, he found Julie with the second fire-fighting team. They were pouring foam down on to the water just behind the second torrent, just clear of the wild disturbance the waterfall was making in the ocean's surface.

By the time that the flames themselves arrived, they were greeted by several metres of oil-free water where the slick had simply been emulsified by the concentrated downpour from the breakwater on the deck above. And, behind that, there were several more metres of foam: light enough to be sitting on the surface, thick enough to be piled in a low mound. Steady enough, even under the relentless wind, to hold the fire back and contain it until it finally guttered out.

In the relative stillness after the terrible crisis, Richard looked down at the intrepid young Captain. The downpour eased. The wind faltered. There was something akin to quiet. 'You need help, Captain DuFour,' Richard said, formally; forcefully. 'You need all the help you can get.'

Richard simply did not expect Julie to be so upset at his sensible and well-meant suggestion. Later, when things calmed down, he would suspect that at least part of her re-action was a result of shock. She had just sent a man to a terrible death after all. He had been a man she had apparently not liked; and her orders had contained just a little spite, perhaps, which made it all the worse. And his death had been unimaginably horrible. A death, moreover, that had very nearly resulted in a similar fiery – almost volcanic – fate for the rest of them.

And who knew what other demons lay in Julie's past that were being exorcized by her dogged independence now? A broken family, certainly. A bitterly lonely adolescence after a seemingly fairytale childhood. A beloved mother suddenly missing – and a hated stepmother stealing her father's indulgent attention into the bargain. A comprehensively spoilt only child, who, at a stroke, seemed to have become a kind of a social handicap – something to be sent away and forgotten, even by the father at whose side she had stayed at her own insistence, imperiously stated to the divorce court judge himself. A father whose errant attention she had tried to catch again with a dazzling career at a distant boarding school, a far-removed residential college and in the globally wandering merchant marine – Charles DuFour's family trade, just as it was Richard Mariner's.

That sad background Richard did know about at least, courtesy of Robin, his wife – and her conversations with her own stepmother, Julie's conscience-stricken, divorced, re-married, all too absent birth-mother Helen DuFour. He knew of it, though it simply didn't occur to him to include any of it in his suggestion that she ask for help now, at once. And consequently, her reaction took him aback. Caught utterly off guard, he was put in mind for an instant of those awful Parisian women during the Reign of Terror, who sat knitting at the foot of the guillotine stridently calling for the heads of more *Aristos* to fall.

'Help?' spat Captain DuFour. 'Why do we need help, Captain Mariner?' Her face glared up at him, aglow with sudden outrage, running with rain as though she had been crying hysterically. Her eyes burned, their black pupils huge in the overcast. As though he had proposed something shocking and obscene rather than obvious and sensible.

'Have we not restored power?' she demanded fiercely, hoarsely. 'Have we not put all of our navigating equipment back on line? Have we not regained control of the cargo?' She gestured across the hose-coiled deck, away over the foam-walled, smoking ocean. 'Have we not overcome yet another crisis without allowing it to become a catastrophe?

'We do not need aid from any quarter,' she continued, almost jeeringly. 'We need to complete the inspection of my command. We need to bring the engineering areas under the same control as the navigation and cargo-handling areas and we need to come back under way. What is it you English say? Under our own steam? Yes indeed. We need to do this *under our own steam*!'

'But the radio, Captain. You are still out of communication . . .'

'Yes indeed. At least partly due to your chopper beheading my radio mast. *Enfin!* I will only need to communicate when I wish to report that we are under way and safely back on course! This is all I wish to say to anyone. And when it has been achieved, we may unpack your precious Hagenuk Marinekommunikation 4000 Series radio transceiver, and announce it to the entire pre-programmed world!'

Julie turned on her heel and marched briskly towards the bridge. The gale patted Richard on the back hard enough to make him stagger. Though, as another English saying goes, he thought wryly, you could have knocked him down with a feather.

Another squall came pelting on to his shoulders and the deck parties all around him began to pack their equipment away. It Richard stirred himself into action as well. For everyone at this end of the deck must have heard the stormy exchange. And reports of it would have spread through the ship by pour out with the same alacrity with which the fire had spread out from the meteorically-falling Lucien just now. As he moved, he unconsciously began to hum a half-forgotten melody, mangling some words deep in his head as he did so.

> Ah! Ça ira, ça ira, ça ira!
> Les aristocrates à la lanterne.
> Ah! Ça ira, ça ira, ça ira!
> Les aristocrates on les pendra . . .

The battle hymn of the Republic; French Republic, 1789 style.

It was, perhaps, typical of Richard that, in spite of his revolutionary considerations, and the dark thoughts generated by a lively sense both of frustration and embarrassment, it did not really occur to him at that moment that the gossiping crew might split into two increasingly fractious camps. One remaining faithful to their trenchant but misguided Captain; the other group inclining to Richard's own more practical and sensible course.

And, for all their talking and speculation it didn't really strike home to either of the Captains that there really might be someone still aboard who would use the situation and the uncertainty – and the increasing desperate tension – to further their secret, murderously destructive schemes.

Richard's first port of call in the bridge house was the Captain's cabin. That was where his kit – what there was of it – still seemed to be. That was the logical place to remove his wet gear and, perhaps, adjust his sweat-soaked overalls before reporting to the navigating bridge.

And that was where he found Julie doing the same.

Richard walked in without thinking and found her standing in the centre of the cabin angrily stripping off the vivid wet-weather jacket. The zipper had obviously stuck – or impatience had got the better of her – because she was pulling it over her head like a cagoule. Like everyone else aboard he had met so far – except for the late Captain Giscard and the enigmatic Mr Song – she was wearing white overalls. But her exertions had pulled the buttons wide all the way down to the tightly secured belt, and the damp cotton gaped now, revealing extremely well-filled white lace underwear so sheer that it showed more than a hint of pink and rose.

Richard turned at once to exit but his oxygen canisters thumped against the door frame and somehow jammed in place. The yellow top was hurled aside. Its owner emerged, tousle-haired, red-cheeked. Her face was still wet, too, he noticed as he turned round, as though the squall had followed her in here.

'Yes?' she demanded, as though the thumping of his air tanks had been a courteous knock at the door.

'I've come up to change,' said Richard. 'I didn't realize there would be anyone else in here.'

'That's OK. Come in.'

If she was unduly discommoded by the exhibition of her underthings and a good deal of what lay under them, she chose not to show it. On the contrary, she leaned forward and began to wrestle her hips out of the wet-weather trousers. Square, solid hips that belied the unfashionable, wasp-like narrowness of her waist.

'I was going to get my kit off,' he said, still hesitating. 'My stuff's still in here. I thought you wanted to go down . . . go down into the engineering sections. I'll need a change of suit and fresh tanks if I'm going to come and watch your back.'

'Very well. Come in. I will help.'

It occurred to him at once that she might be trying to make amends here. To get him back on side after her earlier outburst, which might well have come as a surprise to her as well as to him. Getting as close to an apology as a tyro Captain in her situation might dare to come, under the circumstances.

As Richard finally accepted Julie's brusque invitation, she booted the pile of streaming yellow clothing past him. It slid into place beside by the door as though placed there with care and consideration for the steward to collect and take care of. The energy expended on the brutal disrobing seemed to have calmed her a little, though the wrestling bout needed to rid her of the trousers seemed to have pulled the rest of her buttons wide. From collar to gusset only her belt stayed tightly secured.

A lesser man might have dwelt upon the vividly intimate revelation that she wore a very chic all-in-one white lace teddy that clung like a second, gossamer, skin and failed almost entirely to protect her modesty. Richard focussed his bright gaze carefully upon her wide hazel eyes and tried to disregard all the rest.

Certainly, her look and her tone were much less likely now to make him think of *La Revolution* and *Madame Guillotine*, though the 'Ca Ira!' still lingered somewhere just below his conscious mind as he marched into the centre of the room.

'Turn around,' she ordered, and he obeyed willingly enough. She used the next few moments to loosen his tanks and fasten her buttons alike. 'Yes,' she said conversationally. 'This would all be useless for the time being in any case. The tanks are empty and the suit itself is torn. How did you manage that? Ah. It is the seam that has split. I see . . .' She pulled the straps off his shoulders and set the compressed-air tanks aside.

'I tried to tackle Lucien,' he explained, 'but I tripped over Raoul's hose and that was that, I'm afraid. I might have saved him I suppose, but it would have been a long shot. I'm so sorry.'

'Thank you for the attempt, at least,' she said, her voice quiet and dead. 'It was brave. You were lucky the only damage done was to the seams on your suit.' Then she began to pull the suit-top back off as well, as he unfastened it at the front. 'But fortunately under the circumstances, we have plenty more such suits to spare,' she continued, easing the whole thing down until it settled towards his ankles. Then, quite abruptly, she crossed in front of him and squatted there to help him out of the all-in-one foot sections. And he realized the state of his overall buttons was scarcely any better than hers had been. Thank God for our belts, he thought.

'Our only problem,' she concluded, squinting up at him, 'will be size.'

'That was the largest size we have,' said Third Engineer Honore lugubriously, his watery eyes gleaming in the newly-restored light of the upper engineering deck like those of a beaten spaniel.

'But we have several more in that size,' added Raoul more enthusiastically. 'Get one from the store, Antoine.'

The engineering cadet shrugged, nodded, twirled the toothpick from one side of his mouth to the other and lounged off obediently.

It was half an hour later and Julie was doggedly continuing the inspection of her command. Continuing, as she had said, with the engine room. But the engine room, of course, was still flooded with deadly CO_2 from the inert gas fire-fighting equipment; so she and Richard had stopped off here to get suited up again before they went on down.

'And tanks?' Julie asked as Antoine vanished to get Richard's new suit.

'Now that we have power, we have the compressor back,' answered Raoul breezily. 'But after your inspection, Captain, I expect we'll be pumping out the areas flooded by the IG System, so they'll be excess to requirement in any case. Except for emergency use.'

Antoine returned with Richard's second suit, as though bringing the latest men's fashion across the showroom at Yves St Laurent. He had brought one for Julie too and as the conversation continued so they began to put them on. Antoine, coolly accommodating as if clearly doing them all a favour, went off for the compressed-air bottles, which continued to be the subject of conversation.

'Just so long as you keep them primed and ready,' answered Julie, unimpressed by Raoul's sudden access of youthful enthusiasm. She began to climb into her suit legs, easing her feet into the foot sections – and Richard followed her lead. 'The whole point about an emergency is that you never know when to expect one,' she continued.

'Indeed . . .' said Raoul. He slid a thoughtful palm across his bald head, frowning. Apparently, he had never considered this. A dangerous thing in an engineer, thought Richard, pulling the leggings into place.

'So you must always be ready to meet one,' Julie persisted as though talking to a backward child as she shrugged her shoulders into the suit and started to secure the airtight front. She did this very carefully and Richard wondered whether he was the only one to discern the slightest trembling in her long, pale fingers.

'Absolutely,' agreed Raoul. 'Like the perfect lay. You never know when she'll arrive so you must always be ready for her, eh?' He twitched his hips suggestively and leered across at Honore, upon whom he was clearly used to exercising his wit.

'The perfect *lay*?' enquired the Captain, her voice as honeyed as the purr of a hungry tiger.

Raoul realized that he had, in some way too obscure for him to understand, put a foot wrong here. He gaped, looking a little like a landed fish. He massaged his shining scalp.

Antoine arrived at that moment with the compressed-air sets and spared his boss's blushes. 'I have brought a double for our guest, just like the one he wore earlier, and another for the Captain,' he announced. 'One of the smaller ones . . .'

Julie took the single compressed-air bottle in place of Richard's massive twin-set. 'It is at full pressure,' Honore assured her as he helped her shrug it on. He showed her the reading on the regulator gauge as though certain she would doubt his word. 'As long as you complete your inspection of the engine room in less than fifty minutes, you should be fine.'

'Then we can get the pumps started,' repeated Raoul ebulliently, apparently having forgotten his faux pas, heaving the big bottles up on to Richard's back. 'And get this stuff back in the stores where it belongs.'

'Indeed,' agreed Honore gloomily. 'That's when we'll really start breaking our backs with heavy labour. You can't imagine how hard the work will become young Antoine. Or even you, Raoul. But I've seen it and I know what I'm talking about! Once the engine room is pumped out, I tell you, it'll make *Papillon* look like Perpignan. Devil's Island look like Deauville . . .'

'One step at a time,' riposted Julie with the slightest hint of unease in her voice – enough to make Richard at least think that Honore's dark suspicions might just be well grounded after all. 'We have to check the engine room first.' She pulled her headpiece into place and began the noisy process of settling it safely and securely.

So that she probably didn't hear – but Richard, a second or so slower than she was, did hear – Honore observe with a spluttering hiss of spiteful fierceness, 'Yes! That's our best hope after all. That the Little Captain joins that old sodomite slave-driver Captain Giscard and stays down in the engine room frozen like a statue at Maison Rodin out of sight and out of mind for the rest of the voyage!'

Eight

Air

The last piece of kit that Antoine fetched for them both was a clean-air monitor. These devices were about the size of a mobile phone and were hand-held though secured to their wrists with lanyards. At first, Richard supposed they must be hand-held radios, short-range versions of the bulkier walkie-talkies they had carried to the fire in the forecastle head. He had discovered during that adventure – and the earlier restoration of power – that the suits had no built-in communication.

'We can shout to each other down there,' called Julie. 'It will be quiet enough, God knows, until we turn on the pumps. But these little devices may well keep us alive. They will at least allow us to monitor the air.'

Richard looked at the devices with suddenly clearer eyes. They looked like old-fashioned cellphones, with a sizeable LCD screen above an array of buttons. But they were not, in fact, communication devices at all. They were poison gas monitors. The display on their screens was designed to give an accurate reading of the state of the air through which they were passing; with particular regard to the two crucial areas of oxygen content and breathability.

On the one hand, danger signals would flash if there was too little oxygen in the immediate atmosphere to sustain life. On the other hand, danger signals would flash if there was sufficient oxygen to sustain life – but it was accompanied by dangerous amounts of toxic gasses. Thus the alarms would flash – and sound – in the CO_2 atmosphere pumped out by the IG System. They would also sound if there were appreciable amounts of CO – the odourless, tasteless, deadly carbon monoxide which seeped from improperly vented gas systems and hung around at the sites of fires. Or, indeed, if any other dangerous gas was present.

Julie went on ahead, hunched over her monitor, checking its settings carefully. Richard followed close behind her, deep in thought, leaving Raoul and Honore to suit up with the help of the capable Antoine. It was a crucial part of Julie's plan that the two Captains try and discover what had gone wrong in the engine room, Richard realized, but as Honore had lugubriously observed it would be down to the engineers to put it right.

The Captain had to be fully aware of the situation down here because she needed to schedule the work – especially as it needed careful preparation. Such as pumping out the inert gas from the fire-fighting system. Such as reassigning and detailing – briefing and training if need be – some of Leading Seaman Chow's and maybe even Mr Song's GP seamen. And over and above this, Julie was on the lookout for signs of sabotage. Precisely what she was expecting to find – or why – lay at the outer edges of Richard's speculation at this moment. And, indeed, Richard could see all too clearly that there had been fires. Fatal accidents. A ship left incapacitated, powerless, incommunicado, helplessly adrift in dangerous waters. These things were self-evident. But secret plots? Sabotage? Murder? Only time would tell – but time was the one commodity they had precious little of.

These thoughts were more than enough to bring Richard and Julie to the top of the first great flight of steps. Here they hesitated, putting their headgear in place, checking airtight seals and double-checking regulators and air-pressure gauges. Chanting the routine to each other as though buddying-up for a deep-sea dive. When Julie's face was the palest glimmer, like the side of a white fish behind the thick glass in the aquarium of her headgear, she nodded.

'Let's go,' she said. Her voice was muffled but clear enough for Richard to detect a tremor that matched the trembling of her fingers earlier. He did not think less of her because she was afraid. On the contrary – it was all the more impressive that she was sticking to her duty in the face of her nervousness. Especially as she so firmly believed that she had so much to be nervous about.

But to be fair, in situations such as this, fear was good. Fear was what made you double-check, then check again. Fear was what kept you careful – and care was what kept you alive. Had Captain Giscard or his Chief Engineer been nervous enough to suit up before going into the generator room, they would have been fine when the IG System kicked in, and their men along with them, as likely as not.

As Richard adjusted his clean-air monitor so that it hung clear of his thickly-gloved hands and the rungs they were uneasily grasping, and swung himself out on to the ladder above Julie and began to follow her downwards, his heart was lightened then burdened again almost at once. He was relieved to see once more the clever little airlock Honore and Raoul had made outside the door of the generator room. But no sooner did that testament to their ingenuity and ability register than he caught sight of the pile of corpses all too neatly arranged outside it. Testament to what? A faulty set of priorities in the face of the disaster after all?

Or, perhaps, to an overpowering need to get at the dead men – and the contents of their pockets – before anyone else could. The thought was as sudden as it was decidedly paranoid. But, under the circumstances, the paranoid course seemed safest. According to the old saying, a paranoid is only someone who knows what is *really* going on. Which thought put him firmly back in Julie's company again. Thus he rejoined her mentally, just as he caught up with her physically once more.

At the foot of the steps Julie hesitated and Richard stood beside her. She looked across at the airlock. 'That was a good piece of work,' he observed.

'Yes. But Cadet Antoine designed it.'

'Still, Honore and Raoul did well to build it.'

'Yes . . .' There was uncertainty in her voice. Something else she knew but he didn't as yet. Another source of paranoia?

The ladders beside them began to tremble, giving off an almost bell-like sound. Richard glanced up. Honore and Raoul were on their way down. Confident in their own work – over-confident, perhaps – they had not yet bothered to put on their headsets. Both of the Captains, careful to protect even unreliable and second-rate crew members, checked their monitors to make sure it was safe to be down here without breathing apparatus on.

It seemed that the engineers' pointed confidence in their work was well-placed. But Richard frowned, looking around the cavernous room and down through the heavy mesh grille of the floor. The generator room had been opened and closed Heaven knew how many times recently. And each time it had, an airlock full of CO_2 – maybe ten cubic metres each time – had gone somewhere. The inert gas was denser than air – so it had gone downwards.

Richard looked at his feet, lost in thought once more. It seeped, flowed and penetrated even more effectively than water. It gathered into puddles – lakes, even – that you didn't know existed until it was far too late. And it was all beneath their feet somewhere – filling the lower areas like rivers in subterranean caves ready to trap unwary potholers. Perhaps it had seeped right to the bottom of the double-hull, down in the propeller shafts or the bilges. Perhaps it had stopped and collected somewhere higher on the way, pouring silently through conduits and airshafts to fill apparently safe rooms and areas with invisible odourless death. Perhaps it had joined the inert gas already filling the main engine area. Perhaps it was lurking somewhere else, just waiting: undetected, unsuspected.

Richard had not slept properly for more than one hundred hours now. He had travelled more than ten thousand miles – much of the journey in cramped and stressful conditions. He had been concussed not once but twice, been subjected to Julie's peculiar brand of nursing and been within inches of a human volcano and had seen the Southern Ocean catch fire. No wonder his mind was wandering a little. Only action, indeed, was likely to keep him focussed. Action or the strongest black coffee they had aboard.

Julie turned away from the ladder-foot and walked confidently across the open area past the pile of dead men. Richard followed her, keeping one eye on the clean-air monitor. The last time he had used anything like this, he had been trapped aboard a Russian submarine, and the machine in his hand had been a Geiger counter searching for pathogens that had been different but no more obvious and no less deadly. Radiation or gas – if it killed you it killed you and that was that. The trick was to stop it doing so.

The area they were crossing so purposefully opened out into a gallery edged with a safety rail like the circle in a theatre. But instead of looking down on lower circles, stalls and stage, this gallery looked down a hole that was three full decks deep. The main engines sat down here, surrounded by all the equipment and ancillary machinery to bring them to life, to keep them working and to employ their massive power.

Richard crossed to where Julie was standing and joined her, resting his hands on the top of the metal safety rail, thinking inconsequentially that it was a relief to find that it was not cheap rope like all the safety rails on deck. The spectacle below him made him catch his breath – as it always did. It made him forget the rope rails above, the rancid rubber taste that the compressed air was bringing to the back of his tongue, the dryness it was bringing to his mouth and throat, and even the steady heartbeat throbbing in his head.

Unlike most tankers, which satisfied themselves with one huge steam turbine geared down to power one propeller shaft and turn one variable pitch propeller, the *Prometheus* series had two. A pair of Rolls Royce turbines, powerful enough to make Concorde fly faster than sound, sat bedded in the engine room, as dead as a pair of mummies in the British Museum. Each one was geared through several individual reduction gears – each individually housed – to turn an individual shaft and each shaft turned a propeller. The idea was – making assurance double-sure, but at a price in operating costs which was sometimes crippling – that if one motor failed, the other would still allow ship-handling. There were bow thrusters and side thrusters that complemented the rudder settings so that *Lady Mary* would sail straight and true with one engine or the other. With both motors on line and everything up to spec, she was among the fastest and most manoeuvrable tankers afloat. Just as her double-skinned hull and double-bottomed tanks made her one of the safest. Under normal circumstances at least.

Julie was no doubt banking on this – as she could do with some confidence. All things being equal, this system would get her out of trouble yet – and stand by her in the meantime. As the pair of them stood on the gallery looking down, so the engineers joined them. Julie glanced up and saw that their head-sections were still arrogantly back. She still said nothing, but crossed to a gate in the gallery's safety rail and opened it. The gate stood at the top of a flight of steps soaring downwards to the lower galleries; and then right down to the floor of the engine room itself.

Somewhere down that flight of steps, Richard knew, they would pass out of air and into CO_2, as though walking down into a strange sort of swimming pool. The change would be imperceptible – even to Honore and Raoul if they did not adjust their safety gear. Imperceptible, that is, until they became short of breath and dizzy. Until they started to experience chest pains. Then it would rest with Lady Luck as to whether they could turn round and climb back up into clean air before they fainted, fell and died choking like Captain Giscard. Julie stepped out and began to descend. Richard followed her. They had reached the limit of their bravado at last; Honore and Raoul put on their headsets and started going through the diving-routine checks that the two captains had done one deck up and a long time back.

The steps were not as sheer as the ladder down to the generator room. It was possible to walk down them as though they were steep, skeletal stairs so Julie and Richard faced forwards as they descended, looking out at the motors for the first flight, then in at the gallery wall. The walls were festooned with winches, chains and maintenance equipment. They were hung with the multicoloured cylinders of fire-fighting equipment, below which sat trolleys also laden with the larger cylinders – water and foam, powder and so forth.

Then the final flight faced the motors again – the pair of sleeping monsters hulking high above the heads of anyone descending to the deck of the engine room itself. Each one seemingly the size of a house when you got close up beside them. And, as they needed to be closely inspected in the normal run of things, the sides of the motors were covered with what appeared to be permanent scaffolding – stairs, ladders, metal-floored levels, all allowing the crew to climb up and down them, checking gauges, monitors and LCD displays. Much like the companionways that hung on the outer walls of the bridge house high above.

But neither Richard nor Julie was running down the steps from one level to the next, even to encounter such wonders as these. They would have been moving slowly and carefully even had the air been breathable. As things were, of course, they moved with even more care and caution. They had stepped down less than five of the first flight of twenty when their clean-air alarms began to sound. With the image of a swimming pool still strangely in his head, Richard stood for an instant, at the very level that it happened. Hesitating as though he could discern the CO_2 lapping at his chest, raising and lowering the monitor, watching it switch from green SAFE to red DANGER within the sweep of his arm.

And that too suddenly told Richard something. Either the French had refitted the IG System with a new – and very clever – internal monitor or – more likely – they had simply calculated the cubic capacity of the area that had to be flooded with CO_2 to make the engines themselves safe. And if that were the case, of course, then all the CO_2 available to keep things under control down here was washing invisibly around them now. And once it was pumped away, there was no more left to fight a second fire – should another one break out. Not until the engines had been running for long enough to fill the CO_2 reservoirs with a vital part of their waste once more. And that would take some time. Which in turn explained Julie's painstaking care; her desire to check in as much detail as she could before she gave the potentially fatal order. To pump fire-generating, flame-supporting, potentially explosive oxygen back in here – even in the relatively low concentrations found in ordinary air.

With these thoughts sitting darkly at the back of his mind, Richard pulled himself into motion again. Julie was now on the second gallery down, turning to face inwards for her next descent. Richard joined her.

'You've a range of fire-fighting equipment in here above and beyond your IG System,' he reminded her. 'The only class of fire you're not really equipped for immediately on this level alone is Class A and that's because Class A fires involve paper, wood, textiles and so forth – such as you get in the main accommodation areas.

'But you've got a range of pretty blue powder-based extinguishers that will handle Classes B, C and even D, with care. Yes. Class D – those are metal powder extinguishers there. You've got big cream and red foam and water-based extinguishers on the trolleys over there – though you'd have to keep water well clear of your electrics, of course. More useful on deck I admit, but even so . . . And you have the BCF stuff there too. All those green canisters in that corner. It might be a good idea to keep a pretty active engine room watch as you pump out the CO_2, with all that kit ready to hand in case anything does flare up again.'

Honore and Raoul joined them then – it was an inspection of their area after all: it was they who were expected to take the lead and make the report.

'Class D fire?' challenged Honore at once. 'That's burning metals, isn't it? Magnesium and so forth? Sodium? We don't have anything like that down here, Captain. Are you sure you have your classes and colours correct?'

Richard shrugged and let it slide. He glanced across at Julie, wondering whether she had understood the point he was making any more clearly. He wondered how close any of them had actually come to the devices Julie feared might be down here. How close in *fact*, rather than in speculation? He himself had been near enough to Lucien and his final, fatal burden to see it pretty clearly: see it, feel it, smell it. Richard knew perfectly well what all the classes of fire were – and what you needed to fight each one of them, from a

81

safe distance or up close. And there was no doubt at all in his mind what class of a fire that had been.

Class A fires were domestic. Class B were more serious – involving fat, paint, oil; substances more likely to be solid than liquid at room temperature. Class C fires were those involving gasses, including the kinds of gasses oil, kerosene and petrol all gave off. And, as Honore had said, Class D fires involved burning or exploding metals. Class D fires were the sort of fires you might expect to find when incendiary bombs went off. And, coming full circle, of course, he could see Julie's original suspicion.

If there were certain types of chemically generated incendiaries down here, the CO_2 might have put her crew to sleep, but it would not have killed them outright. And when she pumped it out, then fresh air would arrive like Prince Charming come to kiss Snow White. Only the bright-blue fire extinguishers would contain them once air got in down here. The kind that pumped out metal powder to set in solid blisters like solder over the flames and cut off the oxygen that way.

But that was in the future. The far distant, still speculative future. And, looking at the mess on the deck and all over the motors themselves, some of it was in the recent past, of course. Of immediate importance was the tour of inspection through which Honore and Raoul were beginning to guide Julie. Whatever routine she chose to follow was going to be complicated by the mess and wreckage left after the fire itself, he thought.

If the bizarre circumstances were leading the engineers to take this less seriously than they would have taken a full routine inspection from Captain Giscard, Captain Julie clearly had no such ideas. In fact it was the contrary. At the foot of the lowest staircase there hung several sizeable clipboards, each holding several sheets of closely word-processed information, liberally larded with tick boxes.

'Let's do this the quick way,' decided the Captain. She took two down and handed one to Richard. 'Quick, but full and detailed. Honore, you and I will take motor number one. Raoul, you will take Captain Mariner through full inspection of number two. Is your technical French up to it, Richard?'

'Better than my conversational,' Richard answered automatically, taking the clipboard and scanning the familiar terms with increasing confidence, without really registering that she had used his Christian name for the first time in their brief but stormy acquaintance. *'Raoul, en avant!'*

They began to pick their way across the debris-strewn decking towards their goal. Once again, thought Richard, Honore was in the right. There would be a great deal of back-breaking housework to be done in here before they tried to bring the motors back on line. If that could even be done.

Richard almost immediately saw that Julie's calculations also seemed to be absolutely bang on the mark. The routine inspection, each item covered by the ticking of a box on the paper, covered every nook and cranny of the motor, the equipment and the areas ancillary to it: from the fuel lines and power cables coming in, to the casings and the areas accessible only up the steps and ladders festooning the sleeping giants themselves, to the individual reduction gear housings that led back and – eventually – below. Step by step he followed the detailed inspection forms through, missing only those sections that assumed the motors must be in motion, the gears revolving, the propeller-shaft turning. Adding extra – and making careful notes – when he saw evidence of damage: through fire, mechanical breakdown, other causes. He only paused to move the debris of the fire-fight in order to get closer to the check-list items on the deck. It was hard work from the outset and more time-consuming than he had thought.

It was the vague but vital 'Anything Else of Importance to Note' list that was the trickiest, of course. That absorbed more and more time, demanded more and more attention. Beside the fire-damage on the turbine casing there – the almost surreal swirl of smoke effects and flame-sear – was that blast damage? Could some kind of bomb have done that? Richard went closer still to look at the extravagant sweep of black and red – enough to flatter the most talented graffiti artist.

If it was blast damage, he wondered, pencil hovering, had the blast been caused by natural means – say an oil container

83

exploding or a particularly violent fire-fighting method? If it was bomb damage, then was there anything remaining of the device that must have caused it? If, on the other hand, it was something caused by fire-fighting, then where was the equipment that had done the damage? Much of it, seemingly, neatly restored to the trolleys and walls before the IG was switched on. Could the equipment responsible for these marks have been put back with all the rest? That was at least a possibility, for the IG equipment had been properly deployed down here – there were no bodies grotesquely frozen as there had been in the generator room. Everyone injured or killed down here was up in the ship's infirmary-cum-morgue or over in the care of the British Antarctic Survey's medical facilities. But of course, whispered his exhausted, paranoid mind, if there had been time to clear away the equipment with which they tried to control the fire, perhaps there had been time to clear away the most suspicious of the things that had caused it in the first place.

But still, wondered Richard, proceeding with his eyes as sharp as could be, what could have made those dents on this reduction gear housing? It looked like bomb damage sure enough. Or had something simply dropped from that cradle overhead? The chains hung empty and the deck was liberally strewn with smashed machinery. Something powerful might have detonated beside the gear housing – or something heavy might have dropped upon it. There were two suspicious bits of damage so far, therefore. A third would make his mind up for him. What was it James Bond used to say? 'Once is happenstance, twice is coincidence, three times is enemy action . . .'

'Raoul, were you anywhere near here when the fire was burning?'

'But of course, Captain. I was in the thick of things.'

'Did you observe what happened to this gear housing? It looks as though something fell on it . . .'

'No, Captain. As I am sure you can envisage, it was madness down here. The smoke . . . The noise . . . We were in suits such as these, of course. For much of the time the emergency klaxon was sounding and that made communi-

84

cation impossible even for those of us with radios. The air pumps were on full, of course, venting the fumes. I was here, but I could not swear to having seen anything other than smoke and flame . . .'

Richard nodded. He had been in enough tanker fires to sympathize with Raoul's vivid description. Only a detailed forensic inspection would tell for certain how the damage to the engine mounting and the gear housing had been caused. Whatever; it had done its work too well. Unless this whole thing was rebuilt, the motor he was inspecting would remain useless. Only Julie's suspicions made it worthwhile continuing with the inspection down past the next gear.

Providentially, it was at that point in his utter absorption with the task in hand that he looked up. He was on the point of leaving the open area and going into a much more restricted one – well out of sight of the others. It was all very well to do this with Raoul at his side, but it was Julie who was his diving partner – and his Captain. He glanced across at her, expecting simply to catch her eye and signal his intention to proceed.

But at the very second that Richard looked up, he saw several things – each one worse than the last. He saw that, while he had been studying the damage to the gear housing once more, Raoul had wandered away to chat with Honore. He saw that the engineers had both gone over to the far side of the engine room to study something that he couldn't quite make out, leaving Julie and he unattended. She, like her near namesake Juliet, was stood on a balcony. But this balcony was as far as possible from Shakespeare's Verona, halfway up the number one motor.

And then, as Richard pulled in a breath to call the pair of them back to their posts, Honore's distant arm moved and an emergency klaxon filled the echoing area with its deafening, disorientating howling. Just as Julie, alone and out of communication, dropped her clipboard and sank to her knees, regulator pressed to the glass by her wildly staring eyes, left hand to her choking throat. As though the klaxon's overwhelming howl of sound was warning the world that she had suddenly run out of air.

Nine

Kiss

Richard dropped his clipboard and began to run towards the stricken woman. At once he began cursing the restrictive suit and the bulky tanks that made accuracy of movement as difficult as speed. He needed all his attention to pick the swiftest route through the wreckage on the deck, especially as the sound of the klaxon seemed to punch his ears with enough force to upset his balance as he ran. And yet his mind kept leaping ahead, using these few precious moments to get some kind of a plan cobbled together. He knew the worst thing of all to do would be to arrive at her side and stop there wondering what action to take next.

Had they actually been deep-sea divers, he would have chummed up with his own tanks, swapping mouthpieces with her and feeding her his own air. But that would be impossible with the ungainly headsets stubbornly attached to the rest of the suits as they were. Nor did he know enough about the system to get the tanks off his own back and re-attach them to her breathing system. Frankly, he doubted that Raoul or Honore would know how to do it fast enough either. Had the capable young cadet, Antoine, been here, it might have been worth the risk. But of course he wasn't.

So, decided Richard, halfway across the rubble-strewn space between the motors, he was going to have to carry her up to safety himself. Up two and a half flights of stairs. God! If only he had marked the point that the heavy CO_2 took over from the upper air. Then at least he could see the surface of this deadly pool of gas. Better get her up to the generator room level, just to be certain.

If he could manage it before she was fatally damaged.

A spike of agony rammed through his own chest. If he could manage it at all, he thought. With the weight of his own suit and equipment combined with the weight of hers, the added load of her own slight frame was likely to prove the easiest of the burdens. He glanced at his regulator. Pressure seemed fine. He tripped, stumbled, nearly fell. He shouted at himself but didn't hear a word of it because of the howling of the klaxon.

He suddenly remembered the lifts. They would be full of inert gas if they were on this level of course, but with the power on they should be functioning. Getting Julie into a lift and taking her up three levels might well be quicker than trying to carry her up stairs. Like the diving suit it basically resembled, their suits were not designed for great exertion or rapid breathing. Another stab of agony pierced his heaving chest and he really started to be concerned about the air-pressure in his own tanks. And the blood pressure in his veins, come to that.

Christ! Would that bloody klaxon never stop? raged Richard silently. It was worse than the fog horn at the Wolf Rock lighthouse – under whose relentless howl he had nearly drowned a couple of years back, once again trying to save lives against almost impossible odds. But he had had some vital help then – and he could certainly do with some now.

At the bottom of the steps leading up to Julie's prone figure he glanced across to where Raoul and Honore had been standing. But there was no sign of them.

Richard turned and started to clamber up the steps to the balcony on which Julie was lying. As he climbed towards her, he made his first grim decision. The suit was useless to her at the same time as being bulky and heavy – especially with the tank on its back. No sooner did he arrive on the corrugated metal than he had rolled her on to her back, arching her strangely, throwing her breasts into stark relief because of the tank between her shoulder blades. Her face looked almost green through the glass, her eyes half-closed and

87

flickering as though she were a nun in ecstasy, her mouth wide and her lips worryingly blue. She looked exactly as though she were drowning in there.

Richard reached down and ripped her headpiece back. He tore his own open at the throat, holding his breath, and pumped his oxygen out. He scooped her up and pressed her face to the opening as though they were vampire lovers, trusting that life-giving oxygen would be flooding down over her face rather than life's blood.

She gasped and stirred. A good start. Remaining in the same position, crouched over her like a vampire, he eased her back until he could rip her suit-front open. From throat to gusset it folded back and he lowered her at last, sliding his hands into the hot material below her slim waist. Then he lifted. She came out of the useless encumbrance like a butterfly out of a chrysalis. Only her feet remained recalcitrant, wedged in the boot sections. He pulled her upright, rising to his feet as he did so. His hood fell back over his shoulders, the hard-hat banging on his tanks, and her face pressed close to his.

Without further thought, he put his lips to hers and emptied his lungs' oxygen into her mouth. Then he swung her into the crook of his left arm and pulled his headpiece back with his right, sucking in a great glorious lungful of rancid, stinking air. He wouldn't risk taking the headpiece off again. It would be of no help to Julie if he keeled over as well.

The air gave Richard the strength to step on her useless suit and tear her upward, simply popping her feet out of it by main force. Then he was off. He carried her unsteadily down the steps on to the deck and here he paused and then slung her up over his shoulder in a rough fireman's carry. Aided, once she was settled, by the fact that his tanks took some of her weight and transferred it to the strong webbing straps across his chest. Aided also by the weakness of his suit. The strain proved too much for his seams again. He heard and felt nothing as they burst wide, but suddenly there was a good deal of freedom to move that simply had not been there a moment before.

Richard had no sooner straightened than he saw that

circumstances had relieved him of another decision. The path across the deck to the steps was clear – Julie had obviously made Honore move most of the impediments as they came across to begin their inspection of the motors. The way to the lifts was dangerously strewn with debris, however. Time gained using the elevator – should it be working – would be more than lost in the care needed to get to it. And that thought was emphasized even as it was born by the fact that Honore and Raoul reappeared – near the lifts themselves. Seeing Richard, they began to rush to his aid at last. But 'rush' was a relative word in the circumstances – they had to pick their way slowly and carefully across the deck in order to stay on their feet.

Long before the engineers could get to him, Richard had reached the foot of the skeletal companionway. On the one hand the steps were steep and narrow. On the other, they stood out in the middle of the deck – there was room for Julie's head to hang over one handrail while her feet tapped on the other – and Richard was able to hoist her upwards in a series of gargantuan heaves. Twenty huge bursts of effort, followed by a drunken stagger round the corner past the all too tidy fire equipment, then twenty more in prospect.

Richard's own air ran out on the next level. He felt it beginning to fail – felt the pumping of his racing heart intensify; felt the pains in his chest worsen almost beyond bearing. He sucked in a last, lingering breath until the outer walls of his chest hurt almost as much as the inner workings of his cardiovascular and pulmonary systems. As he swung on to the first step of the final flight up, the bright lights of insidious unconsciousness began to flash across his vision. But still he would not stop.

Richard was working on what his mother called 'Sheer Badness' now. A cross-grained, stubborn, proud refusal to give in. From deep within himself, he called on wells of strength and determination that he never knew he had. And, abruptly, it seemed that those reserves answered his intrepid call. The weight of the woman draped over his shoulders became feather-light. His legs seemed to access an enormous strength as though he had become a super-hero from the waist down. Such was the absolute focus of his reeling mind upon his body and the impossible thing he was demanding of it that it never even occurred to him that Raoul was just behind him, pushing upwards with all his wiry might. The only thing that penetrated the thickening red mist through which he was labouring was a distant, apparently subterranean voice calling, '*Respirez, Capitaine! Respirez!*'

And when he did, obediently, respire, his lungs were filled with air. The half-closed gap at the throat of his headpiece – opened to save Julie, though it had almost done for him – let the healing gasses in. No sooner had the first wild rush of oxygen hit his system like the finest champagne than the open gateway at the head of the flight was there before him. He took four steps past it and sank to his knees.

A lesser man might have stopped there and then. Might have allowed the engineers to do their best with the still comatose Captain. But Richard simply did not trust them. Still unaware that Raoul had come close to saving both of them, Richard shrugged the still, slack form of the woman off his shoulders and laid her on the metal floor. Trained in the brutal routines of first aid to Accident and Emergency level, where courteous hesitation and care for common decencies cost lives, he tore her overalls wide. Still on his knees, still coughing and choking as he fought for breath, made unsteady by the weight of his useless tanks – on top of everything else – he leaned forward over her. He was gulping in great draughts of air in any case, almost hyperventilating his starved lungs. He swooped down between two such gasps and pressed his lips to hers, closing off her nostrils and filling up her lungs. Again. Again. Bobbing up and down like a child's automaton toy.

After the third breath he slewed round beside her and slid his hands on to her chest, feeling beneath the swell of her bosom for the point of her breastbone. Pushing down and down to empty her lungs. He bit off another great chunk of atmosphere and leaned forward once again.

As Richard did this, so his consciousness expanded to take in a couple of pairs of feet. Between the gasps of air and the kisses of life he gave staccato orders, one syllable at a time.

'Warn . . .'
Breathe in . . .
'Infirmary . . .'
Breathe out . . .
'Need . . .'
Breathe in . . .
'Oxygen . . .'
Breathe out.

Slide round. Reach in again. Pump . . . Pump . . . Pump . . .

'But Captain, everyone in the infirmary is dead,' said Honore.

'Get a move on, Raoul. Find Antoine. Go and look! May need a stretcher . . .' The feet pounded off. Raoul's at once; Honore's more hesitantly. The two Captains were left alone with the steady rhythmic beating of the generators.

Richard went through the resuscitation routine once more. Fifteen great breaths. Fifteen long kisses. He slid his hands into her overall again.

'The last man who got this intimate with me was a cadet called Gerard at the Merchant Navy College in Marseilles,' she said suddenly, moving nothing but her lips as she spoke.

Richard froze. His hands remained exactly where they were, abruptly aware that the life he had been fighting to save beat beneath firm curves, all tightly wrapped in hot silk and crisp lace.

Julie's eyes opened. They seemed to be all gold fleck and black pupil. 'My father chased him away with a shotgun and as far as I know he's still running.' Her voice was hoarse, as though she had been screaming.

Richard retrieved his hands. The palms continued to burn. He sat back on his heels. Looked down at her with a slightly twisted grin. 'Parents, eh? Can't live with them; wouldn't be here without them . . .'

'I don't think I'd be here without *you*. Would I?'

He shrugged modestly, then tried not to wince as the movement warned him of strained shoulder muscles. 'Happy to be of service. You want to cover up? The engineers will be back soon and I'm not sure how good for ship's discipline

91

an exhibition of the Captain's lacy underwear would be.'

She gave an almost boyish grin and sat up. She also winced. 'Giscard had drawers full of the stuff,' she rasped.

'Lots of lady friends?' He eased his shoulders, trying not to be too obvious about it, and began to unbuckle the air tanks as a kind of cover for his uncomfortable movements.

'I think he liked to put it on himself. Under his uniform sometimes, so the gossip goes.' She watched him. The lightness of the husky words belied by a frown of concern.

'Maybe that's what Honore and Raoul were checking when they were so careful to move the bodies before they did anything else.' Richard pulled off the tanks and laid them aside, glancing across at the line of corpses still lying by the airlock door as he did so. 'Maybe they wanted to make arrangements to spare the blushes of his family.'

'Perhaps.' She sounded no more convinced than Richard was himself. But she sat right up as she uttered the word and began to pull the front of her overall closed. It was then that Richard noticed with some chagrin that all the button holes were torn and most of the buttons were gone.

The lift whined into motion, the clatter of the cables in the shaft and the rumble of its winches just audible over the pulsing of the generators.

'That's sensible,' said Richard easily. 'They'd never get a stretcher down that ladder.'

'Nor a body up it either – on a stretcher or not. Who's the stretcher for by the way?'

'Well, if *you* don't need it, I could do with a bit of a lie-down myself . . .'

'We can do better than that. I can say the magic words that will get you up in a flash!'

'Really. And what words are those?'

'Come up to my cabin, Richard . . .' She leaned forward seductively and whispered in a throaty, still-broken voice. 'There is hot water there now and . . .' He leaned down again, as though resuming the kiss of life. But it was his ear not his mouth that brushed her lips. 'I have the best *French coffee* aboard,' she promised. 'And the most massive *cafetière* . . .'

They had it with cream, and Richard really loved it, though he usually preferred it black. And moreover, it was tea time, not coffee time. But he simply could not resist the strong black coffee she brewed for him – nor the fresh, thick, sweet cream that came in a jug from the galley fridge.

Its very existence amused him strangely – as though he were tipsy or a little hysterical. When the power failed, of course, the refrigerators had not warmed up. They had stayed a degree or two above freezing – while everything else aboard had cooled down instead. The crew might be frozen to the marrow, but the butter, eggs, milk, cream and cheese were fine.

So were the fruit and salads – which was as well, for Mr Song brought tonight's menu for Julie to approve when he brought the cream. Onion soup, steak and salad, Camembert, fruit – celebratory, but simple and quick to make. 'And this is very fortunate,' observed the Chief Steward dryly. 'I have been seeking you to ask approval for this since I removed the *nems* and sandwiches. In future we must approve the day's menus at our nine o'clock briefing, Captain. The galley will hardly function otherwise. And the cook will certainly jump ship at the next port.'

'Yes, Mr Song,' agreed the Captain meekly, failing to point out that the next port of call was likely to be just about the loneliest, coldest and remotest spot on earth – Kerguelen Island.

The Chief Steward bowed and left. Behind him lingered that faint air of disapproval. What did the Captain mean by playing around in the engine room when there was important business to be completed – such as approving the menus and keeping the cook happy?

'What next?' asked Richard after a moment during which the creamy fragrance of the coffee was transformed into restful warmth in his stomach.

'Pump out the engine room,' she answered, curdling his cream at once. 'Station watches beside the extinguishers to keep an eye open. Make sure Antoine is there to keep and extra eye on Honore – especially – and Raoul. Make sure we are there for the most important part of it also. Leave

93

the bridge watch with poor Sophie for the time being and get Emil down there into the bargain. And Chow and the best of his team. Just in case. But I saw nothing obvious on my inspection. Nothing that looked like an incendiary device.'

'That will all take a couple of hours.' Richard glanced at the face of his old steel-cased Rolex. Took another sip, feeling his heart begin to pound as the caffeine hit his system. 'Done before pour out. Then what?'

'Start the motors.' She spoke in a tone that suggested a certain imbecility in him for asking the question in the first place.

'Not the one I inspected,' warned Richard. He explained about the damaged gear.

Julie frowned. 'The one I inspected seemed fine. We will start that one, then.'

Richard's head was shaking almost automatically. 'You said it yourself,' he reminded her. 'The rudder is lying hard over. That's why we're swinging north of east under the influence of a steady westerly. If you engage the propeller you'll likely chew everything to bits down there.'

Julie sat up very straight. Her eyes narrowed with a potent mixture of thought and irritation. 'We will bring the rudder to midships and then we will start the motor and engage the propeller,' she said.

'You can try,' said Richard. 'But you'll be lucky to move the rudder at all. The servo motors that control it aren't the most powerful in the world. They're designed to govern its angle when the ship is in forward motion and the only force exerted on the rudder blade is being generated by the propellers and the wake. What you have now is the force being exerted by – what? – a quarter of a million tons being moved at more than a mile an hour. My maths isn't up to it so I can't tell you exactly how many newtons or whatever that is. But I bet it's more than your little rudder motors can begin to overcome.'

'Ha! I see what this is! You only wish to put obstacles in my way. You do not want me to retrieve this situation at all! You merely wish to reach for your precious radio. Your oh so powerful Hagenuk Marinekommunikation transceiver!

94

Typical man! This is all about the size and power of your equipment.'

'No. I swear. What you are trying to do would be nearly impossible under most circumstances. As things stand, you're limited by situation and by time. Look at the alternatives. No. Don't. There aren't any. Not realistic ones at any rate.'

'Not so, Richard. For a start, after I have pumped out the engine room I could start the motors but disengage the propellers and try to manoeuvre with thrusters in the first instance. Maybe swing her round enough to take the pressure off the rudder. At the same time we could work on fixing the damaged reduction gear. No. Better! Move the whole gear over from one motor to the other, then start the propeller that is not going to damage the rudder. Yes! I will demand of Honore that he estimates how long this would take . . .'

'With the state of his team, from the look of it, I'd say it'll still take more time than you have at your disposal. Look, I can get an ocean-going tug here in thirty-six hours or so if you'll let me try. A massive thing with a bollard pull of 250 tonnes and more. If she can't pull you clear or slow you down she could at least help the thrusters swing you round in time.'

'So. You have a tug already on the way, do you?'

'Yes. I thought you knew. Giscard knew. My wife Robin is aboard, she's been running south from Durban for the better part of a day.'

'Salvage! That's what you are after. What is this hull worth in salvage? And the cargo – under what is it – under Lloyd's Open Form? Well, as we are bringing families into the matter, Captain Mariner, consider this. *La Dame Marie* may sail under the flag of Les Terres Australes et Antarctique Français but she is owned by men, not territories. And the chief of the consortium that owns her is Charles DuFour. My father. Did Captain Giscard tell you this as you came hurrying south? Of course not, for he did not know it. Papa is, what you say, the sleeping partner. Nobody knows this but I. And now you. But consider, my brave Captain Mariner, what follows from it. If I allow this vessel to be salvaged then I will ruin my own father as a result.'

95

'So, rather than risk your father's fortune, you will risk running a fully laden and dangerously unstable oil tanker up against the side of a volcano in one of the remotest regions on earth! Risk blowing them both to kingdom come and maybe the risk of causing another Krakatoa; another Vesuvius; another Mount St Helens. Risk doing untold damage to one of the most carefully protected and delicate environments that exists! Risk adding more than twenty lives – including your own – to the death toll already headed by Giscard and his senior officers!'

'But yes!' she hissed back. 'Of course! While there is still a hope that I can salvage the situation myself and save my father from ruin I will naturally risk all these things!'

Richard sat back and drained his coffee cup, his mind racing to reassess their position here in the light of the new information. He really wanted to strangle her. Shake her at the very least. Shake her until her teeth rattled and she got some sense of proportion into her passionate calculations.

But of course, according to her own lights she was right. There could be no arguing with that. He did not own *Sissy*, the tug that should be speeding south with Robin anxiously aboard. He could not guarantee that the men who did own her would not demand salvage – under Lloyd's Open Form, as she had said.

Further, he knew that if they did begin to call for help, then *Sissy* would only be the start. Unless she was every bit as powerful as they said, he would need to be calling for more tugs. They would need an ocean-going fire-fighting vessel as well. The tug captains would insist on that as likely as not. Even if nobody bothered to mention to them what had happened when Lucien went overboard this afternoon and set the sea alight.

Furthermore, thought Richard, he hadn't seen all of the surviving crew yet – any more than Julie had managed to complete her inspection – but he knew that somewhere aboard there were men who still needed medical attention. That too needed to be called in, if it could be done in time to save them all transferring to the infirmary, one by one, as they died. And of course, if his gathering suspicions were true –

there would be a lot more wounded and dying aboard as soon as the engine room was pumped out.

The situation could hardly be worse. But it called for subtlety now, not violence. Diplomacy and perhaps a little British pomposity.

'You're right, Captain DuFour,' he said formally, putting his cold cup down at last. 'I came here to try and save your vessel and your lives if I could. I did not count the cost – in salvage or in anything else. And if we start to call for help then that is all it will save; the hull and the lives of the crew. Not your father's business – nor your country's reputation. Not *Compagnie Maritime DuFour* of Marseilles – whether your father is sleeping partner or not. Nor Les Terres Australes et Antarctique Français. But *La Dame Marie*, and you and me and everyone aboard. No matter what the price in pride, dollars or euros. And it may be that the price is too high, as you say. It may even be that the price will remain too high until the whole damn thing goes up in your face. But you are the Captain and that is your decision. You know my advice. But you have my support.'

To offer anything less would be utterly pointless, after all, he thought to himself as they rose together and went out of the dead Captain's cabin, side by side. And, short of killing her or being there when she died, the only way he could continue to push forward his own plans was to be there when she saw the light and began to change her mind.

Ten

Fire

R ichard stood on the middle gallery in the engine room looking down at the motors, his mind racing. On one level, far above his deep, almost desperate thoughts, he was struck afresh by how much mess there was down there. How much of it was black, burned, smoke-damaged. He was wearing his third safety suit of the day. It was just as restrictive as the others had been, but this time at least he wore his headpiece open.

The clean-air monitor hanging from his left wrist remained reassuringly silent, though he would have been hard put to hear it with the throbbing grumble of the generators joined now by the thunder of the air pumps sucking the CO_2 out of the place.

Richard wore the monitor on his left wrist this time because he carried a big bright-blue canister of fire-fighting metal powder in his right. His eyes – almost the same colour as the canister – were narrow, searching among the mess and debris on the deck for the first suspicion of smoke. Left and right, they swept, searching each quadrant of the area before him automatically.

He would be lucky to see it until it grew quite serious, though, for those first few vital warning wisps would simply be lost amid the mess and damage below – almost all of it smoke-coloured, smoke-shaped, smoke-smelling. His mouth was clamped in a thin line and his nostrils were narrow – set, not just with frustration but against the acrid stench of the place, for now that it was being pumped out he wore his headpiece open, like the others. And this was a new stench he was breathing for the first time down. A stench which made him long for the rancid rubber of the compressed-air system on his back. Much as the complexities of the current situation made him wish most poignantly – and in spite of all the reasons for acquiescence he had given himself of late – that he was in command of this mess himself. Or in a position to take command.

Richard was not used to performing the good lieutenant's role and supporting his Captain right or wrong. He had chaired his own companies, commanded his own vessels, rescued ships, corporations – countries, even – but always by leading from the front. By seeing the right course and taking it. Forcing through his will, his vision, with the same brutal self-discipline with which he had carried Julie up the companionway to safety.

But now he felt trapped. His efforts seemed cheapened. His dash to the rescue – not to mention its cost in effort, time and money – devalued. And, he rather suspected, Helen DuFour – at whose request he was fundamentally acting – would be a great deal less than ecstatic to know that he was saving the skin of her errant and faithless ex-husband rather than the life and career of her estranged but still beloved daughter. Helen would be outraged to learn that her long-lost darling daughter would die, and allow a number of others to do so at her side, rather than risk *La Compagnie Maritime DuFour* of Marseilles.

Not, in fact, that Richard proposed to allow her to destroy her ship or kill her crew if he could help it. It simply didn't matter whether Julie was motivated by her public proclamations of duty to France and desire to keep her country's honour bright in this God-forsaken sphere of old colonial influence. Or whether she was moved by the private motivations she had described to him an hour or so ago. She was still wrong. All she should have been taking into account here was the safety of her ship and of the crew fighting to bring her safe to port.

Or most of the crew were fighting to get her to port, thought Richard, side-tracked for a moment. For Lucien's death actually did seem to prove that there really was sabotage involved – and *that*, of course, meant, just as he had so readily speculated when it had seemed rather less likely, there must either be bombs placed earlier and ready to go off now or saboteurs armed with more of them still aboard.

The revelation that Julie's father was somehow involved might well broaden the field of possible reasons and likely suspects, too, for Charles DuFour had made more enemies than his estranged first wife in his long and variously distinguished shipping career. Richard had never met the man – nor seen a clearer photograph of him than a grainy, ill-focussed image in the business pages of *Le Monde*. But he knew all about him – and from sources more reliable than the bitter woman who had begged him to come here and rescue her daughter.

Charles DuFour had the sort of reputation that meant he might not be above sabotaging his own ship for the insurance money. Richard's current standing and fortune were largely based on the fact that he had thwarted just such an attempt in the first *Prometheus*, more years back that he cared to count these days. Certainly, were anyone wishing to ship a legitimate cargo all safe and above board from Alexandria to Durban, then *La Compagnie Maritime DuFour* of Marseilles would be amongst the last places they would look. But if you had a little contraband to move; a little hashish out of Morocco, say, or a cargo of slave children to be smuggled from Banana to Birkenhead.

Richard shook himself and pulled his mind back from interesting but dangerously irrelevant areas. He had to deal with the immediate, not the distant or the speculative. And he really only saw two practical paths forward from here. Either Julie realized the error of her ways and found the good sense and maturity to start calling for help before it was too late or, in spite of his pompous protestations, he would have to find some way of relieving her of command and calling for help himself. Because all they were doing now was running the risk of making a bad situation even worse – and wasting time, into the bargain. He glanced down at his left wrist but his Rolex was hidden under the safety suit. It must be after five, though. If he was going to act he must do it within the next hour. Hour and a half at most.

Richard tightened his grip on the metal-powder canister as though it were some kind of weapon. He looked around the engine room. Everyone else was looking downwards, searching for that first tell-tale sign of smoke. But when Julie had ordered her reluctant crew back down here, she had promised they would be done by 1830, and returning to ship's routine by then. A pre-prandial drink at pour out then a good steak dinner. That would be his own deadline, he decided. He would have to act at pour out, when everyone who counted – who could walk and who was not on watch – would all be together in a situation when the actions he was considering would not simply add to the danger. That was it, he thought. One way or another he would act at pour out.

Of course he felt uneasy at having promised one thing while he was considering another. But the horns of the dilemma were no less sharp for that. His apparent acquiescence had taken them, not down here immediately as he had supposed it would, but up on to the navigation bridge at once so that she could test what he had been saying. Clearly she was not as sure of herself as she seemed and needed to try for a small victory in the face of his massive opposition.

It was strange to be standing beside the unpredictably mercurial Julie at the helm, Richard himself at her right shoulder and Sophie Bois at her left, looking down the length of the deck but feeling their movement all reversed in many ways. Watching as the Captain took the wheel firmly in her trembling hands and looked down at the rudder monitor.

'Coming to midships,' Julie had said icily, and turned the wheel. Or rather, tried to turn it – for the little helm remained absolutely still. She heaved with all her might, grunting with the strain. 'Help me,' she ordered Sophie, and the game little cadet threw herself bodily into the task, grunting with the effort. To no avail.

Richard closed his eyes then, feeling his way into the fabric of the ship with his mind as the women heaved at the helm. Did he know this vessel? he wondered abruptly.

Had he captained her? Ordered the disposition of that very helm? Commanded the power settings of those motors – Full Ahead; Reverse All? Dictated the pitch of those propellers? He felt at one with the stricken vessel, as though he were linked to her – was part of her himself. What did they call it? 'The Sympathy of Command'? Something like that. He and *Lady Mary* were intertwined as though she had been his when she sailed as *Prometheus* – and knew him still as he knew her.

He could feel the twisting of the helm giving orders now – sending strong electrical signals to the servo motors deep below the main engines – safe from the fire but probably still awash with inert gas. He could almost feel the motors themselves striving to answer the increasingly strident demands, whirling and sparking and heating – on the verge of burning out. Fighting to move the immovable. A metal sail, the better part of a hundred square metres in area, held over by the force of all that water pressing down on it at a kilometre an hour.

Abruptly, he was in motion across the bridge. As the women strained at the helm he tapped the buttons of the control computer, guided the cursor, clicked the mouse. His nimble fingers called up the engine monitor programme, which reported automatically on the state of every engine aboard from the huge motors in the engine room to the smallest winch on the forecastle head. Then the navigation subset, which reported on bow thrusters, side thrusters, rudder motors and so forth. Then the steering servos, which reported on the rudder motors only.

'According to this you're in the red already, Captain DuFour,' he said, his voice flat and chilly even to his own ears. 'There is a major damage countdown running. And a fire warning, which I pray is redundant at the moment. That's there because the motors have already overheated quite seriously. In an oxygenated atmosphere they'd probably be aflame. As it is, they will begin to melt within a couple of minutes. If you don't stop pulling that helm over, you will totally destroy your ability to steer the ship in ninety seconds . . . 89 . . . 88 . . .'

'Very well!' snapped Julie. 'Enough of this little game. Let us pump out the engine room and see how we proceed with the serious business instead!'

It was at that moment that Richard really understood her stubbornness and intransigence – and began to calculate just how far he would have to go to out-think her, out-manoeuvre her, to save the situation and everyone involved in it in spite of her.

Very well, he thought grimly. Turning the helm had been her little test of what he had said. Pumping out the engine room would be his little test of her.

'La! La bas. Feu! La bas!'

Richard tore himself round, looking away from the blackened wreckage below towards the crewman calling the warning. It was Chow and he was pointing as he shouted. Richard swivelled back again and saw at once the thread of grey, rising unsteadily from the deck. He was in motion at once, swinging the canister up and hurling himself down the skeletal steps. By the time he reached the deck – as he had had to watch where he put his feet amongst the dangerous rubbish – the smoke had thickened and was mounting the air clearly enough so that he was able to keep it in view every time he glanced up. Abruptly he became aware that he was by no means the only person running towards the danger. Antoine was making a run for it, with an unexpected overplus of youthful enthusiasm and a marked lack of his usual laid-back cool. And, indeed, Fourth Engineer Raoul seemed keen to join in as well, with his headgear banging between his shoulders and his pink skull gleaming in the brightness. But it was Richard who won, by a length. A length of time in this case – long enough for him to arrive beside a pile of oily rags at the base of the wavering column of vapour. Eyes narrow, he kicked at it experimentally and it fell apart, bursting into a brief flicker of flame. It was nothing more than a piled of smouldering waste after all.

Richard relaxed his grip on the trigger of his precious metal-powder extinguisher, content to shake his head for a moment over the miracle of persistence which had kept the rags smouldering, even under the weight of inert gas, through three or more freezing days and nights.

Antoine had a foam extinguisher that took care of matters immediately, with one swift squirt. The rags seemed to flatten and shrink beneath the little hill of foam. Raoul kicked them anyway, derisively.

'Be careful with that, though,' said Richard, a little hoarsely, to Antoine. 'We don't want to be sliding around like skaters if anything big goes up.'

Antoine nodded.

'Down and out,' called Richard. And the three of them grinned at each other almost foolishly.

Until someone called, '*La bas* . . .' again and they were racing off once more.

And so they fell into a kind of routine. The watchers on the upper levels would spot the smoke and call directions. They were led by Julie herself, for the intrepid Captain was realistic enough to see that her physique was not really equal to the task of leaping through filthy rubbish like a mountain goat while carrying a deceptively weighty extinguisher.

Teams of fighters – Richard's team, Emil's team and Chow's team (theoretically commanded by the disgruntled Honore) would race each other to see who could get to it first. Who could call 'Down and out!' before the others could.

Piles of rags were most often responsible. Splinters of smashed wood, on occasion – though no one seemed quite sure how such things got down here in the first place. But there were little reservoirs of oil too – lubricating oil for the most part, grease and dirt such as the mixture that started the disaster on the underground at King's Cross in London. Anything combustible that managed to retain enough heat to reach flame point when the oxygen was restored. And, as the oil showed, the burning medium itself did not have to stay hot – it simply had to nestle against some piece of metal that even now retained some of the fierce heat of the original conflagration.

Richard thanked God increasingly fervently as he rushed from place to place. Firstly he gave thanks that none of the fires was serious enough to demand that he deploy his metal powder extinguisher. Antoine's foam and Raoul's portable gas extinguishers were more than equal to the tasks so far.

And Richard also gave thanks to God that he had won one grudging concession from Julie on the way down here – a kind of prize for being right about the rudder. This was that she empty the inert gas down to deck-level here. And here only, at first. It was logical, to be fair, and she had seen the logic readily enough for all her continued rage against him. To pump out the lower areas would require another set of pumps altogether. It would also require that she find some way of setting fire watches and deploying fire teams in those lower areas, in much more difficult and cramped conditions. Moreover, as the attempt to move the rudder had showed, there was no need for the equipment down there to work in a clean-air atmosphere so long as no one needed to go down and tend it. And finally, crucially, the inescapable fact that she would indeed need to deploy fire teams deep down in that dangerously claustrophobic maze below during any further attempt to pump out the inert gas was emphasized with each and every cry of '*La bas! Feu! La bas!*' that came echoing across the cavernous engine room.

At long last it seemed that all the little fires that had managed to hibernate through the last few days were out and the watchers fell silent. The fighters wearily began to pick their way back through the stinking mess on the deck. Richard glanced up at Julie, standing pale-faced by the head of the companionway, debating no doubt whether to press on with tidying-up now or wait until after pour out and dinner as she had promised. She couldn't waste any time if she had realistic expectations of salvaging the situation, but the crew were exhausted and probably even hungrier that Richard was himself, after cold-cuts and sandwiches for days on end. And no coffee, tea or hot chocolate. Morale was likely to be the crucial factor in the next few hours.

Morale was as important to Richard's plans as to Julie's, come to that. But in the opposite regard. She wanted everyone cheered, motivated and back to work. He wanted everyone exhausted, disgruntled and ripe for mutiny. Because that was what it was going to be, of course. That's what he was thinking of fomenting. Mutiny.

105

Richard had spent much of last year in court fighting accusations of corporate killing and was consequently pretty expert in English law nowadays. They no longer hung you for mutiny and piracy in England; he was pretty certain of that. But this wasn't a British vessel – the sign on the funnel saying Terres Australes, et Antarctique Français made that pretty clear. He wondered wearily if they still guillotined you for mutiny in France. You never know, he thought; maybe I'm going to find out . . .

'Feu! La bas. Soigneux! Grand feu!' The shout of warning was different, somehow. The warning to take care, that the fire was big. Richard took a deep breath, the back of his neck prickling with a sudden chill of concern. Antoine and Raoul felt no such qualms evidently, for they both raced off like hares.

Richard ran after them, but his legal wool-gathering and his growing exhaustion slowed him fractionally. And, in spite of the seriousness with which Antoine had apparently taken his warning, the deck beneath his racing feet was dangerously slippery with little pools of foam.

So that Antoine and Raoul arrived at the thick column of dense smoke well ahead of Richard. He was too far away to see exactly what lay at the foot of the grey tree-trunk – looking oddly like a young silver birch as it mounted and began to spread. He saw Antoine kick it, however, just as he himself had kicked that first fuming bundle of rags. And as the cadet's foot hit it, so the thing seemed to explode. A great shower of fire soared away from the swinging boot. It attained form in the air, like a swarm of fire-flies. And it rained all over Raoul, who burst into flames at once as though his white suit was made of fire lighter, not fire retardant. The stricken engineer reeled away, screaming, blundering into the piles of rubbish all around, raining fire-flies and belching flames: spreading fire with astonishing rapidity, like some terrible plague.

Antoine, stricken, hopped on one foot, helplessly. The other foot blazed almost as brightly as Raoul – until Richard intervened. 'Spray your food! Then spray Raoul!' he bellowed in suddenly fluent French. 'Get a move on for God's sake!'

Antoine obeyed the first injunction instantly. His foot vanished in a second shoe of foam and the fire there died at once. But by the time it did so, Raoul was beyond Antoine's range, screaming with animal bellows – far beyond anything human now. And a surprising amount of the intervening debris was ablaze. Smoke was billowing all too rapidly from the burning engineer, from the blazing rubbish and from the incendiary volcano that had started this.

Richard's priorities were clear. He had to trust that Antoine would do what he could for Raoul. He had to pray that the other teams would get on top of the rash of lesser fires before they became any greater. But he himself must kill this one as fast as possible. He hit the release on the blue extinguisher and pointed its nozzle down.

And nothing whatsoever happened.

'*Christ!*' he yelled, in English. The extinguisher had been used – then replaced on the 'ready' rack without being refilled. A cardinal sin that would get the man responsible fined a month's wages – maybe more – on any of Richard's own commands. But he had no time for thought or recrimination. The volcano before him was gathering force. Its heat was stewing his chest within his suit. It was simply barbecuing his face. His eyes were streaming and his throat was burning. That old familiar spike was back through the middle of his chest.

He swung round, throwing the empty extinguisher aside and there was Chow. The seaman was immediately behind him, a familiar blue bottle raised high. Richard reached up and grabbed it. Turning and releasing in one fluid motion, he blasted metal powder over the geyser of fire at his feet. He held it in place, hosing the obscene thing far beyond what was necessary – like a jittery hunter emptying his weapon into a venomous snake that had come slithering suddenly at his toes.

He saw the spitting metal powder envelop the roaring monster that the incendiary had become in the interim. He saw the dazzling meeting of heat and dust, saw the flames of the one melt the powder of the other until it coalesced; trembled like a massive drop of mercury skinned in lively black film. Until it mounted, formed a hillock, choking the fire beneath, and setting almost instantly as the heat died and the metal blister began to cool.

Only when the deadly device was safely entombed did he look up to see the dreadful mayhem all around him. The fire begun by Raoul's wild reeling was burning apparently out of control. Julie was almost alone on the fume-washed, mid-level balcony, shrieking her orders and coughing her guts up in between. Everyone else, it seemed, was down here with portable extinguishers, trying to bring some kind of order. In the smoking distance he could see Raoul lying on the deck, black and steaming, horrifically stark at the heart of a small lake of foam. He had stopped screaming; stopped moving. His bald pate no longer looked like pink plastic. It looked like smoking charcoal. He looked dead to Richard.

Pour out is out of the question then, Richard thought grimly, plunging back into the thick of things. And so was dinner. No one would want to eat steak after smelling the stench of roasting Raoul.

And so Richard did not need to lead his mutiny after all. But at the cost of yet another life. It took them until the better part of 9 p.m. to bring things under control, tidy up a little and get Raoul up to the corpse-filled infirmary where Julie herself checked in vain for vital signs. Given the state of his face and head, it was just as well he was dead. After the inspection, his body was placed in one of the mortuary drawers that were cooled almost to freezing by the restoration of power. And were blessedly airtight.

It took them all that time and all their energy. By the time they began to drag themselves – exhausted – out of the stinking pit that had been the engine room it was obvious that they were not going to get the motors back on line. All they had left to even attempt it were Honore and Antoine, who was only a cadet. Both of whom were simply stunned by what had happened to their friend and colleague.

The best that Julie could hope to do was set a permanent fire watch here and pray that nothing further went wrong. For she had lost her gamble in the worst possible way. She had emptied the engine room of inert gas and discovered the fires were still too dangerous to allow the motors to start. But the inert gas that filled the major reservoirs of the automatic system that she needed to fill the engine room again were a by-product of the motors themselves. Without them, she could not replace it – and would have to rely on the hand-held extinguishers, as long as they held out. Until they too could no longer be refilled.

Captain Julie DuFour might be a loyal daughter and a staunch patriot; a passionate and temperamental woman. But she was neither a fool nor a suicide. As Richard returned his bright blue canister to the 'Urgent Refill' section and began to pull himself towards the lift – the stairs had ceased to be an option soon after the incendiary went out – she appeared almost silently at his side. She stepped into the little car beside him and gestured to Chow behind them that he should wait.

The door hissed shut and he reached for the accommodation deck button. She prevented him, however, and pressed the button for the navigation bridge instead.

'The first thing you have to do for me, Richard,' she said gently, grimly, her voice gravelly and almost masculine in its smoke-thickened timbre. 'Before we wash, or eat, or get our burns and blisters, cuts and bruises seen to, is for you to show me how to assemble and start up that Hagenuk Marinekommunikation 4000 radio transceiver of yours.

'Because I think the moment has come to ask for a little help . . .'

Eleven

Ether

But the Hagenuk did not invade the ether immediately, urgent though its calls for aid must be and in spite of the fact that it had sat there uselessly for nearly twelve hours. This time it was Richard who slowed things down. Slowed them a little at the outset, hoping to speed them in the end.

'This isn't really a one-man job,' he explained to Julie as they surveyed the big box he had carried with him here. 'We have to do a little more than simply unpack it and plug it in, then have a chat with a few people on nearby boats and pop off to bed. And although I can take you through the operating manual at the same time as I get it all up and running – and maybe it's a good idea to do just that – you're not going to be the one on radio watch, are you? And we will need radio watch once it's running. Twenty-four hours a day for as long as it takes.'

He looked around the chart room, where the box sat on the chart table obscuring the charts themselves. 'And, come to that, this isn't the best place to set it up anyway, is it? Is the radio shack completely out of the question?'

'Look for yourself,' advised Julie briefly.

He did so, striding across the watch-dimmed, draught-haunted bridge with hardly a glance at Sophie poring over her radars, busily making up her logs. With little more than a flicker of his cold blue gaze to register the abyssal blackness of the polar night through which the ship was moving in the grip of that relentless wind. There was no brightness out there – not even a flicker of snowflake or a flash of rain

110

rushing up to the clearview to give form to the black wind streaming in from Crozet and beyond and howling through the bridgeworks as it came. Roaring in over the deck-mounted navigation lights and the warning lights which broadcast to the uncaring vastness of the bellowing night, vessel not under control. Like a lost galaxy agleam in the lightless depths of interstellar space.

Or rather, vessel under the control of the relentless ice-black westerly wind.

Arriving at the radio room, he hesitated suddenly before opening the filth-rimmed door with care – as though the sudden access of oxygen in there would set something off again. And he saw at once what Julie meant, even though his shadow in the doorway blocked much of the light from the bridge itself, making the place look like a stinking little coal cellar.

The equipment mounting the walls had been burned so comprehensively that even the metal shelf-cum-table that much of it sat on had been utterly destroyed. The light-fitting and the deckhead up around it was burst and blistered. And all the pocked, twisted, crusted mess had been comprehensively hosed with foam by the looks of things. There was still a sludgy pool of the stuff on the deck at his feet, as dark as a forest pool in winter, full of rotting leaves.

A desperately dangerous procedure given all the electric circuits in here. Unless they had disconnected it all, of course; had found some way to unplug or isolate the entire room. And if they had, then that would explain why it hadn't started shorting out again as soon as power was restored this afternoon. He opened his mouth to ask, but closed it again immediately; not just because of the stomach-turning stench of the place. It would be a waste of time to stop and start asking questions now. He would read the logs of the incident in due course. Or he could always ask the Assistant Radio Operator, of course. What was his name? Jean-Luc. One of the few people left aboard he hadn't met yet. Largely because he had yet to visit the officers' dining area – which had been turned into a secondary infirmary. An infirmary designed to treat live people, started after the original one filled up with the dead. He closed the door and turned, his mind clear and

111

running smoothly, possibly for the last time that night.

'Right,' he said, striding back across the bridge towards Julie who stood framed in the light of the chart room door. 'I think we need to take the mattress off the bunk in the Captain's day room, in behind the chart-room there, and use that as a table for the radio equipment. It's solid wood if I remember correctly, and easily strong enough to take the weight of the radio, the screen and all the ancillary equipment. There's power close by and I can run the UHF aerial out of the porthole above the bunk and maybe get it up as high as the communications mast in due course.

'The radio will only be in the way then, should you want to get charts out of the drawers beneath the bunk. But given our heading and speed, you won't be rushing to do that for a while. It won't be comfortable but it should work. And at least our communications will still be right by the command bridge.

'We'll need at least two on radio watch, as I said – that'll be myself and one other. Jean-Luc, I guess, unless he's still too weak from his injuries – or unless you've any gifted amateurs aboard. We could make it three watches if you have any spare men and that would be very good for me because I've already promised to share some navigating watches with you.'

'Jean-Luc,' said Julie, thoughtfully. 'Yes. I must see how he is. I don't know if there is anyone else aboard who can help. But we can ask.'

'Fine. You check on Jean-Luc and ask around while I get things ready in the day cabin. But it will obviously be most time efficient if I assemble it all and go through the manual with the watch-men who are going to work it with me, watching as I do it. Otherwise it'll just mean going over the same information time and time again.'

'Unless Jean-Luc, or whoever else we find, knows how to work a Hagenuk 4000 in the first place.'

'That would be good,' said Richard, struck. 'Though not very likely, I think. I've had a crash course and I can get it working well enough, but I'm no great expert. If by some miracle Jean-Luc knows more about these beasts than I do then that would be a great piece of luck.'

112

'I will see,' announced Julie. 'And I will ask around the officers and crew for a . . . what do you call it?'

'A ham.'

'A what?'

'Truely. A radio ham.'

Some uncounted time later, the mattress – still dressed in bedding – stood in the corner of the little room. Richard was arranging the transformers needed to change the ship's power into the wattage required by the radio. The radio itself lay anatomized along the hard wood top of the bed itself, the thin wire length of the UHF aerial, still bound in a figure of eight, hanging from the handle of the whimpering porthole above, when a shadow fell across him and he looked up.

Mr Song, the Chief Steward, was standing in the doorway. Richard's stomach growled in the hope of more *nems*, but Mr Song had other business.

'This is my nephew, son to my sister,' he said, in laboured if beautifully accented English, moving sideways to reveal a younger, sterner version of himself. Richard felt the weight of unfathomable eyes upon him, intensely watchful. He said nothing, but straightened courteously, more knowledgeable than most in the oriental rituals. More knowledgeable than most *gweilo* barbarians at any rate, courtesey of his years in Xianggang – as Fragrant Harbour had become when the barbarian British who had called the place Hong Kong handed it back to the inscrutably patient government of the Middle Kingdom.

'This nephew is called Lau,' continued Mr Song after a moment. 'His ignorant school fellows at his childhood home have called him Ether – or more accurately perhaps, the Idiot who Talks to Ghosts – because of his interest in radios. On this ship he is a Trainee Steward. And he does not talk to ghosts.'

Richard tilted his head forward. 'I thank you for bringing nephew Lau's expertise to my notice, Mr Song.'

'He may have sufficient knowledge and talent to be of service to you,' said Mr Song in a tone which suggested that he doubted it.

'Time will tell,' said Richard, equably.

113

And Song was gone, as silently – and almost as sinisterly – as one of the ghosts his nephew no longer talked to.

Richard looked at the intense young man and inclined his head in greeting. 'Ether,' he said. 'Is this a name you still like to be called or is it, like your milk name, a thing long past?'

'It will do as well as any, Captain,' answered the young man in liquid French, so heavily accented that Richard found it hard to follow at first. 'It is better than Stupid Nephew Lau, which is how I am often known aboard this stinking wreck.'

'Have you seen any equipment like this, Ether?'

'Maybe in an advert somewhere or in an American movie one time. Or in big shop window. I have never seen one in the flesh up close.'

'Well, I'm sure you're going to pick up the fundamentals very quickly.'

Richard went back to arranging the transformers and Ether came a little closer, his interest apparently caught. But he was content to watch silently as Richard performed the simple task. Richard found the steady silent scrutiny a little unsettling however, especially under the constant keening of the never-ending wind, and after a few minutes he asked, 'So where *was* this school where your ignorant school-fellows called you the Idiot who Talks to Ghosts?'

Richard flung the question over his shoulder in an irritable, almost insulting tone. It was calculated to be slightly offensive for, as Mr Song had demonstrated, the giving of offence could be taken as a sign of superiority. Ether would be more likely to respect a boss who put him down than a boss who built him up, if his relationship with his uncle was anything to go by.

But when his question got no response, Richard swung round, frowning, ready to add to the offence if the lad was just ignoring him. Swung round and stopped. Ether was standing just inside the doorway, his face frozen in simple terror, his long black eyes as wide as they would ever go, his mouth ajar, lips trembling. And, beyond him, hulked the cause of his distress. For an instant, Richard wondered

114

whether the ignorant school-fellows had got it right and Ether did actually talk to ghosts. In the silence of the moment, the wind made noises that must have made historical seafarers think they were sailing the seas of hell.

In the dim light of the bridge a strange figure hulked silently, as though listening to what the wind was telling him. Richard's first impression of the new arrival jerked him back to childhood. Memories, forgotten until now, flashed into his head of an evening spent quivering in delicious terror behind the sofa in his parents' sitting room while *The Mummy* stalked across the television screen; a monstrous concoction of infinitely ancient bandages, skeletal frame and limitless evil limping, stiff-legged, through some ancient movie – then out into his scariest dreams for a while.

Richard gasped and the strange stench of burning and medication combined at once to intensify the nightmare impression and bring him back to the here and now.

The figure stepped forward into the light and Ether seemed to shrink away as Richard rose to confront it. The stranger wore overalls, scorched, torn and stained. The trouser-cuffs were ragged, flapping around naked ankles above bare feet thrust into battered deck shoes. The overall the figure wore seemed baggy, as though the body beneath it were indeed skeletal, but above the waist the stained cotton stretched more fully. The buttons across the breast gaped to reveal swathes of yellowish bandages. The arms also looked a little tight and the hands that issued from them wore fine cotton gloves that once, long ago, might have been white. But if the whole thing was loose in some places it was tight in others. And not just because of the bandaging. The strange figure stood as tall as Richard himself – putting just as much strain on an array of seams. And, bulked up by bandages, he seemed almost as powerfully built as the English Captain.

Above the open collar, a slim neck much in need of a shave rose into yet more bandages. But the face was only partially covered. The chin was hidden, as though by an outlaw's mask in a western, but the mouth, nose, right cheek and right eye were bare while a skull-cap of bandage extended down the left. At the edges, where bandage met flesh, there was yellow ointment oozing thickly over swollen red and black crusted skin. It was the skin of course that was giving off the smell of burning. And the ointment that was giving off the smell of medication. A smell, to Richard's nose, almost of ether. As though the stranger, as well as having been burned, had been gassed.

And yet when the nightmare vision spoke, it did not have the voice of the walking dead – or even of the critically injured. 'I am Jean-Luc, Assistant Radio Operator, Captain,' it said, in deep, southern-inflected French tones. 'I apologize for my appearance – my injuries are not quite as serious as my bandages might suggest. I have been the subject of ill-trained but over-eager nursing. I understand you have some equipment here with which we may save the day.'

Julie joined them almost immediately after Jean-Luc arrived and watched as silently as Ether, while Richard and the Assistant Radio Operator began to put the Hagenuk together. As they worked – following the manual with meticulous care – Richard talked through specifications, systems and procedures, explaining to the Captain and to his two watch-mates what the radio was designed to do, capable of doing and pre-programmed to do.

Ether never really came out from behind the barricade of his guarded silence and Richard soon found himself praying that he was soaking up the information just by listening. For there would be no way to test how much of this he was actually following until he actually got his hands on the equipment – and there was a lively danger that overconfident ignorance would do untold damage there.

Jean-Luc did ask questions, however. Questions that set Richard's mind at least partially at rest. To be frank, he had been expecting an Assistant Radio Operator to be a youngster. Jean-Luc must be his own age or older, though the bandages made it as difficult to be sure of that as of anything else about the man. But, no matter what his age – or the reasons he had taken so long to get to this place and his current post – Jean-Luc seemed to know about modern radios. And even if he had never handled anything quite like this one before, he nevertheless knew the basics and had more than enough acuity to apply them to this cutting-edge technology.

Julie, too, was quick to see what the Hagenuk was designed to do and what it was capable of achieving for them. 'I'll let the automatic tests run in first,' said Richard when it was all set up. 'God alone knows what the journey here has done to it. If we use the automatic set-ups then the self-correction programmes will all be in place – like the disk doctors on a computer hard drive.'

'Will it be OK to do this without the UHF aerial up?' asked Jean-Luc, glancing up at the wire figure of eight hanging from a porthole handle.

'Should be. In fact it's also for SHF and EHF frequencies but they're not what you'd call overcrowded with traffic normally. So, it'll limit our access to some frequencies up in the higher megahertz and gigahertz for the time being but the computer can run tests on all the others and get us out on to the ether. And the alternative is to get the aerial out of the porthole there, then try and stretch it up on to the bridge deck and the communications mast in this weather at this time of night. It's too risky.'

'Why the communications mast?' asked Jean-Luc. 'I thought your chopper guillotined that pretty well for us.'

'That's true, but if memory serves, there's a booster in the base for one. And even if that's useless, then the metal casing is still an effective aerial extension in itself, isn't it? Even if we just attach it there, rather than relaying it into the actual equipment or on what remains of the mast itself, it'll add to the range we have on some frequencies where we can't rely on the satellite one hundred per cent.'

Jean-Luc gave that peculiarly Gallic shrug which said, perhaps, time will tell.

'That will be a job to do when it's light in any case,' confirmed Julie. 'I will need to complete my inspection up there at daybreak. We can see about doing it then.'

'Not until you've agreed the day's menus, though,' said Richard without thinking. 'You don't want to upset Mr Song.'

'Or Chef,' Julie agreed equably. Then, a little more pointedly, 'It is they who really run the ship, after all.'

Richard glanced up and followed her gaze over to Ether's frowning countenance. He gave a lop-sided grin and shrugged, thinking that he would have to guard his tongue. He already suspected the boy was here more as a spy than a helper. He just had to work out why, exactly – and who Ether was supposed to be spying on.

He allowed the grin to linger and fade. Then he pressed the icon on the glowing screen marked 'Automatic Set-up'.

'I don't know how long this will take,' he admitted. 'But, talking of Mr Song, do you think he could be prevailed upon to bring some coffee and maybe a sandwich or two? We can eat while we go through the next set of operating instructions.'

Black coffee and cold steak sandwiches arrived ten minutes later, but it was one of Song's younger acolytes who brought them. He and Ether fell into a brief conversation as the food and drink were laid out on the little table in the day room, but Richard paid scant attention, dividing his concentration between Julie, Jean-Luc, the manual and the pulsing screen.

Richard and Julie tucked into the coffee and sandwiches for neither of them had eaten since the *nems*, nor had a hot drink since they emptied the cafetiére in the Captain's cabin. Jean-Luc and Ether had both been seen to by the inevitable running of the ship's routine – which had fed and watered them in spite of such distractions as disaster in the engine room and the preoccupations of senior officers. But the set-up programme ran on a little longer than the sketchy meal did – longer even than the discussion of the next part of the manual.

Ether at last had the opportunity to ask Julie, 'Captain? You know about trouble in the infirmary? This boy says Uncle Song not come up with your food as is his duty because of some emergency below.'

'What on earth can go wrong in a room full of corpses?' asked Richard, wryly.

'Perhaps it is the other one,' answered Julie thoughtfully. 'The old crews' dining area where you were, Jean-Luc. How many wounded were in there with you? Six?'

'Yes, six. I was the seventh. But there are more now since we pumped out the engine room.'

'Yes. That is what I mean,' added Ether eagerly. 'The new infirmary. Very full. Very busy. There is something going on down there.'

'I can't imagine what it is, but I'd better go and look,' said Julie. 'It could be anything from murder to mutiny; food poisoning to fire . . .' Her voice was dull, flattened, defeated. Not even the late supper had given her the energy to face yet another crisis.

'It can't be anything too critical,' observed Richard bracingly. 'Or someone would have come for you. Or sounded the alarm at least.'

'That's true. I guess Mr Song wanted to sort it out for himself or he'd have sent up a proper message with the steward who brought the sandwiches. Nevertheless . . .'

'Shall I come?' asked Jean-Luc. 'I know them all down there. I'll be able to sort out what's what pretty quickly. Anything up to – but not including – fist-fighting. Or fire-fighting come to that. I've had my share of fire-fighting for this voyage.'

'Yes. Please come. That would be very helpful.'

Jean-Luc looked at Richard, his eye gleaming strangely, reflecting the last few data screens of the automatic set-up. 'You can call in the cavalry without our aid, Captain Mariner. And, if you need to you can tell us how to do it for ourselves when we return.'

Richard was glad to let him go. Julie was looking worse than Richard himself felt – and that was pretty rough. The Assistant Radio Officer might be older than expected and pretty badly singed into the bargain, but he was rested, after a couple of days in bed, and clearly well enough recovered to be clear-headed and quick thinking. If not, as he said, up to fisticuffs or fire-fighting.

But then, to be fair, neither was Richard himself. He felt very old and weary, and all of a sudden, as the sandwiches and coffee reacted with his exhausted system, he felt more like a bedtime biscuit and cocoa.

The screen that swam before his sleepy gaze said: 'Ready'.

Immediately beneath that one blessed word it said 'Program One' in a nice safe blue box. Richard picked up the radio's

119

big padded headphones and put them over his ears. He centred the slim stalk of the microphone exactly beneath the cleft in his square, stubble-darkened chin. He pressed the screen gently, right in the centre of the box.

'Vessel *Sissyphus*,' said the screen in answer. 'Locating . . . Locating . . .'

Richard had a sudden mental image of the Hagenuk's signal rising from the stygian blackness of this desert wilderness of sea up to the welcoming dish of a low-orbit communication satellite circling just above the turbulent, screaming atmosphere. That ear-like disc amplifying and transmitting the plaintive whisper northward, across the Indian Ocean towards the waters south of Durban where the mighty tug was pounding towards them, her radio programmed to light up like a firework display when this tiny cry came.

'Located' came up on the screen, followed by 'Vessel *Sissyphus* . . .' A string of figures followed, which in time would be of crucial importance, for they represented the vessel's call-code, wavelength and location. But for the moment Richard paid them no notice whatsoever. The earphones filled his head with a dizzying surge of static.

Then he heard an answer to his call. '*Sissyphus* here. Receiving you strength nine, *Lady Mary*. Tone ten, crystal clear. How are things with you? Over.'

And Richard discovered that he could not speak. His throat was aching agonisingly and closed into silence as a wave of emotion overtook him. The voice from the South African tug was that of his wife Robin. He had the clarity of mind to think, Christ, I must be a damn sight more tired than I supposed. He fought to clear his throat, 'Ha hum!'

And she recognized the sound. 'Richard, is that you, you bloody man? Over . . .'

'*Lady Mary* here, *Sissy*. And yes, Robin, it's me. Over.'

And so they fell at once into the familiar routine of radio connection, each completing every sentence transmitted with the word that signalled readiness to receive the reply. Richard, at least, almost mindlessly clicking the little button on the stalk of the microphone up and down from receive to transmit and back again.

'What have you been doing down there? We've been waiting for your call for more than eighteen hours.'

'It's a long story, Robin.'

'Well we'd better save it for later. Now who else have you been in contact with?'

'No one. This is our first broadcast.'

'Say again? I can't have heard that right.'

'It's right, *Sissy*. This is our first contact. *Lady Mary*'s first contact in – what? – three days and more.' He couldn't think of any explanation that wouldn't generate more questions than it answered, so he said, 'Over,' and pressed the button.

'Okay . . .' She drew the word out, a habit she had while thinking fast.

He could see her – even without closing his eyes, he could see every curl of her bright-gold hair, the steady depth of her eyes, the determined jut of her chin. She would be sitting, like him, before *Sissy*'s radio equipment and he suspected she had probably been almost constantly on radio watch, waiting for this moment to come; ready even though it had arrived in the small hours of a stormy night.

'Okay . . .' she said again. 'Can you give me a breakdown of your current situation. please?'

'No propulsion. Drifting down on Kerguelen at about one mean knot under a westerly wind blowing at a steady force seven; anemometer says fifty knots plus wind speed. Big following sea. No way on the ship. Proceeding backwards with bridge house acting as a sail. We have power, light and heat. We have just about enough fit crew to work the ship but we have no chance of repairing the motors. The engine room is burned out as are many of the work areas. IG System off line. Repair and refilling of hand-held fire equipment high priority – highest now that we have contact. We set fire to the sea itself this afternoon and were lucky to put it out again. All fires aboard now out but we can't guarantee they will stay out.' He paused. Better not broadcast the fears and suspicions he shared with Julie for the time being. 'Worst injured as of this morning sent off with the BAS chopper that dropped me here. More hurt since then. We have dead and wounded

121

aboard. Wounded both walking and bedridden. But I assess that without help there is nothing we can do here except stay on top of the situation and try to limit any further damage. I'll go through precise headings and so forth in due course – we'll need to if we're going to rendezvous in any case – but at this speed, we'll hit Kerguelen Island in ninety-six hours or so. Over . . .' He flicked the button up into the receive position.

'Okay . . .' she replied. 'Then I have some good news and I have some bad news . . .'

But even as Robin voiced the old cliché, Jean-Luc re-appeared in the doorway, his horror mask of a face worse than it had appeared even at first sight. 'We have trouble,' he said, overriding Robin's words on the radio. 'We have very big trouble indeed . . .'

Twelve

Pulse

'You're sure the captain wants me to come down, Jean-Luc?'

'She sent me up to ask you, Captain Mariner.'

'Very well then. But you will stay here with Ether, please. I am in contact with the ocean-going tug, *Sissyphus*. Robin, do you hear this? I'm leaving the Assistant Radio Operator in charge.'

'I hear you, over,' said the radio. Richard nodded, tearing the headphones off. He pushed the Over button hard down, unknowingly clicking it into a third setting: open transmit mode.

Jean-Luc eased himself into the seat and took the headphones with his cotton-gloved fingers, trying not very successfully to fit them over the bandages. At least both of his jug-handle ears were unwrapped, undamaged and available for use – an important thing in a radio operator, thought Richard, turning to leave the day cabin. As he did so, from the corner of his eye he saw Jean-Luc impatiently pull the whole skull cap away. At least the headphones fitted now over the spiky black of his hair. The last thing Richard heard as he crossed towards the lift was, ''Allo? 'Allo? *Sissyphus*? Do you receive me? Over? 'Allo? 'Allo?'

The frustration of being called away from his first successful communication – and one with his beloved wife at that – was bad enough, thought Richard bitterly. But to be called for just as she was getting to the first crucial pieces of information was almost more than he could bear. All the

123

way down in the lift, he found himself hammering on the metal wall, restless with tension and impatience, in the rhythm of his racing pulse.

He burst out of the doors at the bottom and into the A-Deck corridor like a whirlwind. Outside the door to the makeshift infirmary beside the corpse-filled main infirmary stood Mr Song and the ship's Cook deep in earnest conversation. The fact that Song seemed to have called the cook before he called the Captain should have given Richard – no mean detective – a solid hint even before he got close enough to smell the stenches on the tainted air.

He stopped beside the pair of them and faced down their sudden silence. 'What do you think?' he demanded. 'Food poisoning?'

'Infection,' answered the Cook at once. 'A gastric infection proceeding from . . .' and he launched into a stomach-turning series of suppositions. If there's one thing worse than a hypochondriac, thought Richard struggling to keep up with the increasingly nauseating technicalities, it's a French gastronomic hypochondriac.

'Mr Song?'

'Poison seems likely. But not food poisoning. Some chemical poison perhaps . . .'

So, thought Richard. Standing by your friend, the Cook.

There were all sorts of ways that Chief Stewards and ship's cooks could be bound together in hatred or in amity. Some of them were legal; many of them were not. There were, in fact, whole histories of less than kosher activity by the men who manned the galleys and their colleagues who served the food. At least one ex-Chief Steward of Richard's close acquaintance, a man called Twelvetoes Ho, had left Heritage Mariner Shipping to become the Dragon Head of a Triad in Hong Kong. And Long John Silver, after all, seeking Flint's pirate hoard on Treasure Island, had gone aboard the *Hispaniola* as the Cook.

But the information they had given him – self-serving though it might be – was more than enough to prepare him; coupled as it was by that particular, peculiar stench. 'It smells like dysentery to me but that might just be the combination

124

of uncontrolled emissions from both ends of your patients,' he said, stepping into the foetid little room but lingering close by the door. 'Though Mr Song inclines towards poisoning of the non-food sort.' The light was low, as befitted a sickroom. Julie was just one of several shadowy figures stooping over the sickbeds, taking pulses and moving on; passing bowls and bedpans into the bargain. 'We'll need to disinfect ourselves pretty thoroughly on the way out,' he continued. 'And someone'll have to get a solid list of symptoms then go through all the medical books you've got aboard. While I try and scare up a doctor as well as everything else we need. You'll have to get some willing nurses – if there's anyone strong enough left – and then set up a quarantine area until we find out for certain one way or the other. Did Jean-Luc actually come in here with you?'

'I stopped him at the door,' choked Julie, faintly.

'Thank God for that. I can't imagine how we'd get him disinfected with all those bandages and yellow gunk. Mind you, if it is anything like dysentery, then he's got it anyway. We'll have to keep a very close eye on him and stay clear of him ourselves, just in case. Bugger! I've just thought. I may have to boil the Hagenuk.'

'What?'

'Never mind. Was there anything specifically you want me to do?'

'You've done it, I think.'

'Really? What?'

'Given me a sensible set of priorities to follow. And given yourself another job – of finding a diagnosis, a treatment, medical advice, a doctor or a hospital ship. Whatever's easier. No. Whatever's quicker. I'll see you back on the bridge in half an hour at most. By then I'll have sorted out the symptoms so we can check in the medical books or call for help. I'll have arranged nurses and set up quarantine.'

'And taken a shower,' he added. 'Don't forget. Use disinfectant wash or antibacterial soap. Or both, just in case. I'll wait to hear from you before I start talking to doctors because they'll need symptoms if they're going to give us any worthwhile advice. But I'll check for medical facilities nearby. And I'll send Mr Song and his partner in crime back into the galley with every cleaning device known to man. Better safe than sorry.'

'Rather you than me. Cook's a bit touchy about how he runs his galley.'

'Don't tell me. I know. If there's one thing worse than a temperamental chef it's a temperamental French chef of Chinese extraction. There's probably a Wok and Cleaver Triad somewhere that he'll send out after me.'

But both Mr Song and the Cook were unexpectedly amenable. Or rather, they seemed to be so at first. 'It is logical,' admitted the Cook with a courteous bow. 'Even though this is plainly an infection of some kind, or a case of chemical poisoning as Chief Steward has said, I must nevertheless ensure that the galleys do nothing to spread things wider or make them worse. Rest assured, Captain, that my men and I will scrub our areas from deck to deck-head – every surface, shelf and drawer. And all the crockery and cutlery aboard will go through the ship's dishwashers twice. If we start right now, we may be able to serve some breakfast before noon tomorrow. Always assuming Mr Song and his men can ensure that the supplies we are using and the service they are giving is equally as clean.'

'Naturally, Cook. We will assist you where our responsibilities overlap – in the area of dishwashing for example, and match you where we are solely responsible. And yes. Tell the Captain there may be breakfast from, say, noon tomorrow . . .'

But Julie appeared then. She leaned in the doorway like an angry ghost blown in by the wind. It was just possible to see a pulse throbbing at her temple – enough of a danger signal to bring both her temperamental crewmen into line. 'Breakfast will be as per ship's routine,' she grated. 'I will see you at 0800 with the day's menus, Mr Song and you will be serving *lunch* from noon, Cook. And you will perform your miracles of cleanliness not only in half the time you propose – but with half the men into the bargain. I want at least three of your strongest and brightest *each* to get in here and help with the nursing. You will select them and send them to me here within the next ten minutes, gentlemen. Captain Mariner, I will see you on the bridge in half an hour at the most. I will have set up everything by then and I will have made a list of symptoms. And yes; I shall have showered.'

Richard hesitated outside the lift doors, torn. He was burning to get back to the radio for all sorts of reasons. But it would be simply stupid to give good advice and then refuse to take it himself, especially in such a critical situation as this one. When the lift doors remained shut, therefore, he soon ran out of patience. After a count of about ten he turned and pounded all the way up the companionways, beating the rhythm of his anxiety with his heavy footfalls. As though he could batter the racing of his pulse into the very fabric of the ship. He ran out on to C Deck and without even pausing to look around he jogged down to the Captain's cabin which he still seemed to be sharing with Julie DuFour. He ripped off his overall as he went in, then had to wander round in his underwear looking for a new one. He discovered rather more than he wanted to about the late Captain Giscard's fixation with ladies' underwear as he checked in likely-looking drawers.

When he tried the wardrobe, it was the emergency medical box on the upper shelf that took his attention at first. Luckily, there was a selection of overalls in various sizes hanging on the brass rail immediately beneath it, so he took out the largest and proceeded. He would have to stick with his own socks and underthings unless he wanted to try some lace-topped, self-supporting nylons with neat black seams and a salmon-pink Janet Reger thong with diamante fastenings.

A piping-hot shower was just what the doctor ordered in any case, and he soaped himself lustily, body and head, careful only of the extremely tender lump on the back of his cranium and the little square bandage that seemed to be super-glued in place over it. Within five minutes he was out, as sleek as an otter, and towelling himself vigorously. Five minutes after that, he was as disinfected as he ever wanted to be and pounding back up the inner companionway towards the bridge, too impatient to wait for the lift.

Richard sensed that things were not quite right as soon as he came on to the bridge, for there was no sign at all of the ever-present Sophie Bois. Until now, her utterly reliable presence on bridge watch had been the only fixed star in a wildly whirling universe. Frowning, he looked around the gloomy cavern of the deserted bridge, but there was no one there to blot out the colourful constellations of lights. No face or figure to catch ghostly brightness from the pulsing displays. 'Sophie? Cadet Bois?' he called, quickening his already rapid pace across towards the chart room. But only the relentless keening of the banshee wind answered him.

It had just occurred to him that Sophie might well have been called into the day room to give some information for broadcast to *Sissy* – the ship's last recorded position, say – when that hope too was dashed. As he strode through the chart room, he could see in the steady glow from the Hagenuk's screen that the day room too was empty.

No. Not empty. There was someone lying on the floor, part hidden by a combination of overturned chairs and fallen mattress, part hidden by shadows. He hit the light switch as he ran in through the door and in the forensic brightness saw a body lying face-down in a modest but worrying pool of blood. Under the mattress and the chairs, surrounded by the signs of some kind of scuffle, the body was lying right across the middle of the room, as though trying to place itself between Richard and the Hagenuk somehow. He froze, calculating, eyes everywhere. This might very well be murder. It was at the very least assault. There would be police here, in due course: gendarmes trying to build some kind of case.

But his first duty was clear – to preserve life, if there still was any; not to preserve a crime scene until some all too-distant investigation in the far, far future. Even so, the first thing that he checked, with long, careful scrutiny, was his precious radio. Only when he was as sure as he could be from looking across the room at it that it was still OK did he proceed with more immediate matters.

Richard knelt, disturbing as little as possible. He shuffled forward a little and leaned carefully forward, thrusting his fingers under the angle of the body's jaw. And, after an instant or two, he felt a faint throb of life. He pulled out his fingers, wiped the yellow gunk thoughtlessly on his clean overall, crinkling his nose against the dizzying stench of ether once again, and reached forward to roll Jean-Luc on to his side so that he could check for the source of the blood. And he did not have far to look.

The most serious wound was on Jean-Luc's temple – ironically on one of the few unbandaged parts of his face. It was ragged and looked deep. It was still pulsing blood, suggesting that one of the little arteries running round the outside of the skull had been ruptured. An offshoot of the anterior temporal artery, as likely as not. But when Richard gently probed the damaged area with a careful finger, he felt reassuring swelling rather than worrying softness in the thin temple bone itself. A glancing blow, then, on some of the overturned furniture likely as not. The cheek below it was white, suggesting clinical shock, and the eye between, hollow, dark and restless. When he pulled up the eyelid, the pupil looked suspiciously dilated to him. More than shock, perhaps: maybe concussion. More than might be expected from the wound on the temple, no matter how bloody it was. Richard checked further, therefore. And so he discovered another, much more serious bump. A great welt running right across the back of the cranium. Not pumping blood this time, but oozing plentifully into oily, matted hair. But Jean-Luc's vital signs were steady. And that nasty little gusher showed no sign of slowing its bright arterial pulse. The bandage completely obscured the mouth, but it was being sucked in and blown out in irregular ragged gasps.

Richard looked up, as torn as he had been fifteen minutes earlier outside the lift. If he had come straight here instead of going for a shower, he might have been able to prevent this. Whatever 'this' actually was. But there was no time for recriminations, what-ifs or self-doubt now. He had to run with what he thought was best. And his immediate course of action seemed quite clear, if worryingly against routine. He had to leave the bridge untended and look for treatment – if not help. He had to leave Jean-Luc here because there was no way he would have been able to carry him far – even had he dared risk the damage to the earlier wounds. He briefly considered calling for help over the ship's intercom – but dismissed the thought stillborn – there was enough panic about as it was.

As Richard calculated his next move, he grabbed the skull-cap of bandages from beside the Hagenuk and used it to put some pressure on the temple wound – then he was off. Whether there was concussion or just clinical shock, blood loss was a bad thing to combine with it. He had to get back here with the medical kit and staunch that artery. That was the highest priority. At the moment, it was the only possible priority.

The lift did not even acknowledge his summons, yet again in use somewhere below, and so he simply plunged down the stairwell beside it, racing down the companionway that had brought him up here. Down one deck he leaped, skidding round the corner and running along the corridor to the Captain's cabin – and the medical kit above the overalls on the wardrobe there. Such was his hurry, he didn't even pause when he hit the door. He threw it open and charged in. Eyes fixed on the wardrobe door, he was halfway across the room before a glimmer of pale light in the corner of his eye broke through the blinker of his tunnel vision.

Julie was standing in the shower-room doorway, starkly emerging from her shower, like Botticelli's *Venus* rising from the sea. But without the convenient clothing of long hair. Such was Richard's shock that he froze in mid-stride; the only part of him still moving was his suddenly thudding pulse. Such was her own surprise that she stood there too, eyes and mouth wide. She was holding a towel but it was motionless in the act of drying her hair and she made no move to hide any part of her body with it. She made no move to hide herself at all, in fact.

It was not the perfection of the nakedness in the doorway that made it slip, like a subtle poison, into the subconscious of his exhausted mind; it was its imperfections. The way, for instance, that the dusting of freckles across the tops of her cheeks and the bridge of her nose was echoed on the upper slopes of her breasts. It was the bewitching intimacy of her navel, an upturned little cup atop a decided valley reaching down the middle of her lower abdomen. It was not the athletic perfection with which her toned thighs sat in the solid square of her pelvis he noticed most. It was the great purple bruise across her right hip, which told of danger faced and pain bravely borne. It was the fact that on her left upper thigh, sweeping across to the eggshell swell of her belly itself, there were scorch marks like those on the engines below. Traces, still, of the yellow gunk that had also tended Jean-Luc's burns, and the red weals that told of a recently removed bandage. Which explained the lack of steam, too. Her shower had been cool – those burns and bruises could hardly have withstood much more in the way of heat.

She did not cover herself, but she stepped back, turning away. Revealing for another second that lingered in his mind the fact that the scorch marks swirled like some weird body paint, right round her left hip and across the pallid tenderness of her bottom into the bargain.

'Why are you here?' she asked as she moved.

'Jean-Luc is hurt. I have to stop his head bleeding. It's an artery . . .'

'Jean-Luc! Throw me that overall. I'll come up at once.'

He did as she bid him, tossing the crisp cotton of a clean overall from the bed through the doorway as he fell into motion again and crossed to the wardrobe where he pulled down the first-aid box. When he turned, she was coming out of the shower room once more, closing the buttons across her breast. The rapidity with which she had dressed told him that she had not paused to re-bandage her hurts – and distractingly suggested that she had not put on any underclothes either. She stepped into some deck shoes and held the door open for him.

'You need to get those burns seen to again,' he said, fighting to sound distantly paternal, as they hurried up the corridor.

'Are you offering?' Her own tone was difficult to read. Certainly not teasing or playful. But hardly serious either.

'I'm trained and capable. But wouldn't it be better if someone of your own sex did it?'

'I'll ask Sophie when we have time.'

Sophie, thought Richard. Yes. That was something else he would have to discuss with her soon. And Ether, come to that. But one crisis at a time.

Such was Julie's concern for Jean-Luc that, when the lift refused to answer their summons, she, like Richard, went bounding up the companionway instead. Such, indeed, was her worry about the state of the Assistant Radio Operator that she did not seem to register the fact that Sophie was no longer at her watch post.

Jean-Luc was lying exactly as Richard had left him. The two Captains knelt side by side beside him, crowding the entrance to the little room. Richard opened the first-aid box and started sorting out the bandages he needed. Julie, meanwhile, went through the same sort of routine that he had done earlier, checking pulse at his throat and pupil beneath his eyelid.

'Slide the bandage back over his head, would you?' asked Richard. 'I'm going to disinfect the wound then try some styptic and a pressure bandage on the artery itself. Phew! What is that yellow stuff everyone's burns are covered in?'

'I don't know exactly. Some stuff the First Officer La Motte had. We've been using it ever since he got it out. It helps the pain but I don't know if it cures the burns.'

'It smells of ether . . .'

'Does it? I hadn't noticed. Is that important?'

'I've no idea. Hold his head steady, please. Let's just get this bandage into place. There . . . Now, let's move him out on to the bridge. We can bring the mattress out too and make him comfortable on that. Then if you can keep an eye on him there, I'll tidy up in here and check on the radio.'

Five minutes later, Richard was back in the chair – though it creaked beneath his weight more than it had done last time he sat in it. The earphones were back in place – as was the thin stalk of the mic – and as soon as he touched the screen it all came alive. It had slipped into saver mode, and seemed set on transmit rather that receive.

Richard touched the button on the mic. It was set in an unfamiliar position. He clicked it over to receive and at once he heard. '*Sissy* here, *Lady Mary*. Are you receiving me?

Over?' The incoming voice was at once bored and worried. Robin had clearly been repeating the message over and over for some time.

Richard pressed transmit and spoke at once. 'Loud and clear, *Sissy.* This is Richard. Is that you, Robin?' They fell at once into the familiar standard routine.

'Richard. Thank God. What in heaven's name is going on over there? You've been broadcasting on an open channel for more than half an hour though no one's been communicating for a good while and we haven't been able to raise any answer until now. Over.'

'Broadcasting? What?'

'It sounded for all the world like a fight. What is going on?'

'I'll tell you later. Tell you what though. Has your equipment on *Sissy* got a hard drive like this Hagenuk?'

'Yes it has. Why?'

'Then it's like the children's new Sky TV box at home. It will have recorded what we broadcast, won't it? You can keep the fight, as you called it, and play it back to me when I have time to investigate matters a little more closely.'

'Sparks here says we can do that, no problem.'

'Good. In the meantime we have more problems to discuss. But I cut you off. You had good news and bad. Have you passed that along to anyone aboard here yet?'

'No. What do you want first?'

'Hit me with both at once. It'll save time.'

'Okay. The good news is we have scared up another tug that may be able to get to you in time. Her call sign is *Oscar Whisky* and she's out of Bunbury, South-East Australia. She's less than 1,500 miles north-east of you. Her top speed is eighteen knots so she could be with you in three days.'

'Less if she's coming from the east – that's the way we're drifting. What are her specs?'

'That's what's so good. She has four engines and two variable props the same as us. She's a bollard pull of 150 tonnes if need be; that's 100 tonnes less than *Sissy* of course, and nowhere near enough to be of use to you all on its own. But the really good bit is that she carries four massive fire monitors delivering water and foam from an extendable hydraulic arm and mast. And I do mean they're massive. Each monitor is capable of delivering 1,200 cubic metres per hour for water – more for foam, depending on density. How does that sound, Richard?'

'Like the answer to a maiden's prayer. We can set fire to the whole Southern Ocean and she'll still be able to pull us out from the sound of things. Now, what's the bad news?'

'It looks like there's something else going to get to you before *Sissy* or *Oscar Whisky* can.'

'And what's that?'

'A really nasty Southern Ocean storm. It came past the BAS base at Rothera more than twenty-four hours ago and they've recorded force twelve conditions on the Beaufort scale. It was still building then, though the low at its centre is pulsing around 920 millibars. This is mostly computer-generated from satellites, you understand. No one's sitting around in the middle of it trying to take accurate measure-ments. Everyone's running at full power trying to get out of the way of the thing.'

'Everyone who has power. Which rules us out, of course,' said Richard, interrupting her. 'Tell me the worst.'

'It's currently up into force thirteen super-hurricane, they say. I doubt it myself. Storms that severe are very rare indeed. But now that you're back on line you can check it out for yourself. There is certainly a total white-out over land. Huge seas. Wind speeds gusting up around 200 mph from the north-west. Over.'

'How long have we got?'

'It'll be with you within the next forty-eight hours. We'll keep you posted. Over.'

'Over and out,' he said, without even bothering to depress the little button.

Thirteen

Passage

Richard was still sitting there, deep in thought, when Julie came back from transferring Jean-Luc down into the sickbay again. Although she had summoned up a little team of acting medical orderlies to help her move the unconscious radio operator, she returned alone to find Richard still sitting thoughtfully in the creaky chair, apparently having sat there like a statue in the meantime.

He hadn't been idle, however. He was one of those people who think best while physically active and so in the interim he had completed tidying the area and checked the equipment, satisfied that there would be no murder enquiry after all. He was beginning to suspect that this was all probably the result of some ill-natured brawl rather than a coldly premeditated attack, though under the circumstances he was unwilling to leave the Hagenuk unwatched. Although it was quite possible that the attack on the radio operator had been a personal thing, it might well have been an attack on the radio itself, thwarted by Jean-Luc somehow. The logic of circumstances made that quite likely – given the lengths someone had gone to in order to destroy most of the other equipment aboard. But then, given that background, a whack on the back of the skull and a cut on the temple seemed pretty small beer in comparison. And the radio was apparently undamaged.

That thought, however, resulted in a further five minutes checking the equipment itself and its immediate environment with microscopic care. Richard didn't want the Hagenuk to suddenly transform itself into something like the inferno that had consumed the ship's original radio – and the men who had been manning it. But there was nothing obvious.

Only time and witnesses would reveal the truth of the matter, he decided at last. And apart from Jean-Luc, there should have been a couple of other watch-keepers there to see what had happened. Though how Sophie and Ether would fit into the picture was something he would only be able to work out when he caught up with the pair of them, wherever they were. Had he not been worried about the security of the radio, in fact, Richard would probably have gone looking for them himself. But, of course, he was worried about them. And Robin's message had given him quite enough to think about in the meantime. So he sat back down in the creaking chair, and immersed himself in speculation.

'Jean-Luc's quite comfortable now,' announced Julie, as she arrived. 'But he had a hell of a trip down the companionways. We had to take him off the mattress and carry him in the end, when we couldn't scare up the lift. Still he's all tucked up and quiet now. But that's more than I can say for some of the others down in the sickbay. Have you got hold of any doctors yet?'

Richard gave a near silent grunt of wry laughter. This was the last thing that had been on his mind. Typical that it should have been Julie's top priority. He sometimes had lengthy conversations with his wife Robin along exactly the same lines. What did they say? What we have here is a failure to communicate . . .

'No,' he admitted. 'Have you got any sensible symptoms to give me when I do?'

'Apart from the obvious?' Her tone was tart. She was used to such failures of communication herself, clearly. Like the odd set of priorities Honore and Raoul had displayed, rearranging the corpses of the senior officers – a task as useful as rearranging deckchairs on the *Titanic* – instead of checking their watch areas and getting ready to try and get them back on line.

'So your patients are still displaying much liquid and semi-liquid emission at both ends, yes?'

136

'Yes. That at the back end not only noxious in odour but in colour. It's the most revolting green I have ever encountered.'

'Right. That sounds unusual enough to be a symptom.'

'But you haven't scared up any doctors.'

'Not yet. I've been putting things back, wondering what in God's name happened, and digesting some other news while keeping an eye on the bridge. Where's Sophie?'

'Off watch somewhere.' Julie looked around, apparently struck for the first time by the fact that they were here alone. 'She's probably eating or sleeping: she's earned it. More to the point, where's Emil? I sent him up to relieve her a while ago.'

Richard shrugged. 'Looks like he and Ether went off somewhere. Perhaps Jean-Luc sent them on an errand just before he was attacked.'

To tell the truth, Richard was beginning to lose track of who was where. Who was in which area and on what watch, especially as some of the designated watch-keepers were now dead. It must be the same for Julie, he supposed. And things were just about to go from bad to worse as far as he could see.

'We'll have to sort out the watches again later,' said Julie, after a moment's silence. 'We have a good deal to sort out later, one way and another. In the meantime, what news have you been digesting?'

'Ah. The news. Well, some of it's good. Some of it's bad . . .'

Julie went straight to the heart of things the instant he finished explaining what Robin had told him. The sickness, the attack – even the non-appearance of Emil and Ether took second place for the moment. Her new-found willingness to discuss things which had been anathema to her until so recently, was a pleasant surprise to him, so he fostered it. 'These tugs, *Sissy* and *Oscar Whisky*,' Julie began. 'Can they pull us clear of Kerguelen, given the opportunity? Have they got the power if they have the time to do the job?'

'They could pull us over into Resolution Passage, yes. But only if they are given enough time, as you say. Even swinging

137

us round that far will be a pretty lengthy job, I'd say. And, now I think of it, I doubt whether they could stop us dead in the water and hold us still while we waited for a more substantial rescue to be mounted or for a new crew to be sent out with the equipment needed for repairs. We'd need to be sitting safe at anchor for that to be a real possibility. And I see no chance of them tugging us into safe haven in Port aux Français or even Passe Royale, come to that. Though we should keep the possibility in mind as something to discuss nearer the time or as an emergency fall-back if push comes to shove. No. The winds, the waves and the currents would all be across our course if we tried that, and the hull would be very difficult to control indeed. I'd say we'd need a minimum of four tugs to be on the safe side. With only two, they'd probably need long lines and a wide waterway to pull it off, and that's exactly what we have not got. Particularly as the weed around the island is likely to make any kind of tug-work almost impossible as we got closer to shore. There's enough kelp in those waterways to clog up even the best protected propellers in no time flat.'

'That would be a way forward,' she said, brightening up, apparently having failed to register his list of difficulties. 'If they could pull us into any kind of protected anchorage where we could sit and wait for the owners to get something arranged . . .'

'Perhaps. But on top of everything I've just said, the nearest anchorages are in environmentally delicate areas, remember – even if they're not all designated as sights of special scientific interest. And as she stands, *Lady Mary* is a dangerous ecological hazard. With the lively potential to be a full-blown biological disaster. We'll only get permission to go into any anchorages near Kerguelen if there is absolutely no alternative. And, I should think, we'd only get permission even then if there is some kind of agreed rescue in place – together with a very tight time scale. And a raft of insurances and guarantees big enough to float an elephant.'

'OK. I see that.' Julie was crestfallen; deflated.

'But if we can get past Kerguelen,' persisted Richard forcefully, 'then we can drift eastwards almost the whole

138

way round the world while some sort of rescue is sorted out. Make it through Resolution Passage and you're safe.'

'Safe from natural disasters at any rate,' allowed Julie. 'But it'd be a bit like being *The Flying Dutchman*, wouldn't it? Drifting for ever through the Southern Ocean.'

Richard continued with his thoughts as though he hadn't heard her. He considered it a major step forward that she was willing to plan for the tugs' arrival now and he didn't want her side-tracked at all. 'I'd emphasize that we'd need both tugs working together even to get as far as Resolution Passage, though. Not only for the power, the bollard pull, but also for the safety aspect. In case the sea goes on fire again. Getting lines aboard and starting towage is the kind of thing likely to spark something off, after all. I should imagine under the circumstances that *Sissy*'s Captain will only come close enough to get a line aboard if there is some kind of fire safety plan in place. And *Oscar Whisky* sounds like the best plan we're likely to come up with. But apart from that, it's the time frame that is the most important.'

'Then it is the storm that is crucial.'

'That was my thinking, yes. Crucial in several ways, of course.'

'Whether we can survive it for starters . . .' Julie gave a dry laugh spiced with more than a hint of bitterness.

'Indeed. But we've a fair chance of that,' answered Richard bracingly. 'It's a big storm by all accounts – but we're a big boat. And we'll at least be facing into it – though with *Lady Mary*'s current disposition, a north-westerly will hit on the starboard quarter at first – until she swings round again. But then there's the question of how much faster a westerly hurricane will push us eastwards, cutting into the time the tugs have got to get us into Resolution Passage before we bump into Kerguelen Island itself.'

'But it is a *north*-westerly hurricane . . .'

'And therefore might push us *south*-eastwards towards Resolution in any case. Start the tugs' work for them. Good thinking, Julie.'

'But there is also its duration,' persisted Julie, caught up

139

in the plans now, and deep in thought. 'That will be crucial. If it hits in two days and lasts for three days . . .'

'Then we're lost,' admitted Richard grimly. 'That will be our five-day rescue window closed because no one will be able to get a line aboard if wind and weather conditions are too severe. It will push us eastwards even faster than the prevailing winds are doing now. Drive us on to Kerguelen with even more force than the one knot we're moving at currently. And that will be that! But if it hits in two days and lasts for forty-eight hours or less, then we're still in there with a chance . . .'

'Ha!' Julie gave a bark of humourless laughter.

'What?'

'I was thinking. If we can manage to get control of the crew and the vessel again; outwit whoever is planting these incendiary devices. Overcome whatever new medical disaster is looming down in the sickbay. Find out who on earth beat up Jean-Luc and why. Then we only have to rely upon the good nature of a Southern Ocean hurricane and we'll be fine.' She look a theatrically deep breath and rolled her eyes hammily. 'Fine, that is, if we can get two tugs down here, two lines aboard at least and get pulled into Resolution Passage without setting the ocean on fire.'

'That's about the size of things, Julie. You up for it?'

'What choice do I have?'

'The same choice you had about allowing me to come aboard this morning.'

'Bugger all, in fact.'

Richard nodded and gave a wry smile. 'Far be it from me to disagree with a lady,' he said. 'Or, more importantly, a Captain.'

Julie reacted to the growing intimacy of their conversation by pulling back at once. Emotionally and physically. 'Where is Emil?' she demanded, rising and walking out on to the bridge itself.

Richard watched her quizzically. The curves of her back, bottom and thighs were outlined by the tightness of her clothing which seemed to be moulded to every nook and cranny, more like paint than cloth. Reminding him all too forcefully that the thin white cotton was all she was wearing at the moment. He frowned, distracted. Here was a woman, it seemed to him, who was not at all disconcerted by physical intimacy. The occasional flash of nudity, even. But emotional intimacy was not so much to her taste. Was this to do with her nationality? Her Frenchness – if such a word or thing existed. Or was it a boarding-school trait, this almost casual assumption that privacy was impossible so they should just get on with the job in hand no matter who saw what? Richard was the product of a boarding school himself and rather valued his privacy as a result of all those years of enforced closeness to numbers of other boys. Or was it part of being the new woman – this almost masculine leaning towards the physical rather than the emotional side of relationships? How many ships had he served on where the common dream of the predominantly male mess hall was the maximum of great sex with the minimum of ties, comebacks and payment? Were women beginning to dream the same dreams these days?

The clean-air monitor he had used in the engine room slipped into his memory. Or rather the Geiger counter it had reminded him of. For at the heart of his adventure on the Russian submarine *Titan 10*, where he had used a Geiger counter, there had been another woman who had been happy to flaunt her physicality while remaining emotionally at arm's length. In that case it had all been an act – for the fair Maria Ivanova had been using her sexuality as a mask. Beneath her distracting availability she had been hiding murderous schemes. A double life that had of course demanded that she maintain an emotional distance designed to allow her to weave her web of lies and deceit.

Was Julie just Maria Ivanova reborn? Richard most fervently hoped not. It would be difficult enough to keep a lid on this incredibly dangerous situation even if he felt he could trust her. If he had to be watching her all the time – as well as everyone else – then they were all as good as dead.

On that less than happy thought, Richard leaned forward and started tapping the screen of the Hagenuk once more,

141

trying to make contact with at least one place where he was certain to find a doctor – the British Antarctic Survey base that had lent him the Westland chopper this morning. Theirs was one of the contacts pre-programmed into the radio's memory. And the radio lit up with all the correct code numbers for 'Contact Established', but the base stubbornly refused to come on line.

Just as this happened, Julie ran out of patience. The chimes of the ship's loudspeaker system sounded. 'Fourth Officer and Acting Radio Cadet Lau to the bridge please. Fourth Officer and Cadet Lau to the bridge at once.'

After ten minutes of useless calling on the radio answered only with a stormy roar of static, Richard gave up on that one and started checking one or two others – including the main BAS base away round at Rothera – but all he got from the south and the west was static. Stymied for the moment, he switched out of the first pre-programmed mode and started sending more general signals.

Because of the nature of the work the Hagenuk was going to be called upon to do, Richard had caused the radio's controlling computer to be programmed in a manner he thought logical, even for general frequency searches. The radio did not search simply by band or call sign, therefore. It did not simply search up and down the frequencies like a domestic radio with a digital tuner going from one strong signal to the next no matter what was being received or where it originated from. It searched by proximity first.

Richard had asked for this on the simple assumption that if he was going to be calling from a ship with little or no engine power, it would be better to establish contact with vessels sailing closest to her in the first instance. For these, of course, would be the vessels most likely to be able to offer assistance should they need it – except for those like *Sissy* and *Oscar Whisky* who were already coming as fast as they could to help. The radio therefore shuffled through location codes first, sweeping in circles that expanded like the radars on the bridge behind him, fifty-mile radius; one hundred-mile radius. One hundred and fifty – and so forth. Richard was just beginning to understand that he had set the gradations – expanding the sweep by fifty miles a time – far too tightly when Julie came back in off the bridge.

'Look at this,' said Richard at once, still fiercely focussed on the job in hand. 'I should have set it to expand at 250 miles a time. Jesus, are we ever at the back end of nowhere!'

But even as he spoke, the radio lit up, displaying 'Incoming Signal'.

'Receiving you strength ten, *Lady Mary*,' said a voice in French. 'This is the Research Station at Porte aux Français, Kerguelen Islands. *Chef du District*, Alain Faure here. You are running late, *mes braves*. We were expecting to hear from you days ago. How are my old friends Marcel Giscard and Michel La Motte? Over.'

'This is Captain Richard Mariner aboard *Lady Mary*,' began Richard at once. 'Receiving you strength ten, tone ten, Porte Aux Français. Good evening, Chief Faure. I'm afraid I have some bad news . . .'

A hand fell on his shoulder. He looked up startled. It was Julie. 'Let me,' she said. 'At least I know the man.'

Richard nodded once and continued, 'I have Julie DuFour here, Chief Faure. She will take over this contact now, over.'

As Julie slid into the seat, Richard discovered that she had not come in off the bridge alone. Ether was standing in the doorway looking a little hangdog.

'Where have you been hiding?' asked Richard, his voice quiet but forceful, leading the newly appointed Acting Radio Cadet out on to the bridge itself.

As he did so, he heard Julie begin, 'Alain, it is Julie here, over.'

'Sparks got hungry so he sent me down to talk to Uncle Song . . .' Ether gestured to the chart table where a pile of sandwiches sat carefully clingfilmed on a plate beside a mug of fragrantly steaming coffee. His sense of wounded innocence made his grip on idiomatic English go from bad to worse. 'Uncle Song and everyone in the galley velly busy. Everything shut for cleaning, they say. Give me really hard time. Took some time to get them to make the food. And the lift is all time busy so I'm up and down the companionways like a fligging yo-yo.'

143

'Was Cadet Bois down there?' asked Richard. 'The Captain sent her to get some food.'

'No chance. Galleys closed for cleaning.'

'She's probably turned in, then.'

'I think not,' supplied Ether unexpectedly. 'Her cabin is open. Empty.' He caught Richard's look askance. 'I do steward work before I become Acting Cadet Radio Operator,' he explained, as though he had been promoted to his current eminence many years since. 'Of course I know her cabin. Many time I take her coffee. Food. Change bedding. Take out laundry.'

'But she's not there?'

'Not now. I just come past her cabin with sandwiches and coffee for Sparks . . . Waste of time.'

'Oh I don't know . . .' Richard picked up the coffee and savoured the aroma, preparing to sip. 'Seems like your time was bloody well spent to me.'

He looked back into the little day room where Julie was deep in conversation with the Chief of Station on Kerguelen. He did not dwell on the bitter irony that ensured that the little outpost on the rocky island lying directly in their path was also the nearest available radio contact – probably by the better part of a thousand miles. He lowered the cup of coffee back, untasted. Then he picked up the plate of sandwiches and carried it all through to the makeshift radio room. He put them at the Captain's elbow and caught her eye until she nodded understanding of what he had done – though she hardly paused for breath.

'That is correct, Alain. Green. What do your medical books say there? Green . . .'

Richard strolled back through the chart room and on to the bridge. Julie's call to Alain on Kerguelen was clearly going to take some time if she was going to check all the symptoms and, likely as not, the weather predictions; he'd lay handsome odds, the anchorages in Passe Royale and Porte aux Français into the bargain.

Without any further thought, Richard crossed to the console and pressed the button by the microphone there. Where he had hesitated to use it before, Julie's willingness to use it five minutes ago put all his second thoughts to rest. The familiar chimes sounded. 'Would Acting Chief Engineer Honore report to the bridge at once please,' he ordered. 'Honore to the bridge.'

Such was the calm authority in Richard's tones that Honore came puffing up without a second thought – without even a whimper of complaint – within five minutes. 'What is it, Captain?' he enquired, civilly enough.

'You have a problem,' Richard informed him almost cheerfully.

'I do? With what?' Honore, of course, was more guarded. He was probably aware of a wide range of possible problems and wondered which of them had attracted Richard's notice.

'With the lift, as far as I can see.'

'The lift?' Blank incomprehension. 'But what is wrong with the lift?'

'It's not answering.'

'Then someone must be using it.' Honore shrugged.

'It hasn't answered for at least an hour. No one I've talked to, since before Jean-Luc was attacked, has been able to summon it. I've tried several times myself. There aren't enough people left aboard to be using it that much.'

'No one can be stuck in it,' calculated Honore, his mind beginning to register the situation and examine alternatives. 'The alarms are working now with all the rest.'

'That's what I thought. Therefore there is a problem.'

'To be fair, Captain,' Honore was at his most confiding. He looked like a knowing bloodhound. 'In the face of everything else, it seems hardly to matter a damn whether the lift is working or not.'

'But if you think about it, Honore, in the face of everything else, even a little fault could have almost unimaginably serious implications.' Just saying this for some reason made the short hairs across the back of Richard's neck begin to prickle. And he realized he had been nursing an increasingly bad feeling about the lift just below his consciousness for quite some time now.

'Very well,' allowed Honore, back to his usual defensive

145

huffiness. 'If you insist, then I will summon Chow and his team back to duty.' No sooner had he said this than he crossed to the console and sent the all too familiar chimes ringing through the ship. 'Mr Chow and his team report to the bridge at once,' he ordered. Then he swung back to face Richard, jowls shaking with something between decisiveness and righteous indignation. 'Now we shall see what we shall see,' he announced.

'We shall,' agreed Richard, cheerfully. The engineer swung round and began to make a meal of carrying the weight of outrageously unreasonable orders across the bridge, like poor Lucien reborn. Richard watched him, a wry grin slowly freezing with burgeoning unease. Then he glanced through to where Julie was still deep in conversation on the radio.

The words, 'Your meteorologists are sure, Alain? Force twelve still? When will it reach us?' came across the sudden silence after Honore's theatrical exit.

Two out of three, thought Richard. I should set up as a mindreader. I hope Alain thinks to warn her about the minefields when she starts on about safe anchorages.

'Watch the Captain's back,' he ordered Ether. 'I'm going to be with Honore and his team for a while.'

Fourteen

Shaft

The actual winch gear for the lift stood in the winch house right at the top of the shaft itself. The winch house was a steel-sided housing about the size and shape of a large sentry box, standing utterly exposed, up on the topmost deck beside the damaged radio mast. By the same stroke of design that put it there, a maintenance bay of about half its size had been placed right at the bottom of the shaft. This lay beneath the lowest level the lift car called at, right down in the depths below even the ship's lower engineering sections, where only maintenance teams ever went – and that was extremely rarely. Between these two extremes there were eight levels at which the lift car was designed to call; at one of which or between two of which, logic dictated, it was stuck.

Five minutes later, Chow's team, Richard and Honore were all standing on the bridge deck outside the doors looking up at the deckhead. In the relative quiet of the corridor, above the quiet electrical bustle of the navigation equipment, the wind raved madly, scant feet away. It sounded as though it were some kind of invisible monster trying to tear off the winch house altogether then peel back the thin metal decking to get in at them. Perhaps this hurricane was heading in more quickly than Robin had predicted, thought Richard grimly.

'Given the current conditions of time, temperature, wind and weather,' Honore decided, with unusual authority, 'the winch house will be the last place we shall check. And even then, we will check it only if we have no other alternatives

147

and have found nothing wrong within the bridge house or engineering sections themselves.'

And that seemed reasonable enough to the rest of them, even to Richard. They all stood assembled outside the lift doors beside the bridge itself and waited while, having established that they were not going up or out if they could help it, the engineer tried to call the lift. And then, when it still did not respond, they went on down the inner companionways instead.

On the C-Deck corridor, outside the Captain's quarters, Honore tried the doors again – again with no success. On the B Deck, close to the junior officer and officer cadets' quarters, he tried once more.

'It is a pity there is no deck-level indicator,' observed Honore as he was leading them all down again. 'That way at least we'd have some idea of where the lift actually is.'

'When these ships were built, they thought a Lift Coming light and a Lift Arrived light were pretty state of the art,' said Richard, a little brusquely. 'Honore, can't you just pull open the doors at any level and see where the car is stuck?' He gestured to the emergency release keyhole at the bottom of the right-hand door.

'My key is with the gear down in engineering,' said Honore. 'If I just pull open the doors without it, then the lift will be out of order indeed. Perhaps permanently. The mechanism is temperamental at the best of times. It doesn't take much to put it off line. And we lose nothing by checking in this way. For at least we can be certain that the lift is not at any level we have passed or the Lift Arrived lights would light up when I pushed the Call button, even if the doors did not open for some reason.'

'Logical,' growled Chow quietly. Richard nodded and shrugged, thinking, what if it's between floors? But holding his peace for now. The actual position of the car would be established five seconds after they opened the doors down in engineering and looked up and down the shaft itself. If they hadn't found it before using Honore's more elaborate and suitably old-fashioned method.

They went on down to the A-Deck corridor, where Richard

148

had fallen for the second time that morning and turned the back of his head into a fountain, as Julie had said. Here the howling of the wind was distanced not only by the bulk of the bridge house above them and the mass of the vessel's hull beneath, but also by the constant retching and groaning of the sick in the makeshift infirmary, the murmur of the crew members designated to nurse them and the hissing, splashing and scrubbing coming from the galleys and eating areas beside them as the Chef and Mr Song carried out their Captain's orders right to the bitter end.

It was the suddenness of the silence, as they moved from the upper engineering deck to the next level down, that was a little overwhelming. It fitted well with the fact that they were entering the most tragic and dangerous area of the ship now, like sinners outside Dante's Inferno looking up to see the words 'Abandon Hope All You Who Enter Here' carved on the lintel of Hell's gate itself. They were one level below the sick and the dying; one level above the little pile of corpses which had once been senior officers still lying outside the generator room.

Certainly, even with the growing grumble of the generators, it was a marked contrast to the bustle up above. And because of it, when Honore pressed the lift button, Richard was able to hear a new sound for the first time. It was the sound of the lift door opening and closing, almost noiselessly, at some distance or some depth. It came echoing up the lift shaft – a hiss of movement, a *clunk* and a rattling hiss of counter movement – so quiet that Richard strained to be certain he heard it over the buzz of conversation as Chow's men speculated on this increasingly patent waste of time. 'Quiet,' he commanded. 'Honore, push the button again.'

Honore obeyed. The sounds were repeated. Unmistakable. 'It's down another level or two,' said Richard. 'And there's something caught in the door.'

'Something,' agreed Honore lugubriously. 'Or some*one*. Someone who isn't moving.'

'Right. Honore, where is your emergency key?'

'It's in main engineering, two decks down.'

'Fine. Let's get on with it. We don't need to check the next level at any rate.' He led the way down the companionway on to the level below, past the corpses, past the lift doors and on.

But the companionways did not follow the lift shaft, as they had done up in the bridge house. There they had clung to the shaft itself like ivy round a tree-trunk. Here they leaped off the metal-grated balconies of the work areas and stepped down through the vast spaces of the main engine room. And at each level the little group came past pairs of GP seamen armed with extinguishers, on fire watch, their faces closed, concentrating fiercely, their noses crinkled against the piercing acridity of the smell. Until at last Richard brought them back to the smoke-marked, blast-seared lift doors beside which hung Honore's full lift-maintenance kit. From here on down, the passages to and from the lift doors became even more eccentric still – dictated in the lower and lowest engineering levels by the needs of the ship, its structures and its maintenance requirements rather than by any mere human logic or convenience.

This was main engineering, the level where the long-dead engines sat. This was the lift that Richard had hoped to carry Julie upwards in when her air had given out. The atmosphere stank of smoke and fire retardant. He had actually hesitated on the stair, two turns above, at the point where the CO_2 had replaced the clean air all those hours ago, tricked by some atavistic fear that the deadly gas might somehow have seeped back in now that the pumps had stopped.

So while Honore reached for his emergency key, Richard reached for the clean-air monitor that hung on the rack beside it. He switched this on and waved it around, dividing his attention between the brightening display on the LCD screen and what Honore was saying.

'It is not here!' said the engineer, apparently stunned. 'The key is not here! But it is always here!'

'Do you have a spare?' asked Richard. 'If not, is there anything else we could use? Would a screwdriver do?'

'No! I have a spare, of course. But . . . Well, never mind. It is here, you see? The spare. Readily to hand. We keep things well organized in engineering. Even without the Chief to bully us! Now, you will see this is simplicity itself. The key fits in the lower door here and releases the catch. Then we may slide open the outer doors – or both outer doors and inner doors if the lift car is here. *Zut!* Will this thing never go in correctly?'

Honore stooped without thought – as he had obviously done countless times before, talking as he acted, and pushed the key homeward. But it simply refused to slide home fully. It shouldn't have been too difficult, thought Richard. They weren't dealing with a Yale or a Banham lock here – just a square opening almost at ground level designed to admit a square steel shaft attached to a simple handle in a T shape. Perhaps there was a problem because this was the spare key. Who knew?

With a muttered curse, Honore went down on one knee – for all his ready histrionics a real audience unnerved him, decided Richard cynically. But still the older man could not get the key at the required angle. He went down on both knees, then pulled out the simple key, and examined it almost stupidly before he leaned down to put it into the simple mechanism yet again. He moved forward, looking more closely at the way in which the square shaft slid into the square hole – ready to twist the handle and release the catch that would let the door slide back as he had said. But having stooped so far forward, the engineer simply kept going. As though his head were suddenly as heavy as a cannon-ball, he suddenly rolled forward, slamming the top of his skull on to the echoing metal of the door. Then, as they all stood gaping down at him, he slumped on to his side and lay there, twitching. The key made a strangely loud rattling noise as it shivered in the gateway of the lock.

Instantly, Richard was down on his knees, holding his breath just in case, and, as he held the clean-air monitor down beside the goldfish gaping of Honore's mouth, the alarm began to sound. Richard, his breath still trapped safely in his chest, killed the flashing, shrieking monitor and dropped it to dangle by its lanyard from his wrist. He grabbed the twitching man by the lapels and prepared to haul him erect.

There was utter silence as he did this, except perhaps for the echo of the noise made by Honore's head smacking the metal door. Everyone was watching silently; most of them, like Richard, holding their breath. Even the generator seemed to miss a beat. So that the sounds from the shaft echoed even more clearly than ever: *hissss . . . clunk! . . . hisss . . . rattle, rattle rattle . . .* And, so faintly as to have been impossible to hear until this very moment: *tip, tip, tip . . . tap, tap, tap . . . tip, tip, tip . . .*

Richard straightened up like the piston of a mighty engine, pulling Honore upward with him. 'Mr Chow,' he said as soon as he felt his face must be up in cleaner air. 'Help me hold him up, please.'

The leading seaman and a couple of his quickest-thinking mates took Honore's weight so that Richard could work on him. Richard took his sagging jaw beneath the twitching cheeks in one firm fist and held the face still, boring into the brown, baggy, bloodhound's eyes with every ounce of his own steely gaze. Seeking to impart some of his will into Honore. Before his conscience forced him to begin mouth-to-mouth resuscitation. Somehow the kiss of life on Honore lacked the appeal it had had when he had used it on Julie DuFour. Time was short too, for that almost hopeless tapping echoed in his head. Whoever was trapped in the door down there was alive and calling for help. Just barely, by the sound of things.

'Breathe,' he ordered the choking man. 'Breathe out as far as you can, then breathe in.'

Honore was just conscious enough to obey and Richard's reward for his quick-thinking advice was to get a belly full of vomit over his shoes. Then the engineer was gasping and coughing as his lungs fought to replace the poison gas in his system with as much oxygen as possible.

'That was too close for comfort,' decided Richard. 'Let's get him up to the infirmary. He needs a check-up at the very least. And we all need to suit up before we go any further with this.' He caught the eye of the capable Mr Chow. 'I'd bet the family fortune, such as it is, that there's inert gas from knee-height here right down to the *Lady Mary*'s keel,' he said grimly. 'And if memory serves, that's another level and more down the lift shaft then more areas and crawlspaces right the way down to the skin of her bottom. Two decks down for the lift, though. And someone's stuck in the doorway right down there. Right at the bottom. In trouble, too. You heard the tapping?'

Chow nodded grimly. 'Tip, tip, tip . . . tap, tap, tap . . . tip, tip, tip . . . That's SOS,' he said. 'How 'bout if I send two men up with the engineer and the rest of us suit up now? My men can alert Captain after they drop off the engineer at sickbay. Then we go down shaft for look-see.'

'That sounds like a plan to me,' agreed Richard.

Chow knew where the suits were as well as any engineer. They were hanging on a long rack in one of the workrooms behind the main engineering area like discarded snake skins. The air bottles were next door beside the compressor used to fill them. It had been the ever-reliable Mr Chow and his men who had overseen the refilling of the compressed-air bottles while Richard had been bringing the Hagenuk to life. So confident and competent was the young seaman, that Richard didn't even think about the engineering officers until he noticed a toothpick on the deck beneath an empty hook and suddenly realized he hadn't seen the suave young Antoine for a while.

In spite of everything, Richard decided, as Chow eased his air bottles on to his back and he checked the pressure gauge, he was going to advise Julie to call a lifeboat drill as soon as this particular adventure was over. That at the least would allow them to do an accurate head count. Then the exhausted young Captain – running hard up against the edges of her competence and experience – could reassign watch duties properly. As she had tried to do once already with such spectacular failure. What was the title of that aria form *Turandot* that Pavarotti used to sing? 'Nessun Dorma'. That was it. 'Nessun Dorma': nobody sleeps. Too bloody right.

'You ready, Captain?' asked Chow, his voice muffled. Richard nodded. His thoughts had taken him through the buddying-up routine as though he, Chow and Chow's two-man team were four deep-sea divers.

153

'We need walkie-talkies and torches, just in case,' said Richard, and Chow nodded once, turning to a metal cupboard beside the suits and opening it to reveal torches and radios piled on metal shelves. Richard hung the radio on its lanyard from his left wrist along with the clean-air monitor and slid the torch's lanyard over his right. Christ! he thought, with all this lot on, we'll be lucky to fit down the shaft at all.

Indeed, the bulk of the torch made it almost impossible to turn the key and open the lift doors, which made Richard rethink a little. Monitor, radio and torch all had clips as well as lanyards. They would fit over his belt and free his hands for climbing, delicate work and so forth. Even so, having clipped everything securely in place, Richard still wrapped the lanyards round and round the belt in the hope that they would hold if the clips failed. Then he knelt and, moving deftly and decisively with heavily gloved but uncluttered hands, he turned the key. As soon as he knelt, the clean-air alarm sounded. It stopped when he stood up again, but when he put his fingers in the gap between the newly-released doors, it sounded once again. If he looked carefully he could see the slightest disturbance along the vertical of the opening lift door. As though the rubber edgings were hot enough to make the air waver.

'The shaft's full of inert gas,' he called to Chow. 'The pumps didn't move it when they cleared engineering.'

Chow nodded and pulled the left-hand door as Richard pulled the right. The steel portals slid wide, screaming in protest as they moved, and the two men staggered slightly, finding themselves suddenly standing at the edge of a cliff a couple of decks deep. There was a hand-hold that allowed Richard to steady himself as he leaned in and looked up. The security lighting – one dull bulb per level – showed him a six-deck chimney culminating in the winch gear up above the top deck. The cables and the counterweights hung idly like ropes in a church's bell tower, trembling ever so slightly in the rhythm of the generators – and under the battering of wind and weather that was beginning to make the huge hull pitch a little. Even as he watched, the loops of cable began to swing almost like pendulums, as a stronger blast – or a bigger sea – made the *Lady Mary* roll.

Richard swung out and round, stepping down with his left foot on to the nearest convenient rung of the service ladder that reached from the top to the bottom of the shaft. It took him a moment to balance himself and grow confident that the little iron rungs welded to the steel wall would accommodate his big boots and take the extra weight of his equipment. Then he was off, down the shaft as Chow swung out into the square, steel-sided space above him.

As Richard went past the closed doors that would open on to the lower engineering deck, he paused again and looked down. A couple more steps and he would be standing on the roof of the trapped lift car. The security light showed an almost featureless box with a winch pulley welded to the centre of it. And a trapdoor just visible beside it. Or rather, behind it. Richard was at the front – the door side. The pulley was in the middle, with the cables running through it reaching up to those gently swaying coils above. And the trapdoor was at the back. That was all that Richard could see at the moment – and all he wanted to see. His mind was a whirl of speculation, of course. Plans filled it – designed to meet every situation; overcome any crisis. But experience told him that he had to take one step at a time. And that first step was a physical one – down on to the roof of the little car itself. He moved – and not a moment too soon. The instant he stood back on the solid steel, able at last to release the rungs, Chow's boots filled the spaces so recently vacated by his fingers.

As Chow in turn stepped down, Richard pulled the cables aside as much as he could and fitted the bulk of his torso and air bottles into the area he had been studying at the rear of the car. Chow and he filled all the available space, so the seaman called up to the others and they waited, clinging to the ladder. Richard went down on one knee, pulled his torch off his belt and looked more closely at the trapdoor under the brightness of its beam.

It looked to be about a metre square. It sat snugly in the roof-space of the car and it looked to Richard as though the

155

hinges were on the underside – therefore it opened downwards. It was secured from this side by a series of rocker catches designed to release the trap from above – or from below. If he pulled six levers inwards here, then six catches would swing outwards on the underside and the door would fall open.

Richard released the first four catches – on the two sides of the door that joined the hinged back. Then he hunched round, changing his position to take maximum advantage of the way the thing had been designed to work. There was a substantial handle on this upper side, far deeper and much more solid that would be needed just to hold the weight of the door itself – deliberately intended to be a foot-hold therefore. Designed to facilitate someone climbing up or down the open door, up to or down from the roof where he was crouching now.

All Richard had to do was hold the handle, release the last two catches on the edge opposite the hinge and lower the door carefully – in case there was any danger of causing someone standing just below it a blow upon the head. Before he did this, he thumped on the metal with his torch. It was a final safety check. Anyone in the lift capable of standing up would have been well aware that there were people moving around all too close above his head for the last few minutes. Anyone capable of standing up would not be blocking the door and tapping SOS, of course. But it always paid to take extra care, he thought. After he had done this, he carefully returned his torch to his belt. It would be best to keep his hands free for this, he thought, wrapping the lanyard round and round for extra safety.

Richard released the last two catches and took the weight of the door in his right hand. He opened it slightly and looked down. He was uncertain as to what he had been expecting – a brightly lit interior with someone lying half in and half out of it. He had already narrowed his eyes in the expectation of blinding dazzle. But there was only darkness. The lift-car lights were out. He took a deep breath of rancid, rubber-tasting compressed air and began to feel around his belt for his torch. But then a bright beam punched past his shoulder and down. Chow, thinking ahead as usual.

The bright beam defined a well of shadow that at first seemed simply bottomless. But then, as Chow moved over to try and get the beam at a better angle, a puddle of brightness suddenly defined itself on a wall. As Richard watched, the golden shape moved downwards, seeming to ooze off the wall and slither on to the floor. As he watched it, so he opened the trapdoor more widely and so the torch beam, widening in sympathy, at last lit up a figure lying just as Richard had imagined it.

The figure lay face, down, all except its legs in the lift car itself, the door moving relentlessly in and out against its knees. There were air bottles on its back and the air lines seemed to lead into the headpiece alright. The arms were reaching out towards the walls, gloved fingers spread. The left hand was nearest to the door and beneath it gleamed something metallic. It was easy to see how whoever this was might have tapped SOS with it, though they seemed still now. The body, in fact, seemed too still.

Richard let go of the trapdoor and it swung back to click into place. He slid his hands along the sides of the opening until he could take his weight on his massive shoulders, then he swung his right leg in, seeking that step the better part of a metre down. His body blocked Chow's beam at once but of course Richard would hardly have been able to look down no matter how well it was lit below. His torso and equipment might fit through the hole – but they would only just do so. There would be no space to look down into the little car once he went to the next stage of his climb. He found the step and shifted his weight carefully, straightening his back. The next task he faced was to get his body through the trap, with his air bottles and all the other equipment he was carrying. Luckily his waist was still lean and, even though his chest was deep and his shoulders wide, he was able to fit the air bottles into the square.

'Clear?' he shouted up at Chow.

Light played over him. 'Clear,' shouted Chow.

'I'm going on down then,' he said. But in fact he paused, trying to remember exactly how the body was lying across the floor below him. He took all of his weight on the ball of his right foot, eased himself down until his leg was folded up hard against his belly. He pointed his left foot like a ballet dancer, exploring the vacancy beneath until he felt something solid at the extremity of his boot's rubberized toecap. It must be the faintest touch of the tanks, he thought. He swung the leg wide, let go his hold and stepped down. The muscle up the back of his right thigh tore. His right foot nearly wedged in place, then blessedly it slipped free. His left foot hit the floor and he staggered back, unbalanced both by the size of the step and the weight of the tanks. Had this been a bigger room he would have fallen. But as things were, the wall held him up, though the whole car rocked with the impact and the sound was like the crack of doom.

The beam of Chow's torch flooded the area at once as the seaman surveyed the scene. Richard crossed to the fallen body and took it by the shoulder, turning it over the little way that it would go. The faceplate was starred with a web of white cracks – almost shattered, but apparently holding together – just. The inner surface of the glass was impenetrably covered with blood, as though the face mask had been painted with thick gloss. It was impossible to see the state of the features behind the scarlet mess. But it was just possible to see golden curls.

'It's Sophie,' called Richard, looking up.

The torch beam wavered as Chow swung into position, just as Richard had. Richard shuffled over, pulling the body with one hand and wrestling out his own torch with the other. As he did so, the metal object Sophie had used to signal fell out of her flaccid grip and Richard picked it up. It was Honore's missing emergency key. Richard slipped it into the space on his belt vacated by the torch.

'OK?' he shouted.

'OK,' called Chow. 'Clear?'

'Clear.'

As soon as he called, Chow started swinging down. Cursing the thick gloves, which, like the boots, were an integral part of the suit, Richard fought to find the torch's switch and flick it on. The beam went out through the half-open doors and into the stygian tunnels outside. Richard got a glimpse of rounded walls hung with sagging cables; of distant security bulbs like dying stars in distant galaxies, leading away into incalculable distances; of a rabbit warren of interlinking passages and crawlspaces leading under, round, between the enormous cargo tanks themselves right down the length of the ship; of cold, damp, dripping wetness, filled, he knew with invisible, odourless, deadly gas. With an almost superstitious shiver he turned back to the job in hand once more.

Just as he did so, Chow leaped down and went staggering just as Richard had. The lift lurched. The whole place echoed to the impact of metal air tanks on metal wall. Sophie's body lurched back as well and then rolled forward on to its face again. The door closed until its edge hit the legs then opened once again.

Then Chow was standing, straddle-legged astride the shoulders. He reached down and gripped the straps that held the tanks themselves, pulling himself erect and dragging the body upwards until it was sagging against his chest like a broken mannequin. The little lift car was extremely crowded now. Chow's team arrived on the top and two more torch beams cut into the space around the three down here. Richard glanced up. The one shining his torch most effectively was almost hanging from the cable, just where it fed into the pulley. He was reaching down, Richard realized, hoping to catch Sophie's body and help pull it up – for Chow himself was wedged now and couldn't pull her further without changing his hand-hold. The second seaman was leaning right through the cables themselves, adding the brightness of his torch to that of the other three. Richard pulled in an automatic breath to warn them that they were in an extremely dangerous position. But just as he was about to, the doors wheezed closed behind him. He turned, distracted. Poor Sophie's feet were still in the way. The doors juddered open yet again.

Without a second thought, Richard stepped back, outside the car. He stooped to push the feet safely into the lift car as the doors hissed closed again, but just as he did so, Chow gave another, gargantuan heave and the feet slid in before Richard could even reach them. Richard had acted automatically, without thinking ahead. Without any thought at all, in fact. It could hardly have been more different to his usual way of doing things. And it had all the hallmarks of disaster. He could see all too clearly what would happen next, however, and he stepped forward to prevent it. But his foot skidded in a little pool of oil and instead of stepping purposefully back into the lift, he skidded down on to one knee in the dank little passageway outside it.

'Chow!' he yelled in helpless fury. 'The door! Stop the door!' But he was too late.

With the feet moved clear, the door at last could close. And so it did, with relentless efficiency. But the instant that it did, the simple little programme that controlled the lift's movements clicked into place. The car had been called from every deck in the ship and the instant that the door closed the lift began to rise, automatically answering the summonses.

Richard was on his feet now, punching the lift button on the outside with all the power at his command. Had Chow been quicker thinking – or been nearer to the open door button, he might have been able to stop it himself. But he was hindered by the body he was holding and stood no real chance at all.

The lift's programme engaged, it began to head for the bridge deck where it had first been summoned. The winch pulled. The cable tightened. The pulley turned and Chow's man was lucky not to lose his hand. He was quick thinking enough to let go at once, falling dangerously to one side, smashing his arm and fracturing his elbow. His mate was not so lucky. The cables tightened around him like pythons, trapping his torso. The cables were made of woven metal filaments and were well greased and fairly well maintained but they were old and had seen hard use. The cable scraping across his air tanks scored the metal of their surface like a file, stripping away paint and dullness to reveal almost quick-silver brightness; screaming as they did so like cats in a blender.

The cable grinding down his chest and arm simply snagged the straps of the air tanks and the loose material of his protec-tive suit. Despite his best – most panicked – efforts to pull

160

free, the sharp little hooks of metal pulled it all inexorably into the pulley wheel. The horrified seaman sank to his knees, transfixed as he saw the cloth he was wearing gather itself between the greasy metal jaws. And he realized all too clearly that his arm would follow next. Then his shoulder. Then his chest and head.

With a simple bellow of terror, he wedged the only thing he had to hand into the machinery, trying in vain to tear himself free. His flashlight. The torch was gathered into the pulley with everything else as the lift car rose past the closed doors of the lower engineering section and on up towards the bright promise of the opening at the main engineering section itself. But then, just as the seaman felt his skin beginning to join the cloth of his clothing being ground in the metal mouth of the mechanism, the steel barrel of the torch at last wedged tight.

There the lift car stopped; still five clear feet below the opening. Too high to be accessed from the lower engineering deck doors. With two men trapped on the top of it; one man and a corpse inside it. And Richard shut outside the lowest doors, trapped away down in the gas-filled mammoth maze that made up the bowels of the ship.

Fifteen

Space

The first thing Richard realized was that he had left his torch in the lift. That became obvious as soon as the doors closed, shutting him out in the strange, dripping darkness lit only fitfully by the widely-spaced bulbs of the security lighting. Then he realized that if he waited calmly things would be just fine. He calculated that Chow would go up to whatever deck the lift was programmed to serve, then he would simply push the button and come back down here for him. Chow might stop off to get Sophie to the makeshift infirmary – or to the main one that was serving as the morgue – but all Richard had to do was to wait here and things would be fine.

But then Richard heard the bellows of terror from the roof of the rising lift car, the cat-fight screeching of the cable on the air tanks and finally the squeal of tearing metal as the torch went into the pulley. He heard how the rising hiss of the lift's steady progress came to a thumping, grinding unscheduled stop. He didn't recognize all of the sounds for what they were, of course, but he could guess what most of them were from the danger about which he had tried to warn the men on the roof. And he certainly recognized the last one.

Even so, Richard stepped forward and pressed his ear to the doors immediately in front of him, hoping against hope that he would hear the opening and closing of lift doors high above. The sounds so like the ones that had brought him down here: *Hisss . . . Hisss . . .*

162

The sounds that would assure him that everything was all right after all. But of course they never came. On the other hand, with shocking unexpectedness, the other sound came loud and clear: *Tap . . . tap . . . tap . . .*

The sharp tapping was so vivid, so close at hand that Richard leaped back, spinning around. And the culprit sprang from his belt and went tapping, tinkling and skittering across the slippery metal decking at his feet. It was Honore's missing emergency key for the lift doors. The one that Sophie had tried to signal with and then dropped when he had rolled her over in the lift. The one he had tucked in his belt, and which had clearly tapped against the door just now when he had pressed his ear against it.

At once Richard was scrabbling after it, his eyes fixed on the shadow into which it had vanished. It could well be the answer to his predicament, he thought. With it he could open the lift doors down here at once and gain immediate access to the shaft. If he was lucky, the lift would be stuck in such a position that he would be able to climb past it and out on to the deck. If it had stopped halfway up the doors into the lower engineering sections, for instance, he could open the doors down here, climb up beneath it, open the doors up there and slip out on to the safety of the familiar deck. If it had gone up further, he might even be able to make it through the already open doors into main engineering where the air was clear and breathable above knee-level.

It took Richard several moments down on his knees, his fingers made clumsy and insensitive by the cumbersome gloves, to find the key. In fact he found something else first – a work bag about the size of the shoulder bag in which he carried his laptop computer at home. The key had fallen on top of it and the blackness had been all but invisible in the shadows. Richard opened it, hoping to find a torch at least, but it only contained simple maintenance tools such as anyone might use to check up on anything in the engineering sections. Sophie, no doubt, had been carrying it when whatever happened to her had occurred. Richard put it down in the light beside the lift door and turned his attention back to the key. He experienced none of Honore's difficulty in sliding the metal shaft home into the lock and he turned it with decisive force. The door sprang back a little and he pulled the key free, then rose. He spent a moment tucking the key back in his belt and then he slid his fingers between the edges of the door and pulled it wide. As soon as it was open, he reached in for the rung on the ladder that he knew would be convenient to his hand, and he swung his torso in. He looked up at once. The light in the shaft was marginally brighter than that in the tunnels and crawlspaces around him. The bulbs were just as dull, but there were more of them. There was certainly sufficient light for Richard to see the floor of the lift car and make a rough estimate of where it had ground to a halt.

Without a second thought, Richard swung fully into the shaft and began to climb. He didn't have all that far to go before his head touched the bottom of the car itself. He hung on the ladder and looked carefully around. He could see eighteen inches or so of the lower engineering deck doors. Even if he could open them, he calculated grimly, there was no way for him to get out through the narrow gap. Even if he took off his tanks and relied on holding his breath, he would hardly fit through. And it would be incredibly dangerous to take off his tanks of course, because this deck, like the one he had just been trapped on, had a poisonous atmosphere. It was incredibly frustrating. Even more so because the bottom section of the lift car was in fact almost hollow. Under the floor upon which Chow was still standing – he assumed – there was an open box structure eighteen inches deep which folded inwards into little ledges about a foot deep supporting the cross-beams and braces that strengthened the floor and held the box structure solid. If the car had ended with the floor at Chow's feet there would have been plenty of room for Richard to squeeze out. He reached up and tested the structure. It was steel, and solid. There was no way past it. No way out, even on to the gas-filled corridor of the lower engineering section.

Julie would have to be quick to mount a rescue, he thought grimly. She'd have to rely on Honore pulling himself together. And she'd have to rely on the fact that Chow and his men had made a good job of filling the air tanks or there would be some very dead sailors here before she got them up and out.

No sooner had Richard thought this through than he was reaching for the radio on his belt to make contact and alert the Captain to this latest disaster. But then he stopped. Trying to make a sensible report from halfway up a maintenance ladder in a lift shaft full of inert gas was simply asking for disaster, he thought. So he tapped the radio for reassurance, like a departing driver patting the pocket he keeps his car keys in, and began to climb down.

Tapping the radio did have an effect, however. It dislodged the emergency key and the heavy metal T tumbled down the lift shaft; banging and clanging like a discordant little bell until it landed in the depth of the maintenance bay at the bottom of the shaft with an oddly muffled thump.

Richard stepped out into the corridor again and pulled the radio from his belt. He thumbed the open channel, just as he had done when Lucien set the sea alight. 'Captain,' he said. 'We have a problem. Over . . .'

The radio hissed quietly. The open channel remained undisturbed for a moment, then it suddenly spoke. 'Captain busy. This is Radio Operator Lau. Who speaking, over?'

'Ether. This is Captain Mariner. There really is a big problem here. I need to speak to the Captain at once. Over.'

'Captain on Hagenuk talking to Kerguelen. She say do not disturb, over.'

'Ether, unless you get her attention then five more people are going to die. And I will be one of them. Now, move! Over.'

A moment or two later, Richard's radio spat at him. 'Yes?' Julie was clearly not pleased.

As fully but succinctly as he could, Richard explained the situation to her. Halfway through his report he was interrupted by the arrival of one of Chow's men who had clearly taken his time in dropping Honore off at the infirmary and going on up to the bridge. But the seaman's report added weight and immediacy to what Richard was saying, and by the time he had finished, Julie was galvanized into action.

And the first thing she did took care of the suggestion Richard had planned on making to her the next time they met face to face. She sounded the emergency alarm and summoned everyone who could walk to their emergency stations.

'Stay on the open channel,' she ordered Richard. 'I'll need to keep monitoring you as well as the others in the lift. How's your air pressure? Over.'

He checked. 'Fine. Over.'

'OK. If you don't know your way around down there, it'd probably be a waste of time trying to find your own way up. And if you stay where you are at least I'll know where to find you. If push comes to shove I can either send someone down to you or get Honore – or Antoine when I find him – to talk you up. If they're not too busy getting everything else sorted out, of course. But in the meantime, don't do anything energetic. You need to conserve your air at the very least. Over.'

'Right. Though remember, if things get hairy, if you owe me one full mouth-to-mouth resuscitation. Out.'

But Richard was simply not capable of sitting, conserving air and energy, passively waiting to be rescued. The first thing that distracted him as Julie's rescue attempt got under way was the fact that he had lost the emergency release key. He went back over to the open doors of the lift shaft and for the first time, instead of looking up, he looked down. At his feet was a space the size and shape of an ample double grave. It was there for several reasons – to accommodate the floor of the lift car, which was quite thick and hung with cables of one sort or another. It was there for maintenance purposes, like the well in a garage workshop that allows access to the underside of motor vehicles. It was there as a storage area.

It was clearly capable of being used for all of these purposes. But Richard realized at once with a kind of creeping shock that it was being used for something else as well. It was being used as a hiding place by whoever was responsible for the sabotage aboard. Every available cubic centimetre of spare space seemed to be packed with incendiary bombs. By no means would everyone aboard have recognized the canisters for what they were as swiftly or as certainly as Richard did. But he had burned the appearance of the device that killed poor Raoul deeply into his memory during the moments he had sprayed it with fire-fighting metal powder. And he had not a scintilla of a doubt now.

His first reaction was to look over his shoulder in case whoever had hidden these things here was creeping up behind him – just as they had probably crept up behind poor Sophie at the start of this, he thought. But there was no one there. Then, with the kind of care that lion-tamers use, he stepped on to the ladder and climbed down into the little pit. The bombs were tall and round with flat tops. They stood rank by rank, all neatly piled on top of each other, like tins of beans in a supermarket. Or more accurately – given their size – like cans of beer in an off-licence.

There was a clear area in the centre with a pathway to the ladder's foot just large enough to allow someone to access and organize the stuff down here. When Richard stood in this central space, the walls of bombs around him came almost up to his shoulders. But now that he was down here he could see that there was more than just the bombs themselves. Several spaces had been cleared among the regular piles to accommodate other things. The first of these was a torch. Richard pulled it out and examined it. It was bigger and more powerful-looking than the other torches he had seen aboard. And, as well as a focussed beam, it had a section down one side with two long neon bulbs. He switched this on and the whole well lit up with day-bright white light. Thus he discovered that the bombs were a restful blue in colour for the most part. He was tempted to pick one up and examine it more closely, but he hesitated. His eyes were caught instead by several other cupboard-like spaces. One contained a handgun. He pulled this out and looked at it with knowledgeable interest. It was a Glock pistol; a 34 by the look of things. It was fitted with a red dot sight. Richard automatically checked that the safety was on then went to put it in his belt. That action reminded him what had brought him down here in the first place. He switched the torch over to full beam; the golden blade of light brought the grubby white of his boots to blinding brightness. The floor of the little space was metal, but he remembered that the key had not made a ringing sound when it landed. He went down on one knee and began to search more closely. And there, right at the bottom of the hiding place, wedged between two stacks of incendiaries there was a wad of papers sticking out just far enough to have caught the metal T as it fell. Richard was tempted to pull these out and to examine them at once but his mind, as ever, was questing too far ahead to let him stop now – even for something as important as looking through the papers.

Richard's thought processes went like this – though they leaped from one step to the next without looking at the detail. This was the main cache of arms, bombs, plans and back-up for the people trying to destroy *Lady Mary*. They were still aboard, therefore, and almost certainly following some kind of plan. It seemed unlikely that they were stowaways, as it seemed logical to Richard that a stowaway would have kept these things in whatever hideaway an unsuspected extra passenger or two might need. And, of course, a stowaway hiding down here would have been very lucky indeed to survive when the inert gas started flooding in. No, this stash made it much more likely that the saboteurs were crew members. They would not be likely to be found amongst the dead and wounded either – therefore they would be up and active now. They would have been summoned to their emergency stations by the alarm Julie had just rung. But no sooner would they get there than Julie would tell them why they had been summoned and their first action after that – covert if possible, but desperate and swift – would be to come down here. For an emergency with the lift such as what was actually happening now was the only thing that might cause their hideaway to be discovered.

True, these thoughts did not address one or two problems – not least of which was who had attacked Sophie and left her wedged in the door down here? Logic might suggest that she had been attacked by the saboteurs, eager to protect their secret arms dump. But if that were true, why leave her body there, put the lift out of commission and risk the chain of circumstances that had in fact happened?

Whatever. That could be dealt with later, Richard decided. Like the question of the stowaway. What he needed to do now was to get this stuff up and out of here and find somewhere else to hide it. Then, if possible, wait and see who turned up to claim it. A course of action he felt able to consider because he was now in possession of the Glock. And because he had not told Julie – so she could hardly have told anyone else either – that he had managed to open the doors of the lift shaft down here, whoever came down would not be looking to attack Richard himself. Not in the first instance at least. And finally, if no one turned up after all, then he could go through the papers and look for clues. But first things first. Where in God's name could he hide a couple of dozen incendiary bombs? He looked out along the passageway. He had no real idea where it led to or whether there was anywhere secure and suitable nearby. He looked upwards at the still lift. And he smiled.

Antoine turned up ten minutes later, after announcing his approach by calling out as loudly as suited his sangfroid, to find Richard waiting by the closed lift doors, Sophie's work bag nonchalantly over his shoulder. If the chilled cadet thought it strange that Richard had got hold of the bag he made no comment. If he knew the thing well enough to realize that it was bulging more than usual and seemed heavier than normal, again he made no comment. Instead he simply looked at the Englishman as he shone his torch beam up and down him, probably assumed that his faceplate was slightly misted with the sweat of increasing nervousness, and said, '*Ca va?*' as though they were friends who had bumped into each other on the Champs-Élysées.

And, in reply to Richard's nod, he added, '*Bien. En avant!*'

Richard was grateful for the cadet's guiding light, for, although he counted himself as being pretty knowledgeable about the *Prometheus* series, he would have got himself lost down here in no time flat. To be fair, he found it hard to concentrate as he followed Antoine. He was busy dividing his mind between the need to learn his way up and down to and from the upper decks and at the same time to look for any promising hidey-holes down here. For he had not quite given up on the notion of a stowaway set on sabotage. He planned to come back down for a good look around if such a thing should ever prove possible. Experience suggested that it was inevitable that whole areas at this level – such as the one they were crossing – would be full of deadly gas. But, by the same token, it was quite possible that there were also still areas of fresh air where someone very careful and well supplied with clean-air monitors – and well insured with breathing equipment – might survive. But how proscribed would they be? Trapped in little pockets, reliant on huge numbers of air tanks. It seemed inconceivable. Unless, of course, they had managed to worm their way up the whole length of the ship. Up to the forecastle head, for instance. Into the paint lockers or workrooms there. Was it a coincidence that the only new incendiary attack had happened away down there?

Richard's mind, already split, came near to shattering into distraction as they found the companionway at last and started upwards into the more familiar lower engineering areas. He simply burned to get the work bag somewhere private and go through the papers it contained. After he had hidden the flashlight and the Glock, of course.

Richard was, in fact, so distracted by his thoughts that he did not notice the second figure standing ahead of him, waiting at the top of the stairway, until he all but collided with it. Like Antoine and Richard, it was wearing a protective suit, and the dull lighting made its face mask look like mirror until they were all standing side by side. Then a movement of the head and a trick of the light pulled features into prominence, and Richard caught his breath with simple shock. For it was Sophie Bois, apparently back from the dead.

'What have you got there, Captain?' she asked at once, while Richard was still off base with surprise.

'Your bag? I found it beside the lift when I got shut out.' He held on to it, mind whirling, trying to come up with a convincing reason to refuse to hand it over when she asked for it.

'My bag? What makes you think it's my bag? I'm not

170

likely to be doing engineering work! Well, not in the past at any rate. I must do some engineering now, I think. We all must. Come, we must hurry! The Captain says!' She turned away as she spoke and she and Antoine hurried off up the corridor ahead of him, side by side, clearly acting under orders he did not yet know about.

Not Sophie's bag then, thought Richard with relief. And not Antoine's either, or there would have been more than that urbane greeting. Not Honore's either, for he had said only that his key was missing, not his whole maintenance kit. If it belonged to an engineer, it must have been Raoul's, then. Or the Chief's, or Le Blanc, the First Engineer's. But Richard had actually only assumed it was Sophie's because he had supposed it was Sophie in the lift – and clearly it had not been. It must have been Emil, therefore, with his face mask webbed with cracks and painted with blood. Emil, the slightly-built Fourth Officer, whose hair was almost as blond as Sophie's was. Emil, who was effectively the First Officer since Lucien had plunged so spectacularly overboard. But why would Emil have been down there? And why did he have the engineer's bag with him? And what on earth had happened to him? And why?

Time for speculation ended abruptly and the meaning of Sophie's wry exclamation became clear the instant they arrived on the main engineering deck. Richard switched off his compressed air and pulled back his headgear at once, striding across towards the bustle around the open lift doors.

'There you are, Richard,' called Julie. 'Good. We are running out of time here.'

Had Richard been thinking of pleading tiredness or strain as a cover to smuggle the precious bag away and put it some-where safe, her words would have wiped the idea from his mind. Not so much the words as the palpable relief with which they were uttered. He looked around, frowning. No sign of Honore or even of Jean-Luc. Julie was very much on her own here. On her own and beginning to feel the strain.

He crossed to her side and looked down. The predicament was clear at once. There were two men still down on the roof of the lift car. And the car could not be moved until

171

they were clear. But there was no space to work with both men trapped down there. So Chow and Emil were also trapped until these two were freed and the car freed into the bargain.

But that was only the start of it. The man with the broken arm could not get out of the way; the weight of his equipment made it clearly impossible for him to climb one-handed. The ladder was too narrow to allow anyone to go down and help him. His mate, trapped in the winding gear, could not be moved unless his protective suit was taken off. And when the suit came off, so would the air tanks. So that would have to be done in such a way that he had a realistic chance to get to the ladder and climb to safety while holding his breath. Which in turn could not be done because there was simply no space to get to him until the man with the broken arm was moved.

'Rope,' ordered Richard. 'Antoine, you know these areas best. Bustle about, man. We need rope – at least four metres. Thin enough to make a noose, thick enough to bear the weight of a body. Sophie, go and help him.'

Antoine and Sophie vanished. 'She suspected she would soon become an engineer,' Richard told Julie tersely.

'She probably thinks she's going to hang somebody after those orders,' she countered.

'Ha!' Richard crossed to the rack and hung his bag on the hook that had not held Honore's key. Then he strode back and swung out on to the ladder, headgear still back. But he did not breathe until he was sure his clean-air monitor was staying silent. 'Right,' he called. 'I'm going to lower a rope. It will go over your tanks . . .' He gestured at the man who sat cradling his arm. 'You'll be able to help with that even though your clothing's trapped,' he told him. 'Once the rope's in place we'll haul you up. Then we'll have space to get down and free the gear.'

He had hardly finished speaking before Antoine and Sophie hurried back with the piece of rope he needed. 'Captain, would you please arrange a tug-of-war team while I practise a little ropework,' he said. Then, for no obvious reason he slid his headgear back into place and secured it firmly. He held his hand out for the orange nylon, looped it, double-looped it, wrapped the end around the loops, fed through and pulled tight. He pulled the noose to the length of his arm. A moment or two later the noose was settling over the air tanks of the man with the broken arm and the team was taking the strain.

The seaman yelled – it must have hurt like hell, thought Richard guiltily. But he swung up, tanks on top, his body hanging like a turtle beneath them – and his harness held. Richard, on the ladder, reached down and grabbed the top of the straining webbing, then heaved him up and back to sit on the edge where the deck fell into the shaft. A moment after that, he was on his way to the all too busy infirmary. And Richard was already halfway down for a closer look at the trapped man, the clean-air monitor at his belt sounding its warning that he was in a dangerous atmosphere.

As soon as he arrived on the roof of the car, Richard strained over to look down through the trapdoor. Chow was still standing like a statue but he had allowed Emil to slump on to his knees. The beams from the torches gave the little scene a weirdly theatrical look, as though the leading seaman were part of a Maoist poster.

'OK?' bellowed Richard. Chow looked up. Behind the face mask, his mouth was working like a goldfish in a bowl. Richard looked around the little space. The man caught in the pulley was half over the open trap – and with very limited room for manoeuvre. But he would have to be moved before there was any chance of even getting a rope to Chow. A further complication then arrived: Richard abruptly found himself becoming breathless. His tanks were beginning to run low too. He reached for his radio. 'Captain,' he gasped into the open channel. 'I need some shears. Some really big ones. And I need the rope down here again.'

As he waited, Richard hit the emergency release on the trapped man's air tanks and pulled him as far out of the harness as possible. He took handfuls of the tightly-folded material and tried to jerk them up out of the frozen mechanism. But the pressure had half melted the torch and the batteries within its crushed length seemed to weld the whole lot immovably together. Even so, when the rope arrived,

Richard swiftly undid his noose, looped the line around the obstruction and tied it tight again. 'Pull!' he gasped into the radio and the rope took the strain – and pulled. The cloth seemed to stretch. Then it slid up, pulling the melted torch free by an inch or so. Instantly, the winch whined, the cables tightened, the pulley turned. The whole car gave a huge lurch upward and the metal jaws closed again like a rabid dog chewing on a bone.

The seaman began to scream. Richard's Cantonese was rusty but it sounded as though the man was saying something about his arm coming off. But to be fair, even after the upward movement, there now seemed to be a good deal more loose material around the wedged section – so it hadn't all been a dead loss.

The shears arrived just as the rope slackened and Richard was able to change his tactics. First he cut the webbing strap and allowed the air tanks to settle on the roof beside the open trap. Then he set to work, cutting away the newly loosened cloth until the seaman could sit back – with a huge hole in his suit, centred on his armpit, that reached from his elbow to his hip. But at least he was free. Richard handed him the noose of the rope.

'Hold tight,' he ordered. He put the shears to the airlines just above the tanks. 'Deep breath!' The scrawny chest ballooned, ribs straining. He cut down hard. One line went. The seaman started to shake. He cut down hard again. The second went. 'Pull!' he croaked into the open channel. His companion took off like an angel heaven-bound; his flying foot hit the tanks and it was only by a massive effort of reaction and strength that Richard caught them and stopped them falling on to Chow's upturned face. He was not so lucky with the shears, however. Nor the radio, come to that. But providentially, as careful as ever, he had remembered to loop the lanyard round his wrist.

He straightened up and put the little transceiver to his faceplate. 'Rope!' he demanded. Down it came again and he fed it past the bottles into the little cabin. After some uncounted time, it jerked. Chow was ready. 'Pull!' The word sounded faint to Richard's own ears, for there was a rumbling in his chest and head as though the Flying Scot were pounding past him. A body came up through the opening. As he guided it on up, Richard could see the faceplate was webbed with cracks and painted on the inside with blood. As soon as the feet were clear, Richard reached massively down into the lift car – and felt Chow's fist close on his. Up he heaved with all his strength – what there was left of it. And his effort was rewarded. Chow's arm appeared. Then his shoulder. They hesitated as he put his foot up on the step and then Richard heaved again as the seaman kicked up with all his failing might. Then the two of them stood together on the roof.

That was it. Richard was finished now. Even the ten steps up the ladder were beyond him. But, with Chow at his shoulder, he turned because he had to. With Chow's hand at the bottom of the air tanks, pushing him upwards, he began to climb because there was no alternative. At the top, when he fell out on to the engineering deck, he turned and pushed his hand down, as he had done into the lift car, and once again he pulled Chow up and out.

Only then did he let the rest of them help him to his feet, pull his headgear back and let him gulp the wonderful air. Julie was immediately in front of him. 'Well done,' she said.

He nodded and turned to Chow. 'OK?'

Chow, far beyond framing a spoken reply, simply put his thumb up.

Richard turned back. 'Just for a moment there,' he laboured, 'I thought I'd have to collect on the mouth-to-mouth you owe me . . .'

'Just for a moment,' she countered, 'I thought I might have to give it to you . . .'

Sixteen

Time

The one thing Richard really needed after he got his breath back was time. Time to study the contents of the saboteur's hideaway – now in the engineer's case. Time to think. And, ideally, enough time to get some sleep to clear his mind and ensure that his thoughts would be worthwhile.

Looking around the engine room Richard could see all too clearly that he was by no means alone in his increasingly urgent need for sleep. It was in any case coming up for midnight and both he and Julie were most powerfully aware that everyone aboard had to get some rest soon, or the next few days would become utterly unmanageable. And, of course, tonight and tomorrow were likely to be, quite literally, the calm before the storm.

'Why don't we do a late patrol, Captain,' suggested Richard next, more soberly after their words about mouth-to-mouth. As nonchalantly as he could, he slung the bag over his shoulder, hoping with all the fervour of a shop-lifter that no one would notice anything strange in this. 'Not a full inspection, more a bedding-down visit. See how many of the crew it would be possible to pack off to their bunks. Look. We can start down here as we clear away. We surely don't need fire watches on all the engineering decks . . .'

Julie nodded in weary agreement, as though the brief flash of half-hearted repartee had taxed her physically, emotionally and intellectually to her limit.

They left the broken lift awaiting repair at a later date. They closed the doors on the engineering level as a safety precaution, but left the car stuck and the shaft empty. Then they closed the engine room down for the night. At Richard's suggestion, Julie agreed to reduce the fire watches from three to one: a two-man team who would watch from the upper balcony. They would have a hand-held radio rather than a rank of extinguishers. Though they left a full set, all colours, fully charged, at the foot of the lowest companionway, just in case. The first team would be relieved at four, the next team at eight, the last team at noon. Thus, within each twelve-hour period, the teams would each get eight hours' sleep. And Chow would be in charge, able to decide which watch he wanted to take himself.

The reduction in watch-keepers was a risk worth taking, Richard urged, because there had been no further alarms for six hours and more. The sections of the engineering still running, such as the cargo-heating coils, the generator, the power, heat and light systems, could all function perfectly well under the UMS system for tonight at least. It was what they were designed to do, after all.

It was a risk worth taking, he secretly believed, because any saboteurs still energetic enough to be up to mischief would find their bombs and weapons gone. That would surely cause confusion and concern – hopefully full-blown consternation – in the enemy camp. And confusion, in his wide experience, usually engendered hesitation. And hesitation meant inactivity – until some new plans could be drawn up, at any rate.

Julie's next port of call was the infirmary. She needed to establish whether Emil was actually alive or dead. She wanted to check on Jean-Luc too. As did Richard – who had some questions for both of them. And she had to see for herself whether or not the mysterious dysentery-like illness had passed. Richard followed her, still emphasizing how important it was to get as many people as possible safely into their bunks. They arrived at the old crew's dining area to find Mr Song in charge – and ahead of the game as usual.

Richard was struck by the size of the sickbay and the efficiency with which it had been adapted. Sturdy tables had been turned into makeshift beds simply by putting mattresses on top of them. The mattresses fitted perfectly, as though

177

the tables had been especially designed. It made the beds unusually tall, but that was to the good of anyone trying to nurse the patients lying in them. Heaven help anyone who rolled over too fast and fell out, though, thought Richard. It was a long way down to the lino-covered metal of the deck. But all was calm and quiet now, except for a couple of stentorian snorers.

In an open space between the ranks of beds, a single table stood uncovered, dully lit by a table lamp. Here Mr Song sat with a stranger who Richard soon learned was the Chef. They were playing Mah Jong with unusual restraint, and almost no cursing or rattling of ivory tiles.

As Julie entered, Mr Song rose and crossed towards her like a stately ghost. 'All quiet, Miss Julie,' he whispered in his deep, almost sepulchral voice. 'I sent all boys to bed. They exhausted. No use for more work. Old men like Chef and me, we don't need so much sleep.' He smiled, and Richard thought he saw genuine affection in his dark eyes.

'Emil?' she asked, a tiny tremble in her voice.

'Fourth Officer Emil is unconscious but vital signs all OK. Not wake up yet. Not talk. No idea what happened to him. Could have been attacked; could have fallen flat on face . . .' His eyes flicked up to Richard. Their edges crinkled in the ghost of a grin. 'Most of blood from broken nose. Second Radio Officer Jean-Luc also asleep. Bleeding stopped now. All better in morning, I think. Headache, maybe. Be able to ask him what happened to his head at breakfast time I guess. If *you're* up then. Others all more settled. Third Engineer Honore stopped puking and started snoring happily. Like pig in shit, as the Americans say. No more big vomit or green shit from the rest. I give lots of water – some Dioralyte, like they babies with upset tummies. Medical book say if this was dysentery like we discussed then we should give Ipecac but I can't find any. We have Ipecac syrup on infirmary manifest, but I can't find any. Chef say flat ginger ale be good so maybe we raid the officers' bar later on.'

'That's fine, Mr Song. And I will be up for breakfast, naturally. Eight o'clock sharp. How else will I be able to agree the menus for the day? Thank you. Good night.'

'Good night, Miss Julie,' answered Song. Then he glanced up at Richard. Amusement lingered in his eyes – and almost paternal pride. But it was fading. 'Good night, Captain.'

'Good night, Mr Song,' said Richard. He felt his belt and handed the Chief Steward his radio. 'Emergencies only,' he said. By the time he had left, it was on the table beside the lamp, the medical book and the Mah Jong set.

They were followed up the corridor by the sound of Mah Jong tiles and snoring. Indeed, as they climbed through the dim corridors of the security-lit bridge house, the sound of snoring was reassuringly prevalent. By the time they reached the navigation bridge it seemed that they were the only people left awake aboard except for the pair of men in the infirmary and the couple on fire watch. But no. As Julie went into the big command area, beginning to sag with weariness at last, so Sophie Bois straightened above the collision alarm radar bowl. Her gold hair glittered even in the green light. It made her look strangely aquatic, as though she were some kind of mermaid. 'Nothing to report,' she said.

Antoine turned from the weather monitor, toothpick twitching busily. 'Thirty-six hours or so of strengthening westerlies, then the shit hits the fan,' he added. 'That's the latest we have here at any rate.'

Ether called through from the chart room, 'That's what Kerguelen said before they went off air for the night,' he confirmed. 'They're in emergency-only mode now and would like us *not* to disturb them, please. They are mere landlubber scientists and they need their sleep, they say. I have heard also from tugboat *Sissyphus*. They also signed off for the night. But they not landlubbers. They say to call if there's any problem at all.'

'Thank you,' said Julie, straightening. 'Thank you all. But your bridge watch is at an end for tonight. Off to your bunks please, all of you.'

'But Captain!' said Sophie, scandalized. 'You cannot abandon the bridge.'

'I don't intend to, Sophie. Captain Mariner and I will be here, watch on watch.'

'Antoine,' added Richard. 'Just before you go, would you

179

give me a hand, please?' Julie frowned at him, signalling that she wasn't sure what he was up to, but he gave her a tight grin and led Antoine out, with Sophie and Ether at their heels.

As the digital clock in the top corner of the Hagenuk's screen clicked up to 00:00:00, and the three hands on the old-fashioned analogue ship's chronometer above the helm all pointed precisely upwards, Richard and Antoine dropped the mattress and bedding from the Captain's bunk on to the deck.

'Thanks, Antoine,' said Richard. 'Off you go now. Get in a good eight hours.' Then he turned to Julie. 'It's the least I can do,' he said. 'Given what I've done to the bunk in your day room. You know there are times when even the pilot's chair is not going to do the job for you.' He squatted and tucked the bedding into place. 'You go first,' he ordered. 'I'll wake you at four.'

The Hagenuk did not take up all of the bed-top in the Captain's day room. Richard had plenty of space to spread out the contents of the engineer's bag and take his first really close look at the saboteur's secret hoard under the brightness from the display screen which now read 00:30:00. He had spent an increasingly nerve-racking half-hour ostentatiously checking all the equipment as Julie, with the lack of modesty he was beginning to take for granted, slipped off her work clothes to reveal – thankfully – that sometime during the crisis in the lift she had managed to replace her underwear. She folded her uniform carefully, slid into the bed and then slipped all too slowly into sleep. She was snoring gently now and he could get on with things.

He put the Glock away to one side – but not so far away that he couldn't grab it easily at the first suspicion of movement behind him. He patted the solid pistol, wondering how Jean-Luc had come to be surprised. And why whoever attacked him hadn't destroyed the radio. Perhaps Jean-Luc had fought them off. Perhaps they had been interrupted. Perhaps they would be back to try again . . .

Richard's thoughts were interupted by the scraping of metal on wood and found he had been unconsciously touching the gun as he thought his dark thoughts. That was too noisy, he thought guiltily, and the rustling of paper would seem over-poweringly loud, too, even under the relentless howling of the wind. So he spent a few precious seconds setting the Hagenuk to the World Service of the BBC – with the auto-matic interrupt in place. He pulled the plug of the earphones out and adjusted the speaker volume carefully. Then he checked the programme to make sure it would do what he wanted it to do. It was an even more advanced version of the radio in his Bentley Continental GT at home, programmed to interrupt any station or CD playing with important news or traffic updates. He could rely on its gentle mumble to cover any noise he made – while allowing him to hear any footsteps creeping up behind him. He could be confident that if an important message came in, it would break into the programme and warn him.

Lady Mary was five hours ahead of GMT, so it was coming past tea time on the World Service. Richard listened with half an ear to the last half-hour of *European News* followed by *World Briefing*. He was briefly tempted to set the timer and catch *The Archers*, just as though he were enjoying a lazy evening at home. But a sense of reality caught up with him and he decided against the indulgence after all.

What Richard arranged on the table in front of the murmuring Hagenuk as the time ticked up to 00:40:00, there-fore, was this: the powerful torch – that went over by the Glock; a pair of hand-held transceivers markedly more up to date than those he had seen aboard, these went beside the torch, but well clear of the Glock in case he needed to grab the gun at any time; four cellphones, a make he didn't recog-nize but they looked very state-of-the-art. They were a lot like the ones he had bought for his teenage twins last Christmas, which meant they were probably the best of the best. He placed them beside the transceivers, treating them with extra care, as though they were dangerously venomous. He was all too well aware that the explosive devices deto-nated by terrorists in several European capital cities over the last few years had been set off with signals from cellphones.

He had just studied the cellphones and put them aside

when Julie started screaming. The sound was so stark, so sudden, that had he still been holding them, he would certainly have dropped them. He threw the chair back, testing it almost to destruction, and ran through on to the bridge. Julie was sitting up, her form quite clear in the dim lighting. Her eyes were as wide as her mouth, staring with such fixity, that Richard himself looked at the point where her horror was focussed, expecting to see something monstrous. But there were only shadows. His run slowed to a walk.

'Julie,' he said, speaking French without thinking. 'It's all right. It's just a nightmare. Don't worry.' The fixed look did not waver, but the screams choked off. He realized she was still sound asleep. 'Lie down, Julie, it's all right,' he said.

She said, in a voice of infinite horror and sorrow, 'Papa!' and lay back down.

In the sudden silence, Richard listened, struck and disturbed, as the screaming was taken up by other sleepers lower down the bridge house. It was their first sleep after witnessing horrors without number, he thought. But still, it made him shiver, as though the Southern Ocean wind had come in here with its Antarctic chill and its eternal sobbing.

Richard went back into the makeshift radio room and sat for a moment deep in thought. The muttering of the BBC World Service announcers could not quite cover the continued sobbing and occasional scream. But after a while the sounds faded – until at last it was impossible to distinguish them from the howling of the wind outside.

Then, at last, Richard turned to the papers. These were a mixture of cheaply-produced magazines and pages printed from the Internet. They were written in a range of languages, mostly English and French. The printouts had a range of web addresses, none of which were in any way familiar to him. It would have been easy enough to type them into his laptop at home and track them down that way, he supposed. But following up this stuff was less important than trying to work out who it belonged to and what it might reveal about their plans and motivations. For, in combination with the cell-phones and the incendiary bombs, the chilling sample –

182

folded, re-folded, much thumbed and well used – made very disturbing reading indeed:

THE REAL FRIENDS OF THE EARTH

They call it **eco-terrorism** and say that it is a crime. They call us **eco-terrorists** and condemn us with the other martyrs willing to **kill** and **die** for the causes they believe in. They have made us what we have become. **The fault is theirs.**

Would Al-Qaeda exist without the rape of Iraq? The atrocity of Afghanistan? The perversion of Pakistan? Would there have been a Provisional IRA without a Bloody Sunday? Would there have been a PLO without the empire-building of Israel, the invasion of Gaza and the desecration of the West Bank?

Would there be heroic brothers and sisters willing to go beyond even the Animal Liberation Front to target so-called researchers, their laboratories and entire universities without the systematic torture and murder of helpless animals by the drug and cosmetic industries? Would the executions of abortionist doctors and nurses take place without the relentless genocide of unborn babies in their millions?

No!

Then who will stand up against the **rape** of the **world**? Who will go as far as it takes to stop the whole of our planet, the lives of every species and the future of our children being sacrificed on the altar of corporate greed, political expediency and spineless failure? Who will take any meaningful initiatives in the face of this overwhelming lust for power and profit?

Who will be willing to **kill** and to **die** in the face of the destruction of the already pathetic UNFCCC

183

treaties? The toothless Montreal Protocol, diluted and emasculated with revisions at London, Copenhagen, Vienna and Beijing? The laughably less than useless Kyoto Protocol which America, China, Russia and half the businesses on earth dismiss out of hand in any case? The refusal of rapist nations and multinationals to admit their relentless destruction of our precious planet from the rainforests of Brazil to the ice shelf of the Antarctic?

We say that they are killing millions of our children in future generations as surely as any army of abortionists. Destroying our animals, wiping out complete species, in far greater numbers than all the so-called scientists and cosmetic companies of the twentieth century put together. They are desecrating not just **our** countries but **all** countries. And they must be stopped before it is too late. No matter what the cost.

Producers, refiners, purveyors, transporters . . . From the greatest country, corporation or company ripping out the hearts of our precious, irreplaceable rainforests to the most insignificant tanker pushing this filth into the pristine reaches of our last virgin environments, they must be stopped.

Who is brave enough to **kill** to protect humanity's last and only heritage? Who is heroic enough to **die** to protect it?

Richard shook his head, glancing up at the display on the gently whispering Hagenuk. 01:33:04. He sat back until the chair creaked. Eco-terrorists, he thought. Now what in all his wide experience had he discovered, and in the recesses of his capacious memory, did he know about eco-terrorists? Maybe Julie was right. Maybe they should just get the two tugs to pull *Lady Mary* into Port aux Français no matter what the dangers from weather, weed-covered rocks and Second World War minefields. Drop anchor – if they were all still afloat – and call for help after all.

Not from the owners. Not from the insurers. From the French authorities. From the RPIM. He smiled, sleepily, pleased that he could even remember the acronym. But all things considered, that was who they probably needed. The Premier Regiment de Parachutists d'Infantrie de Marine. The French Green Berets. The French SAS.

As Richard dozed off – asleep on watch for the first time in perhaps a decade – so the gentle, soporific voice on the Hagenuk completed the half-hour news bulletin:

> *And finally, reports are just coming in from Brazil that the main buildings belonging to Yangtze-Mindanao, the major Far-Eastern financed Amazonian logging consortium, have been destroyed. Early reports suggest that there was a massive explosion, followed by a fire, which completely gutted the plant and offices. Several hundred workers, mainly office staff and management executives are believed to have died, together with several senior members of Brazil's local and national government.*
>
> *The explosion seems to have occurred at a ceremony designed to mark the ground-breaking deal which allows Yangtze-Mindanao to resume logging in the Amazonian District of Brazil, which has long been the focus of ecological concern because of the uncontrolled defor- estation of the area . . .*

'Incoming Message', flashed up on the screen. The gentle tones of the World Service were replaced by an insistent buzzing. Richard's eyes opened wide. Blinked owlishly as they came into focus. Began to take in the words on the screen in front of him.

Under the incoming message banner it said: 'Vessel *Sissyphus'* with the call code, longitude and latitude.

He reached across and pushed the button on the micro- phone stalk. *'Lady Mary* here. *Sissy*, what's up? Over.'

'Clearly *you're* not up,' came Robin's acerbic voice. 'I've been trying to raise you for half an hour. Do you know what time it is?'

He looked up at the clock in the corner of the screen.

185

07:55:05 it said. 'Bugger,' he said. 'I haven't slept on watch for years. Thanks for the wake-up call, though, over.'

'You must be getting old, my love, over.'

'Like vintage wine. Fuller bodied, deeper, more resonant and precious? Over.'

'Ripe Stilton, more like. Crusty and blue-veined. Over.'

'Was there a message, Robin? Or just more pleasantry? I've a Captain to get up and she's got an eight o'clock appointment she won't want to miss. And you don't know what crusty means until you've been on the wrong side of her. Over.'

'No. It's OK, my love. You get your crusty little lady up and out. Over.'

'Thanks again for the call. Oh and Robin . . . Have a think about eco-terrorists, will you? What do we know about eco-terrorists? And who do we know at the RPIM, the Suretee, Interpol, or the anti-terrorist wing of the SGDN in Paris? Out.'

Having left Robin with more than a little to chew upon, Richard went bustling almost gleefully straight out on to the bridge, leaving the papers, the cellphones, the torch and the Glock where they were. He reckoned Julie would be focussed on getting down to her meeting with Mr Song to discuss the menus. No way would she check the radio herself with only five minutes in hand.

He shook her and she sat up at once, eyes wide, looking round the day-bright bridge. Her gold-flecked gaze settling on the chronometer. 'I knew you'd do that,' she said. Her voice was husky and she smelt of sleep like a child. But, unlike Robin, she met the morning firing on all cylinders. It was an impressive sight in all sorts of ways.

'Knew I'd do what?' He kept the guilt out of his voice. Had she guessed he'd slept through his watch?

'I knew you'd do both watches. You chauvinist!'

'It's a French vice,' he said playfully, more than a little relieved.

'Just because it has a French name doesn't make it a French vice.' As she spoke she came up out of the bedding. She stooped and scooped up her uniform.

'How did you sleep?' he asked, glancing across at her – then swiftly away again.

'Like a baby.'

'No bad dreams?'

'Not that I remember. Why?'

'One or two people below. They were screaming in the night.'

'Probably the wind,' she decided, dismissing his concerns with apparent ease. She straightened, pulling her belt tight. 'Four minutes to my meeting with Mr Song,' she observed dryly. 'You really expect a girl to be up and out on short notice. Dreams or no dreams. Your Robin must move like the start of Le Mans in the morning.'

If only you knew, he thought.

'You'll make it, Captain,' he said.

'If I don't stop off for the bathroom,' she countered, running her fingers distractedly through the jumble of her hair. 'Or pass any mirrors on the way.' And she was gone.

But no sooner did Julie exit the bridge than Sophie entered and Richard was put most forcefully in mind of his earlier thoughts about boarding schools and privacy. If Julie was less bothered than she might have been about physical intimacy, Richard was used to preserving privacy. Indeed, secrecy. 'I've just woken the Captain, Sophie,' he said airily. 'I've been on communications watch all night. As well as keeping an eye on the bridge, of course. I'll need to get on with the eight o'clock updates to get ready for Ether. Bring the logs up to date, would you?'

When she obediently crossed to the console, Richard went into the Captain's day room and gathered together all the incriminating bits and pieces lying around the Hagenuk that belonged back in the bag – only as a temporary measure, of course. Once Emil awoke he might well want to reclaim it – so Richard needed to find somewhere other than the bag itself to hide everything as soon as possible.

Ether's arrival complicated this quite considerably. Fortunately he paused to exchange pleasantries with Sophie on his way in and so Richard had just enough time to slide open the lowest and deepest of the chart drawers under the day bed and shove the bag in there. It was by no means a perfect hiding place, but it would do for the moment. And it was, at the very least, convenient.

187

Richard straightened as Ether breezed in. 'I've just finished talking to *Sissyphus*,' he said. 'You'll need to do the rest of the new watch updates. Try to get hold of *Oscar Whisky*. If you can't get her directly, check with *Sissy* – she has all the details. Then you must check with Rothera and the nearest British Antarctic Survey base as soon as possible. But be aware that they were impossible to contact yesterday: it may be something to do with the storm. And, of course, you'll need to see whether the landlubbers on Kerguelen are up yet. Then we need to know about the progress of that storm and – as soon as you have a moment – we would like to talk to anyone with a competent doctor available in case things down in the sickbay go downhill again.'

Ether sat, open-mouthed. 'Should I write all that down, Captain?' he asked.

'No. You'll get the hang of it. And I'll be in and out to check on you – especially if Jean-Luc's still too ill to share the radio watch with us,' Richard assured him over his shoulder as he went back out on to the bridge.

'How are things?' he asked Sophie immediately.

'I'm still checking, Captain,' she answered a little defensively. 'Weather's still deteriorating . . .'

'But, as Antoine observed, there's still more than twenty-four hours until the shit hits the fan?' he probed.

'Yes.'

'Disposition of the vessel?' he pursued.

'All as before, I think, sir. Same heading; a little north of west. Same following seas – so to speak – same progress.'

'Making about one knot?'

'One knot.'

'Twenty hours since the last sight at noon yesterday. Have we made twenty nautical miles – according to the GPS at least?' he persisted.

'Automatic monitor says yes. I can give you our current position – according to GPS and you can double check it on the chart.'

'That will be the Captain's decision. But thank you. Is Antoine up and about, do you know?' he enquired innocently.

'Yes. That is, I think so. Why?'

'Because with Honore still sleeping – like a pig in shit, I recall – Antoine is the engineering section. And just as I need to check things with you, I need to check things with him.'

'Not so,' said Julie, stepping briskly back on to the bridge, sparking with energy, decisiveness and command. 'And for two reasons, Captain Mariner. One: because I have talked with him already and sent him down to run the necessary checks. Two: because Third Engineer Honore is up, and will soon be on his way down to help him. Though it ought to be the other way round, I know. And, further, Honore is not the only person up and about. Would you assist Sophie with her watch, please? I have to interview Radio Officer Jean-Luc and Fourth Officer Emil about what happened to them last night.'

'I'll come with you at once. You'll need some help with that,' said Richard, stepping forward automatically.

'No! Certainly not. Why should I need help? Help Sophie here as I asked, please. Or help poor Ether: I'm sure you have also given him a long list of things to do.'

And Julie vanished again, leaving Richard simply stunned by the fact that she had no intention at all of letting him join in her interrogation of the two men. Stunned, and suddenly brimming with suspicion once again.

Seventeen

Calm

Almost beside himself with rage and frustration, Richard went through into the makeshift radio room, trying in vain to calm himself down. There was only one chair in there so he towered beside Ether for a while until he realized he was simply intimidating the youngster as he tried with no success whatsoever to raise any radio contact on the entire Antarctic continent. So he went back to the bridge, working on the assumption that Sophie would at least be more difficult to intimidate, no matter how ill-concealed his simple outrage was.

However, he kept close to the radio room, restrained from the habitual pacing across the bridge with which he would normally have tried to calm himself. Held in place by the almost subconscious concern that Ether for some unimaginable reason might open the lowest drawer of the chart chest and discover the case. And so Richard almost by chance was made privy to a snippet or two of conversation of which he – perhaps he alone – really understood the importance.

'*Sissyphus*, this is *Lady Mary*, over,' Ether was saying.

'Receiving you, strength five, clarity five, *Lady Mary*. What's up? Over.' The cheery tones of *Sissy*'s Duty Radio Officer came and went through clouds of static.

Ether might have been a keen radio ham but he wasn't really up to speed with all the procedures and he did not seem to register the fact that the Hagenuk was beginning to lose *Sissy*'s signal. He might well have responded with the same report about strength of signal and clarity of tone as the one he had just received. Instead he answered, 'I've been trying to get a call to the BAS base at Rothera. Nothing but static. Have you been in contact? Over.'

'Negative, *Lady Mary*. We lost Rothera under the storm that's whipping round these latitudes and we haven't had her back. It's clear of them now and heading your way fast but they're still not up, over.'

'Is that usual, *Sissyphus*? To lose contact because of a storm? Over.'

'Sure, *Lady Mary*. Electrical interference. It doesn't happen every time. But it happens. You got satellite TV? Happens to mine all the time. There you are, in the middle of the Bodacious Babes Channel or Naked News when you get a crack of thunder and suddenly zappo! Zilch. Should have gone for cable. Or got one of those extra-special aerials, over . . .'

'Ether!' spat Richard, striding back in so suddenly the young radio operator jumped clear off the creaking chair.

'Yes, Captain?'

'Slide over. I put that engineering bag in the drawer when I came on radio watch last night and I need it now.'

Ether obeyed without a second thought.

Richard tore open the drawer and pulled out the bag. 'If the Captain wants me I'll be up on the top deck to begin with, then down in engineering,' he thundered. And was off, leaving Ether open-mouthed.

'May I tell the Captain why you're going out and down?' demanded Sophie as Richard strode purposefully across the bridge.

'Yes. Did you hear the conversation Ether just had with *Sissyphus*?'

'Most of it . . .'

'Good. Think about it. What we need to do during the next three days is to stay in contact with *Sissy*, *Oscar Whisky*, Kerguelen, any passing ship with medical facilities mad enough to be out here now, and maybe the nearest bases on Antarctica as they come back on line. So that on day four we're in a position to get all our people up from the sickbay and out on deck, bring the cables aboard, and move *Lady*

Mary over into Resolution Passage before she runs aground and blows us all to kingdom come.'

'I see that . . .'

'But the storm that is catching up with us pretty quickly now has a strong electrical element to it – enough to take out a sizeable land-based radio facility like Rothera for two or more days. Strong enough to be interfering with our signals now as it moves between us and *Sissy*.'

'Yes. I see that also.'

'So, like the man said, we get in a special aerial – or we lose our signal at the first crack of thunder and *zappo* goes the Naked News.'

Sophie frowned, and not at the reference to nudity either.

Richard continued, more calmly, 'I have to check on the state of the radio mast after my chopper guillotined it yesterday, then get either Honore or Antoine up there with a team of workmen while things are still relatively calm. Before the weather gets any worse,' he explained patiently. 'We have to make any further repairs necessary to the mast itself, then open up the base of it and root around in the boosters and so forth. Then we have to secure the Hagenuk's extra UHF aerial to the signal systems up there, if there are any and if they're still on line. If I can do that and make it strong enough to remain secure then we might be able to stay in contact with the rest of the world during the storm. If I don't then we certainly won't. And that could make all the difference in the end. Do you see?'

'Yes, I do.'

'Then tell Captain DuFour when she asks.'

'Yes, Captain Mariner. I will.'

'If she turns up within the next five minutes you can tell her I'll be getting on some wet-weather gear, though.'

In fact it took more than five minutes because, thinking ahead as always, Richard found the biggest windcheater he could – the one with the loosest waist and the deepest pockets. There were things he wanted to put in there and he didn't want them to be obvious. The rain had stopped with the arrival of dawn, so the wet-weather gear wasn't strictly necessary. Warm and windproof clothing was, however. The wind was blowing stronger – a steady gale gusting towards storm according to the weather monitor – but it was ripping the clouds away. Richard stepped out into howling iciness given an extra keenness by the wind-chill. In fact the decks under the unsteady brightness were not frozen; but the impact of the busy air was definitely sub-zero. Only in these latitudes could he ever have thought of these conditions as 'Calm'.

It was the scale of the morning that hit Richard first. After the claustrophobic closeness of the night, it seemed as he climbed the outer companionway up past the top of the bridge wings that he could see for ever. The effect was compounded, he was certain, by the fact that there was actually nothing much *to* see. It was as though the ship were sitting in the middle of a puddle of wrinkled, undulating mercury. A puddle so big that it seemed to be ever so slightly curved into the appearance of a huge hillock. As though he could actually see the curvature of the earth.

The horizons all around had withdrawn under the influence of the steady wind and the simple clarity of the air. Although there were still fumes streaming from the funnel, they were largely colourless now – clear and gaseous, visible only where they disturbed the wind like a heat haze. Other than that, his vision was able to sweep out to seemingly limitless distances before the mottled chalk-dust of the sky began to settle on to the corrugated silver of the sea.

The quality of the air was astonishing; in contrast to the foetid atmosphere in which he had spent all his time aboard so far. As he reached the broad red football field of the topmost deck, Richard simply stopped moving and breathed in until his ribs ached, filling his massive lungs to capacity with the salty perfection of the atmosphere. Away in the distance – so far that it was impossible to guess at scale – a single white dot hovered. Some kind of sea bird. And, suddenly, apparently beneath it – but with the spurious closeness of two airliners passing each other overhead – a pod of whales broke the surface, spouting white lace foam.

Richard stood, entranced. The steady thunder of the wind rushing past his ears almost masked the bellowing of the gale in the nearby wreckage of the beheaded mast-top. The abyssal booming as it moved across the opening of the pipes within the funnel. The restless whip-crack of the flogging safety rail – again, broken by that first, near-disastrous arrival on the Westland. He would be looking more closely at the mast and the safety rail in a few moments, he thought, bringing his mind fully back aboard. But, in the meantime, he had other plans.

After a quick glance all around, pulling the focus of his vision in from the far horizon, Richard crossed to the housing that contained the winch gear for the lift. The door that allowed access to the machinery within it was at the back of the construction, facing the ship's square stern – perfectly down wind now. In the relative calm of the little building's wind-shadow he paused, playing one last mind game with the saboteurs and with himself.

He had hidden the incendiary bombs within the hollow bottom of the lift itself – running them up the ladder out of the maintenance pit and packing them safely and invisibly in above the inward-folding ledges that bore the struts which strengthened the box of the car. Hiding them so close to their original cache had been a gamble dictated by circumstances.

Yet here he was, with the whole ship available – within the bridge house and planning to hide the other stuff in the winch house. So convenient. So out of the way. Maybe accessed once in the whole voyage. And that one time would be today, when Honore and Antoine tried to fix the lift – as he was certain that they would. But he was equally certain that he could make sure he was here with them when they did. And, equally, that he could put the stuff somewhere that they would never check. And he knew once the lift was mended or declared defunct no one aboard would – or could – come out here again, especially after the storm hit, until he brought the authorities here himself in due course, and showed them the papers and all the rest of it. By which time, he hoped, his prime suspects would be in custody and able to make no further use of their deadly little arsenal.

Richard was particularly keen to put the cellphones and the walkie-talkies well away from everyone else aboard.

With any luck, their absence would make it impossible for the saboteurs – The Real Friends of the Earth, the IRA of the Arctic, the Al-Qaeda of the Rainforests, or whatever they called themselves – to plan or organize anything in secret. Or to detonate anything else at all. He had no such plans for the torch or the Glock, however. He would keep those close at hand himself. And, now he thought of it, the manifesto from The Real Friends of the Earth as well.

Richard carefully kept in the housing's wind-shadow as he opened the engineer's bag and took out the same square key that opened all the other doors on the lift system. He inserted it and opened this door too. The winch was packed into the little space, and much of the vacant area around it was illusory, for the walls and the insides of the doors were hung with various pieces of maintenance equipment. The way the thing had been designed really focussed everyone's eyes inwards and downwards to the winch itself – so obviously a thing of the lower decks, almost out of place up here. Part of this focus came from the way the cables came out of the machine itself and plunged straight down through the decking. Part of it was the fact that the winch seemed to crouch there almost like an animal, seated massively down on the same solid deck.

And that was just what Richard was counting on. For, knowing these housings of old, he knew that they had a double top. Anyone fighting nature and inclination and looking upwards carefully enough, would see that the sloping square of the roof was more than the simple slab of white-painted metal it seemed to be. There was more to this than a metal plate welded on top of the metal walls. There was a second section, inside and below the roof. Between the two was a little attic space usually packed with flameproof, water-retardant wadding that would help to keep everything in here safely dry and rust free. As nothing aboard this ship had been updated recently, Richard calculated confidently that the wadding would be dried out and shrivelled up by now. With luck there would be a little space, safe and secret, where he could put the stuff he wanted to hide.

As he completed these calculations, Richard was busy

with the other contents of the bag. A little spanner soon loosened the nuts he wanted loosened and the second roof yawned open. He slipped his hand in. Yes, it was dry and warm in here. He reached into the bag again and began to transfer the contents as quickly as possible. Out came the Glock – and went into his windcheater pocket. The torch came out next and went straight into another pocket. Then he pulled out the cellphones – and slipped them up under the padding, one by one. The walkie-talkies, likewise. The papers next. He actually held his breath, seeking to dictate the respiration of the Southern Ocean by the control of his own, as he pulled out the flimsy sheets, and slid the most folded and wrinkled off the top of them. Off the top and into his mouth where he could hold it firmly between his teeth. Then in went the rest of the incriminating bundle, good as gold.

With an unconscious sigh of relief, Richard slid his hand back into the bag, checking through its familiar contents and construction for anything he might have forgotten. Unaccountably, he thought of his daughter Mary, then. But almost immediately even these random thoughts were driven from his mind by an immediate and unexpected find.

Because Richard was searching the bag by touch not sight, he discovered the little extra secret. A square of flexible toughness that felt for all the world like a credit card: slipped into the lining and forgotten. He felt it, but such was his fierce concentration on the job in hand, he did not really register it other than as a vivid, unexpected sensation, because he had not found it at the lower end of the lift shaft. Satisfied, he pushed up the inner roof and tightened the bolts. A careful, narrow-eyed inspection assured him that the winch house showed no signs of having been disturbed. And so he closed it and turned away, removing the folded paper from between his teeth and slipping it into his pocket beside the Glock. And not a moment too soon.

Twenty paces or so took him to the radio mast and allowed him to velcro the pocket shut over the incriminating contents. Julie appeared twenty-five seconds later. 'Sophie told me where you were,' she explained unnecessarily.

He nodded, looking up at the mast as though he had been

doing so for a while now, rather than for four and a half seconds. His hands at his sides as though they had been hanging there while he considered his options – not hiding secrets away and closing clothing innocently over them. He hoped his pockets were not bulging too obviously, though he was holding Emil's bag over the bigger, bulkier torch. 'Those were pretty quick interviews,' he observed.

'Neither of them had much to tell. Jean-Luc says he rocked back on the chair to stretch his legs, tipped over backwards, bashed his head, thrashed about, cut his temple on something – then passed out and that was that. Emil doesn't even remember that much. I think he must have amnesia. It's quite common after a bash in the head, I understand.'

'Oh. So he *was* bashed on the head then, Mr Song wasn't too sure.'

'He must have been . . .'

'Because he's got amnesia now . . . Yes I see how that would work. So, where are they now? Going back on duty?'

'Yes. I think they're both well enough. And we need the extra manpower.'

'We do. Poor old Ether certainly needs all the help Jean-Luc can give him. Where did you send Emil?'

'Down to engineering. He's quite capable down there – even though he's trained as a deck officer. I see you've still got his kit bag. He can help sort out the lift, at the very least, but I may reassign him now I know what you're up to. I expect you could do with him up here instead.'

'If Honore and Antoine are going to do a proper job with the lift then they'll need to be up here anyway,' said Richard easily. 'They'll have to shut down the power, disengage the winch or the override programming before they try and move the blockage from the pulley otherwise it'll just keep winding up every time they start to get it free.'

'Yes. I see that. And this is the best place to do it?'

'Switch off power and disengage the winch? Yes.' He nodded across at the housing.

'I'll call them all up here, then.' Her voice was mellower. The snap and suspicion gone out of it. But she hadn't liked him challenging her right to do the interviews any more than he'd liked having to do it. He wished he had insisted on being there because he simply didn't believe a word of what she had been told by either man. Still, he could do some gentle probing of his own. It would help to pass what little time they had.

'Got your walkie-talkie with you?'

'No. I gave it to Chow for the fire watch last night. Got yours?'

'No. I gave mine to Mr Song and Chef. We'll have to do it the hard way and use the loudspeakers. Do you want to go down to the bridge or shall I?'

'I'll go.' The answer was inevitable. She hadn't got to the stage of letting him give the orders yet.

As she turned away, Richard slipped his hand into Emil's bag, seeking that odd little card again. Fingers busy, he watched her walk away. He let her get to the top of the companionway before he called, 'Talking of Mr Song and Chef, what is for dinner?'

She stopped and turned round. Then replied, 'Kung Po chicken with Singapore noodles.' Then she turned away and was gone. Deep at the back of his conscious mind, Richard started counting, measuring the seconds almost as accurately as his watch – without having to look away from what he was doing.

Richard lifted the bag close to his eyes and looked at the square of fabric covering the credit card. He could just see how, by snipping a thread or two, he could get the thing out. There were no scissors in the bag, but there was a pair of electrical pliers. They did the job nicely. He pushed the card upwards and it popped out of its hiding place like a rabbit from a conjurer's hat.

'Now hear this!' The chimes called loudly enough to make him jump. He had reached three hundred. That would give him three minutes after the announcement. Unless Julie got side-tracked and gave him longer – or sent Sophie up at once and surprised him.

'This is the Captain speaking. Can the Fourth Officer and engineers report to the top deck at once, please. I say again . . .'

Richard started the countdown in his head, 300 . . . 299 . . . He looked down into the bag again.

The card was an official-looking ID card. Emil's ID card, judging from the owner's picture in the corner. But it did not identify the owner of the familiar face in the little photo as Emil Brun. It gave his name as François Gailmard. And it did not give his profession as merchant navy officer. Instead, what caught Richard's eye was a little logo, white on a blue background, that looked for all the world like a curved, cupped hunting horn with a flame burning in its hollow. And there were some words beneath it: *Le Département de l'Intérieur* . . .

The sound was so loud and so immediate that Richard for once did shout out with shock. Working almost on autopilot, his fingers slid the card back into its place as the startled man looked up. Something huge battered through the steady blast immediately above his head and for an instant he thought that somehow the BAS Westland chopper had come back. But no. As he straightened and began to come to terms with his surroundings once again, a huge white wandering albatross came tumbling out of the lower sky to settle, like some emissary of doom straight out of romantic literature, on the top of the winch-housing in front of him. And the instant it did so, Emil's golden head thrust up above the top step of the companionway.

'My God,' called the Frenchman. 'Look at that. It's like something out of Coleridge or Poe . . .'

'It's a bit too big and bright for a raven,' Richard called back cheerfully, walking towards Emil while giving the restless albatross a wide berth and using the movement to finish zipping up his bag. 'But I'll do perfectly as the Ancient Mariner, I guess. At least I would have done last night, the way I felt! How are you feeling now?'

Emil rubbed his head with his hand, almost sheepishly. He did not flinch with pain as he did so, but his nose looked black and swollen.

'Much better. Thank you for coming down after me.'

'Think nothing of it. Yours, I believe,' said Richard, handing over the bag as he spoke. 'The Captain tells me you can't remember much as yet?'

'Nothing, I'm afraid.' The blue eyes twinkled self-deprecatingly. 'I'm not even sure what I was doing down there, you know?'

'Ah well.' Richard shook his head theatrically, keeping the tone as light as Emil himself. 'I hope at least that you can remember whether there's any equipment in the footings of the communications mast here that we can use to enhance incoming signals to the radio.' He turned as he spoke and began to go back towards the wreck of the beheaded mast.

'Ah yes,' said Emil more seriously, falling into step beside him. 'I do believe there is.'

They had just arrived at the mast itself, when Honore arrived on the deck. 'Hey,' he called, outraged. 'Will someone get that fucking great bird off my winch-housing? I've got work to do in there!'

In fact it took both Honore and Antoine to move the albatross. And even when they made it take flight, it simply gave a couple of lazy flaps of its huge wings, sailed easily into the eye of the wind and settled on the top of the nearest Sampson post part-way down the deck. From here it spent the rest of the morning watching all of them with lazy interest as they got on with the work in hand. The pristine whiteness of its plumage seemed to become almost unearthly as the sun continued to shine on it through the silvery overcast above Kerguelen while the grey of the sky behind it gathered, changing through leaden, slate and graphite to simple storm-warning black.

As the morning progressed, Richard became increasingly well aware that more than the approaching sky was becoming dark. The capacious pockets of the windcheater, velcroed tight against wind and rain alike – and against prying eyes – allowed Richard to start the work at least. He clambered easily up and down the ladder welded to the side of the mast. He was able to remove Lucien's makeshift cover unaided and with an ease that told him it would never have survived the coming storm. He hung on to the twisted wreckage of the ladder's top and examined the black gape of the hollow mast, trying to see what equipment had survived in any kind

200

of order. Looking casually over his shoulder every now and then to check that his hiding place on top of the winch-housing remained unnoticed as Honore and Antoine bustled about in there.

He knelt beside Emil as the panels at the base of the mast came off and the equipment was revealed for the first time since the chopper had done its damage and the power had come back on – and could be tested now. But soon he began to feel the weight of his secrets – and more than merely physically. Probably because he was watching Emil so closely himself, as well as keeping a more distant eye on the work on the winch. He began to wonder whether someone else was watching him. One of the other three – or two – or all of them.

Richard's focus on Emil was in many ways speculative, of course. The glance he had got at the ID card before the albatross had arrived had really told him very little. So he watched his every move closely, trying to work out if Emil was really a French James Bond undercover – or whether he was just an ordinary bloke who had an eccentric place to keep his library card. He chatted with apparent vague garrulousness, trying to find the truth about last night, but then his own growing suspicion that he was being watched began to burgeon distractingly out of control. It might be a little paranoid, but it was none the worse for that.

After half an hour or so, Richard finally decided he had better empty his pockets before his distraction led him to do something stupid or dangerous. The other horn of the dilemma, of course, was that if he was going to hide the Glock, the manifesto and the flashlight, he would have to stop keeping his own clandestine watch on the false top of the winch-housing for a while at least.

'You continue checking here,' he said to Emil at last. 'I think we can use a third pair of hands.'

And off he went below, pausing only to exchange a cheery word with Honore and Antoine as they laboured on the winch, seemingly to get Jean-Luc; actually to find somewhere to hide his guilty secrets. That should lighten his conscience at least, he thought. Julie caught him at once, as soon as he stepped into the bridge house. 'How are things going up there?' she demanded.

'We need another pair of hands on the mast, I think. Certainly now that we're getting ready to run the aerial itself up there from the Hagenuk and get it properly secured in place. I don't know how the lift repairs are coming . . .'

'How long does it take to disengage a winch mechanism?'

'I think they're doing a little more than that. I get the feeling that the extra strain of the breakdown has done some unexpected damage to the motor itself.'

'I'd better go up and see.'

Richard watched her go out into the companionway and then he went straight to the Captain's cabin. He had not been assigned any other quarters and assumed he would be using it as a base in the future just as he had in the past. The bunk was neatly made, where he had half expected to see it stripped with the mattress still up on the bridge from last night – Mr Song's men had been busy, clearly. He looked around the cabin as he entertained these thoughts. It was sparse enough – almost Spartan. The bed, the wardrobe and the washstand all basic. Shower and toilet en suite. The toilet without a cistern. The shower head simply sticking straight out of the wall. He sought inspiration in the wardrobe; uniforms and clothing were hanging neatly. The upper shelf held extra bedding and a first-aid box. He pulled the box down and opened it. It was full of the bandages, plasters, pills and ointments you would expect to find. And there was certainly no room for anything else in there.

No help for it then, he thought. He crossed to the chest of drawers that formed the base of Captain Giscard's bunk. After a moment's hesitation, he pulled the lowest one wide. He went down on one knee and started rummaging at the very bottom of the drawer, moving the clothing carefully to one side, hollowing out a hiding place. Only to pause, frowning, his nose wrinkled slightly, before he shook himself into action once again. He really didn't have time for all this airy-fairy thinking. This was a time to get on with things if ever there was one.

Under the starched and neatly folded shirts that seemed

to fill the drawer were a range of underthings. Well, it might not be original, but experience suggested that this was a popular hiding place at least. He just hoped that this was because it was a good one. He tore his left pocket open and pulled out the torch. Then he ripped the velcro flap on the right one wide and pulled out the Glock, putting it beside the torch amid the silk and lace in the Captain's drawer. He almost put everything back again but then he remembered the manifesto. He pulled the folded square of paper out of his pocket, noting almost guiltily that he had marked it with his teeth. He lifted it towards his face for a closer look at the damage he had done to it – and froze.

Maybe the airy-fairy thinking wasn't all wasted after all. He had thought of his daughter Mary when he put the paper in his mouth because he had smelt and recognized the faintest trace of perfume upon it. A perfume he had bought for her the last time he had been in Harvey Nicholls' London store. It was Calme Du Cacharel and they had all been most amused by the name. Calm: so much more suitable for a teenage girl than Poison, Passion or Opium. But it was the same scent that had made him pause and wrinkle his nose just now, for he had smelt it the instant he disturbed the lacy underwear.

And that, he saw at once, meant one of two things. Either the manifesto from The Real Friends of the Earth had been hidden in here quite recently. Or whoever hid the paper in the lift shaft also wore the perfume called La Calme du Cacharel.

Eighteen

Surge

It seemed as if the storm began in many ways during those final hours before the big winds at last caught up with them, bringing the dark rain and the tall seas. And, first of all, the great storm surge. Richard's mind was a storm of speculation from the moment he realized that the saboteurs' Internet manifesto and the lacy silk underwear shared the same exclusive scent. At the same time, the darkening atmosphere on the topmost deck seemed to get more intense when Richard brought Jean-Luc up there. He had not seen the Assistant Radio Operator and the Fourth Officer working together before – so there was no reason he should have been prepared for the naked animosity that instantly sparked between them. Animosity that grew stronger minute by minute. Had the storm situation not been worsening at almost the same rate, in fact, he would have split them up.

But the instant Richard returned to the upper deck, it was clear to him how deeply they were already involved in a desperate race against time and in very real danger of losing it. During the all too short interval in which he had been away, the sky had blackened further and closed down upon the sea behind their trailing bows like the jaw of a vice. A final glimmer of the afternoon sun flashed under the belly of the beast pursuing them, giving a terrible definition to the great ribs of cloud spinning down upon them.

Richard immediately called on Ether to check with *Sissy* because the storm seemed to be accelerating far beyond reasonable expectations. But he was already too late. The tug's signal had become buried under the blizzard of static that the meteorological monster on their tail was generating. And that in turn ensured that Emil and Jean-Luc had to continue side by side whether they hated one another or not, because it was their work that would give *Lady Mary* back her vital contact with the world.

It really didn't matter to the increasingly desperate Richard whether they killed each other later or not, so long as they kept the Hagenuk alive for the next few hours and days. To be fair, Emil and Jean-Luc just managed to keep their animosity in check while Julie was up on deck. But she didn't dare to stay for long, not with the afternoon closing in on her helpless command so swiftly and threateningly. Things got chillier the instant she left but they really went over some kind of cliff when Antoine and Honore shut up the winch-housing and went down to free the pulley on the lift car.

It wasn't that the two men called each other names like feuding schoolboys; or even uttered threats like bellicose drunks. It was simply, Richard realized, that they were on the verge of damaging each other. Permanently. Perhaps fatally.

'Run up the ladder, please, Jean-Luc,' ordered Richard before he had properly understood what seemed to be going on. 'See whether you notice any movement within the mast when we connect this circuit.'

'Certainly,' said Jean-Luc and up he went. Richard and Emil crouched forward, connecting the wires that hopefully would reanimate one of the little dishes stored within the hollow aerofoil mast itself.

'I see it,' called Jean-Luc, but as he spoke, a rush of wind came past, and a heavy spanner clanged on to the deck by Emil's knee. 'Pardon,' called Jean-Luc at once. 'It slipped out of my belt.'

'One last connection here,' Richard observed a little later, 'and the signal enhancement system should be back on line. Jean-Luc, hold this . . .'

'Of course . . .' There came a flash as the assistant took the wire. 'Ahhh! Merde . . .' A burning smell instantly snatched away by the wind. The palm of Jean-Luc's bare hand was blistered and burned. They were lucky not to have fused everything they were trying to fix.

'Oh, was that connected?' asked Emil, all innocence. 'I had no idea . . .'

Richard straightened up. He stood, towering with his back to the wind, swaying just a little as it pounded on his shoulders. 'Look, you two,' he snarled. 'I don't know what this is all about and I don't want to know. But the facts are these. The sky you can see over my shoulder will be over our heads in an hour. That's all the time we have left to finish here. We've got to get as much of this wreck back on line as we can, we've got to connect it to the Hagenuk and then secure it all. That will mean hanging over the front of the bridge house four decks up with the safety rail all broken. It will mean shinning up and down that mast like monkeys on speed. It will present all of us with numerous opportunities to kill or maim each other. If you two want to do that more than you want to save this ship and everyone aboard her, just speak up now. Because we don't have time for this. We really don't!'

And, as if to emphasize the power of his words, the first great lightning bolt pounced down away at the far end of the ship's wake. He saw the jagged reflection in their widening eyes. As though their eyeballs had been made of glass – like dolls' eyes – and had suddenly shattered for an instant. The thunder that followed drowned the screaming of the wind. And a squall of rain hit him hard enough to make him stagger forward.

Richard dropped a line, weighed it down with Jean-Luc's heavy spanner. Jean-Luc went down to Ether and helped him open the porthole and connect the UHF aerial to the end of the line, keeping the spanner there in the hope that the steady weight would give them control of the thin line in the thick wind. Then, as quickly as their care would allow, they pulled it up.

While Jean-Luc and Ether did their best to secure the lower end to the front of the bridge house, then close the porthole as far as they dared, Emil and Richard spliced it to the main line leading down towards the bridge. They had to search carefully among the cables that contained all the information bound towards the radars and the weather predictors. They had to connect the aerial to the one connecting the signal enhancers to the blackened graveyard of the burned-out radio room. By the time Emil and Richard were happy with the connection, Jean-Luc was back. Julie had given him a walkie-talkie and they were able to check with Ether that his signal was now much improved. By the time they had resecured all the panels and done their best to secure this end of the aerial as well, Ether was deep in conversation with Kerguelen, who were warning them that the storm had changed its track a little and accelerated quite a lot.

Then Ether himself appeared, sent up to help them batten everything down up here while Julie shared some more of her thoughts with Chef du District Alain Faure at Port aux Français. The charming French scientist didn't have so much time for social chit-chat this time, Ether observed dryly. He was busy battening down his facility in the face of the fast-approaching Armageddon which would reach them long before it got anywhere near him.

It certainly needed all of them to get Lucien's covers back and properly secured, in the face of the raving winds that were threatening to engulf them. In fact it was providential that Antoine and Honore came up to put the winch back on line and test-run the lift – for Richard got them involved at the earliest opportunity as well.

And then, with the first great sheets of solid rainwater coming down like a series of dark grey waterfalls along the deck towards them, Richard sent them all below. He lingered out here alone for one last look around before he abandoned the streaming decks to the elements and the albatross. He looked up at their work on the masthead. He looked down at the already inundated panels at the mast foot. He checked the doors of the winch house carefully, making sure the roof of the little metal sentry box was secure. Then he staggered away below. His last thought, which took him down the companionway, was, that's the last we'll see of this old red lead weather-decking until we come back out to take *Sissy*'s tow-ropes aboard.

'It's gone south,' said Julie as Richard shambled, streaming with water, on to the bridge. 'Does that mean what I think it means?'

'South of us?' demanded Richard. 'South of *Lady Mary*?'

'Yes. Kerguelen says the eye is just about to pass over the Fram Bank. It's tightened up, apparently, and the winds along the leading edge have strengthened, particularly in the north-eastern quadrant.'

'Well, it'll die more quickly, especially if it's spinning further south still over the continental Antarctic itself – or the ice shelf. That's all to the good. But on the other hand, it'll slow down on contact with solid land or ice – then probably begin to tear itself apart. But that's only of limited benefit to us. The north-eastern quadrant is where we'll be for the next few hours – maybe days, depending on the speed of the storm as a whole. That does mean that we'll be in a strongly north-westerly airflow as the winds whirl clockwise around the eye. Is it still a strong 12 on the Beaufort scale?'

'I guess. If it was in the Gulf of Mexico, it'd be Category Five, apparently. That's the strongest, isn't it? Like that famous one that almost destroyed New Orleans a couple of years ago? Hurricane Katrina?'

'Katrina was a five on the Saffir-Simpson scale – the highest category – over the water. She went to a four when she came over land. But they don't always give them names or categories down here.'

'Do tell! That'll be because no one but the penguins see most of them.'

Richard gave a bark of laughter. 'Could be,' he said.

As they had been speaking, he had been pulling off his wet gear, unwilling to leave the bridge during these early, crucial moments of the mighty battle against the elements they were undertaking. He dumped the yellow gear by the door in the certain hope that the quiet efficiency of Mr Song's machine would be sending stewards up here to clear up after them as well as to see to their other, more bodily needs. Like every other element aboard, Mr Song's command area might well prove crucial. The ship handlers and engineers needed to concentrate during the next forty-eight hours. They needed to keep their minds focussed on the job in hand. They needed to know that if they reached for a cup of coffee there would be one to hand. If they wanted to leave wet or dirty work clothes – or pick up some clean dry ones – these things could be done with the minimum of fuss.

And the worth of the system was proved at once. For even as Richard kicked the streaming pile of gear towards the door and turned to stand with Julie at the clearview, so the hurricane's first great calling-card arrived.

It was a mountain of water more than twenty-five feet in height. By the grace of God it was not steep-sided, like the lesser waves that preceded it and followed it. It simply gathered, inexorably; gaining and gaining as it swept on by them. By them, and, for a terrifying moment, over them.

Richard had been watching for it and so saw it first. The bottom of the sky seemed to gather solidity amid the whirling of the squalls that span along the great depression's leading edge. The spray-laced slate of the storm wind became a solid hill of coal. The steadiness amid the whirling wildness drew in towards the bow, overtaking *Lady Mary* with the majesty of an express train. An express train that was wider than the horizon and taller than a house. 'Hang on to something,' called Richard. 'And remember this one for your grandchildren. Supertankers don't often pitch like rowing boats.'

Even as Richard spoke, the storm surge swept in under *Lady Mary*'s bow. At first, as he had said, the huge length of the tanker tried to ride the great width of the wave. But the hull was simply too long to accommodate the speed or steepness of the great dark hill, pushed up and out by the fierceness of the storm behind it. White water cascaded in over the forecastle head even though the bow was rising like a giant elevator. Then the twin cascades of white water rushed up along the deck towards them, thundering down over the pipework, the hatch covers, the chevrons of the breakwaters, the rest of the deck furniture, joining together in a wall of foam that hit the front of the bridge itself with devastating force.

The whole structure seemed to stagger back as if torn loose of the deck. The windows cracked. The clearview stalled. For a moment everything went opaque: streaming, white, impenetrable. They were blind for maybe thirty heartbeats. And that was probably just as well. For during those heartbeats the whole huge length of the weather deck was under water. The great grey-green ocean simply heaved itself up over the whole length of the deck and, while the crew stood blindly on the command bridge, the bridge house itself was all that could be seen above the water, like the conning tower of a diving submarine. The bridge house and the tops of the two Sampson posts halfway down the deck. And the albatross still sitting calmly on the top of the starboard one.

But then the clearview sprang to life again and dashed the blinding foam aside, just as the forecastle head exploded out of the back of the surge, heading for the sky like a breaching whale. Everyone aboard who did not have a firm hand-hold was staggering backwards – then they were stumbling forwards as *Lady Mary* settled and the massive wave was past.

'Get in touch with Kerguelen, Ether,' bellowed Richard. 'Warn them that the storm surge is heading their way fast. That was the better part of ten metres high and it'll wash Port Aux Français away if it catches them unawares. Then check with *Sissy* and *Oscar Whisky*. If it hasn't caught up with them yet, then it will soon. Julie, we need to do a quick damage assessment before the worst of the weather arrives. I'd be surprised if that hasn't popped a rivet or two somewhere.'

'I thought it was going to break her back. I really thought we were all going to die then,' said Julie, simply awed. Her voice was husky, cheeks were pink and her eyes huge.

Danger seemed to stimulate her, in fact almost sexually, Richard observed. But then he dismissed the thought as a distracting irrelevance. 'Can Emil keep an eye on the cargo? If *Lady Mary*'s back is put in any danger, it'll be from sheer rather than seas. If she's come through that surge, she'll come through anything else the ocean's likely to throw at her within the next forty-eight hours. Unless we lose control of the cargo. Emil needs to watch tank temperature, balance and so on. Is he up to that?'

'He can start out in the First Officer's lading control office where Lucien and the First Officer worked. We'll go down with him, help him set up and start our inspection there, OK? Emil, did you hear that? Off you go down to the lading office and check the First Officer's work. We'll look in on you in a minute or two. Sophie, hold the watch. We'll be as quick as we can. Antoine, Honore, down to engineering. We'll check on you as well.'

The first great gust of wind hit the windows then, almost as hard as the white water had. But it was a glancing blow, with a fair amount of northerly heading in it. *Lady Mary* seemed to reel a little. 'Do we have to go outside, Richard?' asked Julie, breathlessly.

'No. We haven't any safety lines rigged. Not that they would have survived that storm surge in any case. We'll be lucky if the deck pipes have. And all deck plates, come to that. We'll have to assess things as best we can from inside the hull. But like I say, we're getting very low on time to do it.'

They caught up with Emil as he dashed on to the A-Deck corridor. As soon as they arrived there, Richard felt his footing lose purchase and he slowed, looking down frowning. There must be an inch or more of water here, he thought. Then he looked up. Emil was at the lading office door. Richard had an instantaneous flash of memory – looking straight down the deck from the office window at the crinkling wave of smoke that had covered the deck just before Lucien died.

'Door's stuck,' said Emil to Julie, who was just behind him.

'Careful!' shouted Richard. He was just too late.

Emil turned the handle and the door exploded open. It slammed right back, nearly torn off its hinges, throwing Emil aside like a puppet. The windows in the office had caved in under the weight of the storm surge on the deck. It was a miracle the door had held under the pressure. It had certainly yielded now. A roomful of water slammed the door wide and hurled itself out into the corridor, washing Julie back towards Richard, who caught her and hauled her up. Then Emil hit them and knocked them both down. They floundered to their feet and pulled him up. There was a welt running down his face where the edge of the door had hit him. By the look of his overalls it had hit him on the shoulder, chest and hip as well.

The three of them stood for a second, gulping air. 'That's the lading office gone,' said Emil grimly, spitting blood. 'And one of my ribs, I think.' He spat again, blood and teeth. 'And some very expensive dental work. Lucky I had my bag to protect my chest – and a health plan for the rest.'

'We need to go down to engineering now,' said Julie. 'That's where the main lading controls are. Shall we drop you off in the infirmary, Emil?'

'No. You can't afford to lose anyone else. I'll survive. Let's get on.'

Richard sloshed back up the corridor and slammed the door shut. Then he crossed the corridor and stuck his head into the makeshift sickbay. 'Get Mr Song,' he yelled at the young man looking after the patients in there. 'Tell Mr Song to hang "No Entry" warnings on the doors on the opposite side of this corridor. All the areas with windows or portholes looking on to the main deck at this level are likely to be full of water and very dangerous. And anyone in here who can possibly get up and out should do so. We need all the help we can possibly get to keep this ship afloat.'

The A-Deck corridor was no longer full of water when Richard came out again. Of course it wasn't, he thought. The water would all be washing down to engineering – down the companionways and lift shaft. He wondered briefly how the incendiary bombs would enjoy being under water. And than he decided it was probably just as well that the cell-phones were up and away from them. Just on the off-chance that one phone might manage to send a signal in the instant that it fused. Then he put all such thoughts out of his head. *If you can't fix it, don't sweat it*, he thought. He had more than enough to worry about in any case.

Lady Mary gave a rolling heave as a big wave took her on the starboard quarter. 'Let's be quick,' he called to the others. 'I'll bet we've lost all the weather-deck windows. That means every time a big sea sweeps the deck it'll try to force more water into the lading office, the officers' bar, the library, the games room, the officers' dining area and everything facing the wind and the weather. Mr Song will put up notices but we'll have to send up Chow and a team to try and shore the doors up. We don't want the water just washing on through.'

Richard's thoughts were well placed. Engineering seemed almost awash. Level by level as they ran on down, the situation seemed to worsen. They certainly did not want to let any more water down here if they could avoid it. They paused with the nervous-looking fire watch on the upper level, while Julie checked on Mr Chow and then sent one of the men to find him.

Richard walked to the edge of the balcony and looked down into the great hole of the main engineering area. As though it were some kind of underground grotto, engineering oozed dampness. The walls seemed to be running with constant moisture as though they were stone, not steel. The deckheads dripped from above. The decks beneath gathered puddles that turned to tiny streams – that vanished through gratings or down companionways just as Richard had imagined the inert gas doing. And that too gave him pause – especially after the experiences in the lift shaft. Water was heavier than CO_2. It would push the poison gas back up again, reflooding areas they had supposed to be clear and safe.

'Emil and Antoine need to isolate the lading office as soon as possible and then monitor the cargo from the lading room down here,' Richard whispered urgently to Julie when she joined him. 'Fortunately those mid-level work areas seem to be snug and dry for the time being. Honore needs to get the pumps on line and up to full power, though. We don't want this lot collecting in the lower areas if we can help it.'

'I can see that!' Julie answered tersely. 'Where in God's name is all this water coming from?'

'I think we've popped a rivet or two,' he answered. 'In the deck plates for starters, by the look of things. What someone really needs to do is to pop along the walkways between the weather deck and the tops of the tanks to see what's coming in.'

213

'Can't we monitor that from here?'

He shook his head regretfully. 'There's nothing here that will assess that kind of damage. It's one of those hands-on things, I'm afraid. And if the lower areas weren't flooded with inert gas we really ought to be checking them as well. But we'll just have to trust the pumps.'

For the next half-hour they worked in the engineering sections, doing the jobs that Richard and Julie had discussed. But then they hit an obstacle – just at the most important point of all. Richard and Julie were with Antoine and Emil in the lading control room. The cadet and the deck officer had managed to isolate the lading office upstairs so that the water damage done to the circuits in the computers up there would not affect the machines down here. They had run diagnostics on all the circuits controlling the heating to the cargo. They had checked the individual temperatures in the tanks. They were beginning to see about planning for the various contingencies that might require them to move some of the oil around when Emil abruptly broke the tense and concentrated silence. 'I can't do this,' he said. He looked across at Sophie, his face pale and showing an unexpected intensity of strain. 'I simply cannot get my head round this, Captain. I'm going to kill us all if I . . .'

'Here, let me,' said Antoine at once. 'I can see what we need to do. Captain, let me run through this with you to make sure I've got it right. Then we can patch it up to your screen on the bridge and you can keep an eye on me from up there when you're back on watch.'

'You want me to go back up?' asked the shaken Emil, picking up his bag.

'No!' spat the enraged Captain. 'I don't know what I want you to do! Go help Mr Chow maybe. If you feel you can handle woodwork . . .'

'I need someone to come with me,' said Richard. 'If this lot's under control then I need to check along the tops of the tanks like I said. In these conditions that would be a dangerously stupid thing to do alone. I was going to ask for Antoine to help, but Emil would be even better.'

At the starboard extremity of the forward wall of the upper

214

engineering level there was a big bulkhead door like the doors that connect the watertight compartments in a submarine. Ten minutes later, Richard was turning the handle in the centre of this with Emil at his shoulder holding two big waterproof torches. A coil of rope hung over his shoulder over the top of his bag. As soon as they were through they would be tying themselves together as though they were climbers or explorers. Each man had a walkie-talkie secured to his belt, even so; as though they were half expecting to become lost or separated. Richard pulled the door wide and stepped over a sill even higher than the one leading out of the A-Deck corridor. Emil silently followed him in. Then he turned and closed the door behind him as Richard walked along a corridor immediately above the cofferdam and opened the next door forward. It was exactly the same as the last one – except that beside it on the wall at shoulder height there was a sealed box with the words 'Emergency Use Only' stencilled on it. It was the first of these boxes but Emil knew there was one beside every door from now on. Before they stepped forward this time they tied themselves together. Then Richard led the way.

What they stepped into was effectively a long passageway that led above the metal tops of the half-dozen enormous tanks that stretched from here to the forecastle head. Each tank was contained within steel walls that reached from deck to keel – and there were five more doors ahead. They walked over steel grating, through which they could look down past the six inches or so before the metal shell of the tank began. Immediately on their right shoulders, the skin of the outer hull rose until it folded over, two metres above the grating, to form the weather deck itself. But on their left sides, their view went almost the whole way across the ship. The great tops of the tanks rose upwards to the great pipe connections that soared like the truncated columns in a troll's cathedral up through the deck to form the tank tops and connect with the sheaves of pipes up there. Columns that stood at most two metres high – but one metre for the most part and a mere foot in the middle. The whole area was dimly illuminated by the security lighting which was just strong enough to give a weird sense of scale – to make it feel that the whole constricted vastness was closing down to crush them as they moved.

As Emil turned to close the second door, Richard reached back for his torch and flicked it on. He shone the bright blade of the beam up across the glittering, sparking metal to the top of the nearest column. Emil turned back, flicking on his own torch and gasped.

'Yes,' said Richard grimly. It was raining in here. No, worse: it was pouring. The glitter and sparking of the metal was torchlight on cascading water. Had it not been for the over-whelming cacophony of wind and waves outside, the noise in here would have been thunderous. Water was simply flooding over the top of the tank and swirling away down drainage holes that led to the bilge below; holes that seemed to be large enough to swallow an elephant each. Emil stood staring down at the first of these, looking through the grating between his feet as though into the throat of the Maelstrom itself. For a horrific moment it occurred to him that the water running through from the deck might simply be pouring into the interior of the tank itself. And he really could not begin to imagine the damage that might do. He stood there, rapt by the nightmare vision. So deeply disturbed, in fact, that the pains in his head, jaw and chest seemed almost to fade away. He did not actually move until Richard, opening the door into the next gallery, unknowingly jerked the rope. Then Emil hurried forward, suddenly very unwilling to be far away from the reassuring solid competence of his companion.

There was less water coming in to the second area. 'That's a bit more reassuring,' called Richard – though Emil had to strain to hear. 'At least there's only water in that last tank. There's oil in this one – you see the water steaming on the top of it? We really do not want Antarctic water and hot crude to mix if we can help it. Not inside the hull at any rate.' He led the way forward and Emil followed, still frowning with concern.

The next space seemed a serious set-back again. This was especially true as the instant the door opened, eye-watering fumes came washing through. Richard stepped back and closed the door. Emil hesitated, half expecting him to turn and go back to engineering. But no, Richard simply pulled the door of the box on the wall down and pulled out two sets of breathing apparatus. They were much lighter than the equipment that they had worn down in the sections flooded with inert gas. Little more than a face mask with a bottle hanging from it. Richard slipped his on and tested it, then reached for a clean-air monitor which sat in the box beneath it. Emil took more time settling his mask over his damaged face but at last he got it comfortable, then they stepped onwards through the next door.

It clearly wasn't just the deck that was leaking here, Emil thought. Some of the pipework was sprung as well. This was about the mid-point of the hull, he calculated. If the long ship was going to flex anywhere under the influence of that massive surge, then it would be here. And any flexing at all would be bad news in all sorts of ways. When he flashed his torch around, echoing Richard's decisive movements, he saw rainbows rather than sparks. Every surface was marked with liquid colours like puddles in a parking lot.

'Are we losing much?' he shouted to Richard. Richard shrugged. The eyes behind the mask were narrow, their expression distant. Richard was obviously deep in thought.

'Let's press on,' he yelled. Emil nodded. Richard heaved the next door open and stepped through. And it was then that the peculiar physics of their situation overtook the men. The first real hurricane blast hit from the north-east, bringing the second largest wave so far along with it. The huge ship rolled beneath the onslaught. The whole corridor tilted up and over, sending both men staggering back. The door between them slammed shut, severing the rope with casual ease. The railings hit Emil in the small of the back and he simply cartwheeled backwards over the top. He fell little more than a metre but he landed on the point of his atlas bone, just where his spine joined his neck. The bone cracked. It was enough to paralyse him in absolute agony. Every extremity – each individual finger and toe – felt as though a red-hot needle had been driven up beneath the nail. Even thought was impossible for those few crucial seconds. He sucked in breath to shout with outrage at the pain – and choked. His mask was gone. He turned his head – thus discovering the paralysis was not permanent – and saw the weighty little bottle pulling the plastic faceplate away down the slope of the oil-slick tank towards the whirlpool of the nearest drainage hole. Emil realized that he was sliding inexorably downwards himself. The outer edge of the metal grating walkway he had just fallen off began to slide above his head. He gasped again, and choked. But this time he managed a scream.

The door burst open again and Richard stepped back through. One glance was enough to tell him what had happened and with almost superhuman speed he secured the end of his severed rope round the safety rail and leaped over on to the tank top. He landed well and stood for a moment before crashing to his knees. He reached down. 'Grab my hands!' he bellowed. Emil tried, but when he tried to raise his arms, the pain in his neck and shoulders hit him like lightning.

'I can't move,' he screamed. 'Help me! I can't move . . .'

Richard didn't hesitate. Putting all his trust in the strength of the railing and his rope work, he threw himself full length, sliding down after Emil until his own lifeline brought him up short. But all he could get hold of was the engineer's bag. 'Hold on!' he bellowed. 'Hold on to the strap!'

But Emil simply had no real strength or control in either of his hands. Hardly able to move any of his limbs, spread-eagled on his back like a butterfly in a collection, he simply slid down helplessly, hesitating only momentarily as the strap slid off his spastically twitching arm.

'For God's sake, hold on!" shouted Richard helplessly, watching the man he was trying to rescue succumbing to the lethal pull of the drainage system. 'Just grab a hold!' But he was too late. The last chance was gone.

The wave of oil-coloured water gathered around Emil's spread-eagled body and for a moment lent him a butterfly's delicate colours as it sucked him helplessly down the drain.

It took Richard ten minutes to pull himself back up on to

the grating. He staggered through into the clean air of the next section. And, while he sat there, fighting to get back his breath and his self-control, he pulled out the little ID card from its hiding place and looked at it more closely. François Gailmard, it said. *Officier de Douanes et Droits Indirects du Département de L'Intérieur.*

Not a French James Bond after all, thought Richard. But what in God's name was a customs officer doing working undercover aboard the *Lady Mary*?

Nineteen

Storm

Richard leaned back against the shower wall and let the spray thunder over him like the downpour of a tropical storm. It was an hour later – an hour filled with many moments of thought, crouching there on the walkway, cradling Emil's bag like a dead child in his lap. Then a weary scramble back to engineering and a slow climb up the companionways to the bridge. Here he had completed a lengthy report to Julie. She had been more affected by his news than she had been by Lucien's death, he thought. Partway through the report she had moved off the navigation bridge and into the chart room, away from the raving of the wind against the clearview, which had made him report the tragic events in a most unsuitable bellow. Thus Jean-Luc, on radio watch, had heard the final sections of the story. Perhaps that had turned out for the best as she had grown faint at the thought that the poor man had still been alive during that long slide down the oil-slick chute between the massive tanks and into the gas-filled bilges. Even Jean-Luc, who had clearly hated the Fourth Officer, had paled. Richard had left the pair of them consoling each other when he had been dismissed to clean himself up.

As the scalding cascade washed away the mess of filthy water and emulsified oil off Richard's own skin, so it seemed to clear his mind and revitalize his depleted stores of energy and decisiveness. Typically, he was finding that the bitter frustration and simple burning anger generated by yet another useless death filled him with resolution as well as regret. With an invigorating desire to get the matter sorted out, rather than hopelessness, defeat and despair such as he had fleetingly seen in Julie's eyes. After a moment or two he got up, chose the least heavily scented of the toiletries on offer and began to soap himself with purposeful, energetic strokes.

So, he thought. The dead man had been a French official working undercover. Therefore the ship or her crew was suspected of something illegal. Suspected by officialdom at an early date. Certainly there was an enormous amount of illegal action going on at the moment – attempted violent destruction of the hull, leading to arson, assault and murder for starters – just as he had described matters to Julie soon after his arrival aboard. But realizing the true state of affairs now, in the middle of things, was by no means the same as suspecting something right back at the outset. Yet someone in Paris or Marseilles must have suspected that the tanker, her crew – or the company which owned her – was up to no good. That this voyage was going to involve smuggling, the breaking of international agreements, insurance fraud. Or, of course, there might be someone aboard that the authorities were suspicious of. But, whatever – whoever – the French authorities suspected, they must have suspected it early enough and strongly enough in order to be sending undercover operatives aboard.

And the fact that Emil was an undercover man added new dimensions to everything that had happened to him, too. The mutual hatred he seemed to share with Jean-Luc. The matter of the stuck lift and the assault on Emil that seemed to have caused it in the first place. What had resulted from that apparent accident? Perhaps it was possible, up to and including Richard's own discovery of the bombs, that even that apparent coincidence might have been part of another plan. It would by no means have been the first time that Richard himself had been manipulated to further someone else's secret, sinister ends.

But, thought Richard, in the final analysis, somebody had certainly suspected the late Fourth Officer of being more than he seemed, just as someone somewhere in France had

221

suspected *La Dame Marie* was up to more than she was supposed to be.

Richard decided that he had better tear the dead man's bag apart at the earliest opportunity. There might well be more than an ID card hidden in there. He had just reached this typically decisive and active point in his reasoning when *Lady Mary* gave another lurch like the one that had killed Emil. Richard staggered across the shower stall. Then turned and headed for the door, thinking perhaps the bag had better wait for a moment when the hull was not being torn apart by the storm. He didn't want to be looking into Emil's secrets when the call to abandon ship went out.

Five minutes later, Richard was back up on the bridge. The bag was beside the bunk in the Captain's cabin but the ID card was in the pocket of yet another set of overalls stretched too tightly across his massive frame. His main objective was the Hagenuk, of course, but the simple state of the tanker's situation stopped him and turned him aside for a moment; for even during his brief shower, things seemed to have worsened further.

Once again he was struck by the strangeness of *Lady Mary*'s position. He had weathered hundreds of storms in his career, some of them as fearsome as this one. Many in the *Prometheus* series of hulls like *Lady Mary*'s. But he had always ridden them out under power. He had never drifted as he was drifting now. Never backing almost helplessly away from the eye of the wind, with the forecastle head pointing powerlessly into the following seas. It was something he found deeply disturbing, as though he was driving down a busy motorway looking exclusively in the rear-view mirror. And what he saw, looking back along the dully-lit length of her, was a howling whirl of spray and water, rain, spume and tall dark sea. It all came in at more than a hundred miles an hour, beating at an angle from his right towards his left as it roared up and in towards him and screamed against the shuddering clearview like a squadron of giant banshees come to tear them all to hell.

But there was simply no choice except to look back down the screaming throat of the thing, Richard thought. To go

222

out on the after deck and stand at the point he had first seen Julie, Sophie and Antoine, would have allowed him to look ahead only for the briefest moment before the wild wind simply tore him away and the big seas gulped him down. And it would be yet another waste of time and life. There would be nothing at all to see.

Richard crossed to the collision alarm radar and stood beside Sophie, looking down into the bowl in an attempt to set his sailorly unease to rest. Sure enough, the green sweep of the radar beam showed no contacts between here and distant Kerguelen. Even so, Sophie strained to keep it under observation, just in case. He was almost surprised to note that somewhere along the line the over-eager young cadet had grabbed a moment long enough to shower and change. But then the smile of almost paternal indulgence froze upon his lips. For somewhere in her shower and change of uniform Sophie had anointed herself with Calme du Cacharel.

'So, Sophie,' he said without further thought, keeping his voice just loud enough to be heard above the raving of the wind and the crashing of the sea. 'How did a girl like you get to be aboard a ship like this?'

The line was as corny as any old pick-up used by a drunken sailor to a girl in a Portsmouth bar. The cadet looked up, her closed face green and frowning. The light from the radar bowl compounded with genuine fear – and a little seasickness. This was the first time this old hull had ever pitched or rolled to any degree.

'It'll help to talk,' he said gently. She gulped and nodded. Her natural reticence – and perhaps a good deal more – was overcome by a simple need to talk through her sickness and her fear.

'It was Julie. The Captain,' she said softly, glancing across the bridge. 'She was one of the senior students at the boarding school I attended just outside Paris. I never knew her then, of course, for I was in the lower forms when she was going off to college. But one day she came back to visit her old school. I was one of the senior girls myself by that time. She had passed her exams, and had just returned from her first tour of duty aboard her first ship. She gave a talk to the senior

223

students about the sea and her life. She was so much like me in so many ways that it seemed almost inevitable that I should follow in her footsteps, you see. And so I did . . .'

'And your parents didn't object? The sea can be a hard life, especially for a young woman.'

'I am like Julie, as I have said. My parents divorced some years ago. They each have new partners; new families. That was why I came to be at the school. I see it more clearly now than I saw it then. They had fought like wild cats over the house, the furniture, the car. They wanted their *things*. Their business investments. But neither of them really wanted me . . .'

'Still,' he said bracingly. 'You love the sea. You have found a new home and family aboard *Lady Mary* and ships like her.'

'Yes, I love the sea. But . . .'

'But you don't love great filthy hulks of tankers?' Richard hoped he wasn't being too obvious with his probing. He himself had trained as an officer in the merchant marine after all – not as a detective in the CID.

Sophie's face closed. She turned away. Just as she did so, Ether called through from the radio, 'Captain Mariner, I have *Sissy* for you.'

Richard eased himself into the creaky chair, his forebrain already speculating as to what *Sissy* would want while his subconscious pondered deeper, darker things. An update on her position, perhaps. On her circumstances. How she was weathering the storm – and how *Sissy* was doing under the more severe conditions further south and east. But no:

'Have you been talking to this man Alain Faure at Kerguelen?' demanded Robin as soon as the formalities of contact were completed.

'Not personally. The Captain has. Why?' Richard was dumbstruck by her tone.

'You mean you don't *know*? Have you not been listening to the news services? Not even the BBC World Service?'

'I listened last night but . . .' He could not see where this was heading.

'There's a news bulletin coming up. Switch over and listen in.'

Richard's fingers hit the buttons and the machine's memory automatically called up the World Service:

... That was *Sports Round-Up*. In a moment the news. And immediately after that, in five minutes' time, *One Planet* will be replacing its scheduled programme with a special edition from the BBC's *Costing The Earth* team. Assisted Ecocide will look at the problems faced by societies, such as Easter Island, which have managed to wipe themselves out by continued misuse of their environments. Assisted Ecocide will be looking at the way in which society seems to be putting complete ecosystems at risk. In particular, it will examine at the Amazon Basin and its catastrophic deforestation – after the 'spectacular' terrorist bombing at the offices of Yangtze-Mindanao by the eco-terrorists The Real Friends of the Earth.

That must be it! Richard thought, and was just about to switch back to Robin on *Sissy* when he realized she knew nothing about his suspicions, his discoveries, his manifesto from The Real Friends of the Earth that smelt of Calme du Cacharel. He hesitated, therefore, through the time signal and the opening formalities of the news bulletin. Until he found out in no uncertain terms what Robin had been talking about.

... And the eyes of the world remain focussed on the most remote spot on the globe. Alain Faure, Chief of the French scientific station on Kerguelen Island in the Southern Ocean, reported less than an hour ago that they have survived the storm surge and the men and women at the station are now awaiting the arrival of the hurricane. And, of course, the arrival of the stricken French supertanker, *La Dame Marie*, which is still drifting helplessly in the grip of the hurricane itself, apparently on fire, heading towards the volcanic islands. And giving rise to world-wide controversy as it does so.

225

The French authorities have said that as soon as the weather moderates it is hoped that the vessel may be taken under tow and two ocean-going tugs are racing to the rescue. The chances of an environmental disaster on the scale of *Exxon Valdez*, *Amoco Cadiz* or *Torrey Canyon* are remote, they say. And talk of an explosion powerful enough to destroy part of the island and cause a volcanic eruption is simple scaremongering.

However, Senator Ephraim Crook, who speaks for the American Senate on environmental matters, has said that the French have been criminally irresponsible in their handling of this ecological disaster. The situation is just one more proof that they are not really capable of upholding their claim to a complete section of the Antarctic continent, he said yesterday, in a speech to the Antarctic Society in Washington . . .

'It must have been Julie. She's been on to Kerguelen most often, and always to Alain Faure,' said Richard a few moments later.

'Did she talk it over with you?' asked Robin. Both of them were almost whispering, as though fearful of being over-heard.

'No. But I don't see why she's got Faure involved at all. If she was going down the path of maximum publicity, she could just have gone direct. Reuters or RTF. Any French broadcaster would probably have picked it up.'

'Think it through, though,' said Robin more slowly. 'Faure has to have more time than she does. Be more easily available. And anyway, surely she'd have to go through you or the radio operator. Sounds as though Faure's gone it alone. His fifteen minutes of fame. And, of course . . .'

'What?' Richard was still fighting to fit this new piece into the puzzle.

'It's a bit grim but I bet she thought it through. If publicity's what she's after, then Faure guarantees continued coverage. Whether *Lady Mary* makes it or not. Unless the whole of Kerguelen goes up, of course. And then there'll be no end of publicity . . .'

'And the promise of a base,' added Richard, struck. 'Somewhere the news teams can camp out with their choppers and their cameras. I mean, if I got down here, so will they. And of course the news services will kill for footage of this. When the storm clears, it'll be simply spectacular, won't it?'

And, with all the thoughts and suspicions being crunched through the subconscious parts of his mind as though through a never-sleeping computer, it was that one word, 'spectacular', that made the penny drop.

He glanced around almost guiltily. Ether still lingered in the doorway, Jean-Luc stood a little way behind him deep in conversation with Julie. Richard leaned forward until his lips were brushing the microphone. This time he really did whisper. 'Robin, what did you find out for me about the matters we discussed earlier?'

'Eco-terrorists or such? And the forces ranged against them?' Her own voice dropped further – but at least she dared say the phrase aloud.

'Yup.' He hoped that the gruff monosyllable would give nothing away.

'We had a brush with *La Guerre Verte* a few years ago of course, when we got into the business of moving environmentally hazardous materials. But they seem to be out of the picture now. This new lot, The Real Friends of the Earth, are cutting-edge currently. You heard what they did in the Amazon?'

'They're aboard *Lady Mary*. The organization you just mentioned. I think someone in Paris may suspect. Have we any contacts?'

'Are you serious? If they were aboard, then you'd be at the bottom of the sea, my boy. Or blown to smithereens like those people in Amazon.'

'It's not for want of trying, believe you me. Look I'm a bit worried about open channels and such. Especially with the news hounds in full cry after us. See what you can scare up there. I'll keep looking here. Have you got an ETA for Kerguelen?'

'Still the better part of thirty-six hours. Weather conditions allowing. But the perfect storm here's supposed to be spin-

227

ning south and breaking up over the West or Shackleton Ice Shelves. We may pull you out of it yet.'

'That would be a spectacular, wouldn't it? *Lady Mary* out.'

Richard eased himself out of the chair. Jean-Luc replaced him and Ether went down to get some food. Richard replaced Jean-Luc at Julie's side. '*Sissy* will be here in thirty-six hours or so,' he said. 'That'll be four and a half watches – allowing one watch as a standard eight hours. Two and a half day watches handling the ship and two night watches catching up on sleep and preparing to get the tows aboard. All things being equal. We can pull it off if we get half a chance – and if *Sissy* and *Oscar Whisky* can get to us on time.' Richard paused, thinking – as he had said to her right at the beginning – that they might indeed be safe in the assumption that their secret adversaries might let them rest for thirty-six hours after all. Even if they still had access to their incendiaries – or an alternative supply – that still might well be true. For they had a much more effective target in view than the simple sinking of the *Lady Mary* away in the Southern Ocean and out of the public view. 'In fact it sounds as though the world and his wife will be here – given the chance. Well, all the most active news teams at any rate,' he added, looking down into those wide, gold-flecked eyes. There was no surprise in them, he noted. No confusion. She knew exactly what he was talking about. 'Why did you get us up in the headlines?' he asked. 'You do know that we are the top news story? Worldwide?'

'Are we?' She shrugged. 'It seemed to Alain and me that we would get more of what we needed if we managed to motivate one or two more people, you know? He does not want his islands desecrated with the filth in our holds and I do not wish to be responsible for the destruction of his almost perfect environment.'

'But publicity like this will not make the storm pass any more quickly. It won't make *Sissy* or *Oscar Whisky* get here any faster. It won't help us.'

'It might. Who knows? And what harm can it do? Everyone will *try* and help. They dare not do less. You say the eyes of the world are on us.'

Richard paused. He could see two paths in his reasoning and each was as persuasive as the other. Either Julie had been lying and playing a double game all along – she was a member of The Real Friends of the Earth and she wished to engineer the spectacular destruction of her command while all the world was watching. Or she was what she had said – a loyal Frenchwoman and daughter who had found a brilliant way to motivate her sluggish country and take the pressure off her father and his company. For the issue was now the one she had cited at first – the ability of France to oversee these territories properly. In the face of what she and Alain had done, the French government had now promised to help – Charles DuFour was no longer liable for the *Lady Mary*'s salvage.

But of course, Julie's actions had another, hidden price – even if her motives were actually innocent. For if she had arranged the glare of publicity to help her father, she had also, unwittingly, given The Real Friends of the Earth the perfect setting in which to mount their terrorist 'spectacular'. They now had the opportunity to arrange the explosive destruction of a desecrator of another pristine environment under the cameras of the world's press. Live, on prime time.

No sooner had Richard completed the thought, than Jean-Luc called through from the makeshift radio room, 'Captain, I have someone here who wishes to speak with you.'

'Who is it?' asked Julie as she walked towards the door.

'Lou somebody – I didn't catch the name. He says he works for CNN, the American news company, and he wants to interview you live for the *Six O'Clock News Show*.'

'Tell you what,' said Richard to Sophie. 'While the Captain's talking to the press, I'll go down and see how Honore and Antoine are making out with the cargo. Any messages from bridge to engineering?'

Sophie shook her head, frowning slightly. 'I can call down if I have anything to say. You know that. And if you want, you can call up the lading schematics to the computer up here.'

'It's not the same,' said Richard.

Ten minutes later Emil's bag lay in shreds on the Captain's bunk – but its destruction had told Richard little. There were no notes, letters or messages, no convenient little recorder with one or two all-revealing messages. The only thing he found tucked in the lining was a key with an odd little tag on it. He popped this in his pocket then reassembled the bag and put it back apparently untouched and undamaged. Then he did start down to engineering. He walked slowly, giving himself time to think, fingering the key in his pocket as though his digits could think about that on their own.

Terrorists tended to work in cells. Even eco-terrorists, he supposed. It seemed logical to presume therefore that Sophie was not working alone. Her most obvious possible accomplice seemed to be Julie. They were so similar it was disturbing. What motivated one might motivate the other. And rejection by embittered parents often leads to embittered children doing terrible and outrageous things. Perhaps that Parisian boarding school had been a hotbed of sedition and revolution after all. So Julie had to be a very strong contender as a member of Sophie's cell.

But then again, thought Richard, looking at alternative approaches, if Sophie was most firmly at the centre of his suspicions, then who had Sophie most obviously been associating with? Julie, again? Antoine? Emil? Rule Emil out and assume he had been watching Sophie, not the other way around. Jean-Luc? Perhaps. He had certainly been close to Julie too. And to be fair, there was something about the Assistant Radio Operator that did not really ring true. This was independant of the suspicion that Emil might have been investigating Jean-Luc into the bargain – if the men's relationship was anything to go by. And then, of course, there was Mr Song. But the actual warriors of the Terror War tended to be the young and impressionable. The elder statesmen were the tacticians, not the bomb carriers. It had been true of the IRA, the PLO, Al-Qaeda, the Basque Separatists, the Mujehaddin, the Tamil Tigers.

The central question remained Julie's position, though, he thought. If the terrorist cell was Sophie and Antoine that was one thing. If it was Sophie and Julie then that was something very different indeed. And there was only one way that he could see to find out more.

Oddly, because he had only ever seen her in the Captain's cabin – and seen a good deal more of her than he might have wished – he had not really thought of her as having a cabin of her own. But he did now. She had only been camping in Giscard's cabin. Making a point; marking her new territory – establishing a pecking order. Her own cabin was down a level, of course. Near Sophie and Antoine's quarters. Where he was now standing, hesitantly.

The door was not locked and it yielded silently to Richard. He flicked on the light and closed the door behind him. He paused, looking around the tidy little cabin. On an almost spiritual level he tried to read the atmosphere of the place – as though there would be something of her lingering in here. And there was – a scent, faint and unfamiliar. He breathed it in deeply, thanking God she did not seem to favour Calme du Cacharel. Then he crossed to her drawers and began to search through her personal belongings. He did this briskly, impersonally. Lifting, looking and replacing increasingly inti-mate items. But they concealed nothing more than a love of dainty feminine underwear. Which, to be fair, was not news to Richard. There was a desk in the corner and he crossed to this in the faint but fading hope that there might be a diary or some such. But all he found was her graduation picture. A photograph of a very much younger and much less care-worn Julie standing in front of an impressive building. There was the base of a flagpole at her right shoulder and a crowd of faces behind her left.

He put it back. Then, frowning, he picked it up again and brought it much closer to his face, holding his breath so he didn't fog the glass. Utter silence settled on the little cabin except for the raving of the wind and the thunder of the waters outside. The whole hull heaved and shuddered. The door swung silently open and Jean-Luc stepped into the room.

'What are you doing here, Captain Mariner?' asked the Assistant Radio Operator quietly.

Richard turned, holding up the photograph. 'I was just about to come and ask you the same question,' he answered. 'What are *you* doing here? In this picture and aboard this ship, Monsieur Charles DuFour?'

Twenty

Resolution

By the time *Sissy* came over the horizon thirty-six hours later and began to battle her way down towards *Lady Mary* with *Oscar Whisky* in her wake, Richard felt much more in control of matters. As did Julie and her father Charles DuFour. Not completely in control – still a little away from that. Just as the stricken tanker seemed now to be drifting only a little way from the first rocky outreaches of Kerguelen Island itself. They had turned the sound on the collision alarm radar off early last night, too well aware of the way that solid wall of green was marching inexorably towards them across the circle of the radar's bowl. They found the constant screech of the collision alarm, which had been triggered when the enormous contact came less than fifty miles distant, increasingly unsettling and depressing.

The three of them were not certain enough of the crew's mood to reveal Charles's true identity and so he remained Jean-Luc the Assistant Radio Operator. They were not certain enough of their facts to put Sophie and Antoine under any kind of formal arrest though they discussed at some length the wisdom of confining them to their quarters, under guard, after interrogating them both. But even the evidence Richard had hidden in Giscard's drawer did not really present a sufficiently watertight case. The three of them looked at it, discussed it, assessed how it fitted in with the rest of the stuff he had secreted at the top and bottom of the lift shaft. But in the end they agreed that none of it would stand up in court on its own. And so they settled for close observation instead, in the hope of discovering more. On the one hand they were confident enough to do this because the lower levels of the ship remained inaccessible because of the inert gas and the bilge water flooding them; and Richard had hidden their arsenal of bombs safely. On the other hand, they remained frustratingly uncertain about the terrorists' precise intentions, and suspicious that these were still unfinalized: awaiting events, news teams, cameras – publicity.

On another level entirely, they were still unsure whether the lingering rearguard of the hurricane, which still held them trapped in the suffocating bridge house, would allow anything to be done on deck in time to make a difference. A concern renewed every time any of them looked at the radar, now almost bisected by the rough white line that represented the tall black cliffs less than twenty miles ahead. They were still, in fact, by no means convinced that the tanker could be pulled past Kerguelen and into Resolution Passage at all.

But, to Richard's mind at least, a satisfying amount had been cleared up. Julie's ambivalence, some of her more unreasonable decisions early on – deferring to her father's advice instead of Richard's, the way she had obviously been hiding something from him – from them all in fact. The obvious over-abundance of bandages and ether-smelling ointment that had disguised Jean-Luc from his own eyes until they were certain he would not realize who Charles really was. The tension between Jean-Luc and Emil – between the hunter and his prey, both trapped in a situation with no immediate prospect of resolution or escape. Both involved in their own little battle – then suddenly finding that they were part of a much larger crisis. And Emil's disguise also was explained – and his reason for being aboard. Perhaps even his predilection – as a *soi disant* deck officer – for wandering around below decks with an engineer's bag. The ID card came as little surprise to Charles. He had been under all sorts of investigation in his time – and for far worse crimes than smuggling. None of which had stuck, so far. Neither Charles nor Julie had any idea what the little key would open. And that was the end of that discussion – for the time being at least. So, almost all the elements of the mystery, except the central thread of the terrorists' actions, could be largely accounted for by the father and daughter's deception: a simple piece of theatre. A disguise and a series of little white lies to keep the nearly bankrupt businessman hidden aboard – out of the grip of the authorities, out of court and likely out of prison too.

And Richard was happy to focus on trying to keep them all alive rather than looking any more closely at what Charles and Julie had done. That meant, for the moment, that he was also content to leave aside such suspicions as he might be harbouring about the late, apparently unlamented, Captain Giscard and his involvement in the charade and Charles's own ideas concerning the all too convenient loss of his hull. As well as the prospect of any fortune in insurance money that might be due to *La Compagnie Maritime DuFour* if *Lady Mary* in fact did go down. For, on the bottom line, two things at least seemed clear. Charles could never sink the ship he owned if it put the life of his daughter at risk – no matter how much money the loss might make for him. And Julie could never blow up the ship, even if she was some kind of eco-terrorist – if it meant blowing up her father too.

Had urgent action been required at once, then Richard's thoughts would have been a dangerous distraction. But even now, as he stood on the bridge at the unsuspecting Sophie's shoulder watching the busy blips of *Sissy* and *Oscar Whisky* bustling towards them across the last of the dark area in the radar, he was bitterly aware that thinking and planning were all he could do. It was all very well for Julie to be on the Hagenuk in contact with *Sissy*'s and *Oscar Whisky*'s Captains, making detailed plans for the placing of the ropes and the start of the tow. That was something else Richard and she had discussed at length and he was sure she would do what he advised. It was something, indeed, that he and she had discussed with everyone likely to be involved in setting up and overseeing the tow when the weather moderated and the tugs arrived – if these things happened before Kerguelen filled up the radar bowl and they were lost. But Richard simply burned to be taking some kind of physical action. Preferably outside on the weather deck. For – at the very least – setting up a successful tow of a hull this size in conditions like these was a lengthy and exacting process.

Charles was suddenly hulking at Richard's shoulder. 'It looks as though we could be making first contact and taking lines aboard before the end of this watch, if the weather continues to moderate. The Captain asks if you could go down to engineering and see how things are down there,' he said quietly. 'I'll keep an eye on things here until she gets off the radio.'

Richard shrugged. What with one thing and another, he hadn't been down to engineering in a while. And they would have to rely on Honore and Antoine, Chow and their teams to ensure that all the winches, blocks, bitts, bollards, capstans, claws and chain stoppers were ready for when the messenger ropes came aboard. Not to mention a range of sizes, lays and lengths of rope and cable – whether they were using the tugs' tow ropes or not. Quite apart from anything else, he would have to lead a team back down to the workshop on the forecastle head where Lucien died. They would have to get metal and wood to build a series of A-shaped timber shorings to support the aft capstans – or the tension of the tow was likely to tear them straight out of the deck.

They would need to be doing that from the moment the wind moderated into speeds where deck work became possible, Richard knew. Which in turn meant that they would have to make doubly sure now that the work they were doing to keep the cargo safely stowed could be left at a moment's notice; that the lading programmes and the cargo they controlled could be relied upon to sit untended until the hull was safely in Resolution Passage. And, by the same token, Richard had to be as certain as humanly possible that while they were all so hard at work out on the deck, preparing for and then overseeing the tow itself, Antoine got no more chance than Sophie did to set off any unexpected explosives.

'All quiet?' he asked Chow, who was back on fire watch and clearly rested and relaxed. Richard looked down into the pit of the engine area, then glanced across to the glass-fronted area where Honore and Antoine sat on their watch, like characters in a huge television. The capable young

235

seaman nodded once. 'Good,' Richard continued. 'Because we'll be relying on it staying that way unattended soon. I'm going to need you and all the hands we can spare out on deck . . .' For the next few moments he repeated his plans for the tow, treating the capable young seaman as he treated the officers who would technically command him and his team. On a whim, he produced Emil's odd little key and asked the seaman if he had any idea what it would open. Chow shrugged and shook his head. Not even the little tag on the key-ring rang a bell so Richard went down to the lading control room.

Antoine and Honore were, frankly, having a good long rest. The cargo seemed safely stowed. It was back to the correct heat and everything seemed well. The only shadow of a problem – and potential rather than current at that – was the amount of water *Lady Mary* was taking aboard. But now that the weather was moderating and the sea beginning to settle, the inward flood from sprung plates and pipework joints on the deck was falling, there was less water, at any rate. The worrying seepage of oil was going to remain constant however – unless the tensions of the tow caused yet more movement in the long hull: a sideways, yawing movement to complement the dangerous pitching caused by the storm surge. The pumps were coping – if only just. As long as things continued to calm down, they should continue to pump out whatever was coming in.

Richard had no sooner cast his eyes over this situation, and the two men lolling all too easily in their chairs keeping only the remotest watch upon it, than the tones of the ship's announcement system sounded.

'This is the Captain speaking,' said Julie's familiar voice. 'Wind and weather have moderated to safe levels. All hands report to your muster stations. Officers, assemble your teams and prepare for being taken under tow.'

The air hit Richard with the same force this time as it had the last time he had come out of the bridge house. Not so much with its speed or power – for these were waning – but with its clarity and purity as it whipped into his face from the west again. And the fact that it no longer teemed with

236

rain or spray. He looked up at the albatross, still miraculously perched on the Sampson post and he waved at it in sudden excitement. An excitement which he knew might well be dangerously misplaced. The bridge house hulked behind him. The deck stretched away towards the forecastle head. The grey seas gathered in long low combers following the track of the departing storm. There, her upper works outlined against the last of the stormy sky and her bright hull just visible on this side of the horizon, sat *Sissy*. Richard focussed on her, continuing to look west along the wake, such as it was. Because he knew from the actions of the men around him that if he turned and looked the other way he would see nothing but the great black wall of cliffs into which the ship was still relentlessly drifting. To an extent this was an optical illusion he knew – but it was no less terrifying for all that. At sea level, the horizon is about twenty miles distant from an observer of average height. Go higher or look at something taller and the horizon appears to come closer, because you are actually seeing further. By much the same token that the moon and the stars seem equidistant. *Lady Mary*'s main deck was thirty feet above the water, her top deck above the bridge house nearly one hundred. The cliffs towards which she was heading stood a thousand feet, and fronted peaks stood twice as high. Nearly fifteen miles of water still separated them, and they had maybe twelve hours' grace, therefore, but it looked as though they would collide at any moment now.

'My team to the forecastle head,' he ordered, and headed down the deck without looking back. They gathered at his shoulder, led by Ether who had been dismissed from radio duty and replaced by Jean-Luc – Charles DuFour – so that Julie would not be distracted by watching Sophie on her own. They were almost as good as Chow's team, which was going aft with Antoine and Honore.

At the huge spade of the forecastle, they gathered round the hatch which led down into the metal shop. Richard fought a sense of *déjà-vu* as he pulled it carefully open. A sense compounded by the stench of burning that the black gape emitted. The smoke was gone now, however, and the area

237

down there was clear and dimly lit. Richard led the way, eyes busy. There had only been time for a brief safety check cum post-mortem between Lucien's death and the next crisis. But there had been little enough to see in any case: a workshop apparently painted sooty black from waist-height to deckhead, metal and woodworking machines, store rooms, lockers and such, trolleys solid enough to carry equipment and balks of timber down the deck and designed to be rolled up the wide slopes beside the stairways and on to the deck.

'Right,' said Richard, decisively. 'This is what we will need to begin with . . .' As he gave the list of requirements to Ether and the team, Richard strolled around the area, eyes busy. The flashpoint for the incendiary that Lucien had taken overboard was clear – right beside the wood store where it could do most damage. Still giving his list of orders, Richard walked past the flashpoint itself to look at what lay beyond the seared and blackened timbers. Only a wall of lockers, full of the kind of equipment best kept under lock and key aboard any kind of ship. The sort of things that – like kitchen equipment – could all too easily double up as weapons in a fight: saws, drills, chisels, knives and such. All safely secured by the look of things and neatly tagged with some kind of identification system. Still talking, almost oblivious to the bustle of activity behind him, Richard looked at the lockers more closely. It was only when he found the tag that he realized he had been looking for it. The instant he saw it he knew it, for it was a perfect match to the tag on the ring that also held Emil's little key.

Richard glanced over his shoulder. Ether's team were busily loading trolleys with lengths of wood and piles of machinery and tools. They would be calling for stuff from these lockers too, in time. Richard slid Emil's key out of his pocket and pushed it into the lock. It turned at once and the metal door swung open. It was the key-locker of course. All the keys to all the other lockers hung on their tags on the back wall. But Richard was not looking at these. He was looking below them to what was lying on the narrow floor of the shallow locker. There were some documents folded neatly and sealed in a plastic bag. On top of the bag was a cellphone.

Richard picked it up. It was not like the ones hidden in the winch house. It was older, less expensive. More like Richard's own phone. It wasn't from the Stone Age, though. It still had Internet access, photo messaging, video and a camera. It wouldn't work, of course. Not down here. That's why they needed something like the Hagenuk. Emil wouldn't have been able to call in, upload, download, text – make any kind of contact with the outside world. *Would he?* Richard pushed the buttons and switched the little handset on.

As soon as the battery power came on, the screen lit up. At first Richard thought Emil must have had a personalized screen-saver, a photo of his father perhaps. But then he realized the truth. It was a photo of Charles DuFour. A publicity portrait – very formal, very public. Frowning, Richard scrolled down the picture gallery in the little machine. The next photo was much less formal. A candid shot – probably snapped secretly – of Charles and Captain Giscard deep in conversation. Then there was one of Charles, Giscard and Julie. *Lady Mary*'s bridge house towered unmistakably in the background. The pictures were clearly proof for Emil's ongoing investigation. That was interesting. Richard needed another word with Charles, perhaps. But his fingers were as busy as his mind, continuing to scroll on down the pictures. Captain Giscard and Julie again, still aboard the tanker, but this time in conversation with Charles disguised as Jean-Luc. It was surprising how different he looked. No wonder no one recognized him.

However, the next photo brought Richard up with a jolt. It showed Sophie Bois. The young cadet was unaware that she was being snapped with one phone because she was engrossed in doing something to another one. Next came Sophie and Antoine together, equally engrossed. They each held cellphones this time. Two of the four cellphones Richard had hidden up in the winch house, in fact. Richard felt his scalp crawl. His hand shook just a little. He took a deep breath to steady himself. Then crawling, shaking, breathing even, stopped. For the next picture showed Sophie deep in conversation with Lucien. The engine loomed behind them, slightly out of focus And the last in the scary little series

239

showed Antoine and Lucien cheek by jowl with grumpy old Honore, outside the infirmary door.

'You see what this means?' said Richard tensely. He was so fearsomely focussed on the picture and Charles and Julie's reaction to it that he hardly registered the height and closeness of the island cliffs ahead. Illusion or not, it was a sight that scared him almost as much as those last two photographs had done. As he talked, he took but the slightest notice of the teams of men labouring on the poop deck below, carrying out his orders to prepare for the tow ropes to come aboard. He looked exclusively at the father and daughter standing at his side. They both stood looking almost dumbly at him. Which was why this conversation could not possibly have happened on the bridge in front of Sophie. Why Ether was back at the Hagenuk and Chow was on the bridge while the Captains apparently oversaw this crucial stage in the preparations for rescue from the very point that Julie had stood when Richard first had come aboard. 'First of all, Charles. No more beating about the bush. Was Giscard a transvestite? Did he fall in with your plan because you held that over him?'

'No! He agreed because we are old friends. Who said he was . . .'

'Honore did, now I come to think of it. And Antoine agreed with him. Antoine . . . And it was Antoine who kicked the incendiary over poor Raoul and set him on fire when we were trying to clear the engine room. Raoul was the only officer in engineering who wasn't in on this by the looks of things. Or he was by then, with the Captain and the Chief dead. Could Honore or Antoine have triggered the IG System in the pump room do you think?' he asked Julie. 'That really cleared the decks.'

'It's possible. But why? Why would they do such a terrible thing?'

'Because their "spectacular" had gone wrong. Think about it. Your crisis with the incendiaries happened at the same time as that explosion in the Amazon. Almost to the minute if my calculations are correct. The two locations actually mentioned on that sheet I found; the Amazon and the

Antarctic. Don't you see? They were designed to be two halves of one event. But something went wrong. You got on top of the fire before the cargo went up and the ship went down. They had to improvise. Clear everyone out of the way so they could move. Try to get their Plan B into place. Or their Plan C if you take Lucien into account . . .'

'Lucien? I see that he was part of the conspiracy according to Emil.'

'If he was, Julie, then his main aim was to blow up the ship whether he died or not. I'd suggest to you that setting the sea on fire all around it was a pretty spectacular way to do that. And it would have succeeded, too, if we hadn't had that providential downpour that put the fire out. What else? The sudden illness in the sickroom. That was pretty convenient, wasn't it? Lots of crewmen getting better – getting well enough to go back on duty, fill up the place with suspicious eyes just when the inert gas was going out of engineering and Honore and Co needed a little privacy . . .'

Richard swung round to Charles again. 'And back to you. You didn't fall off your chair. You were hit on the back of the head. Who did it?'

'The only person I saw was Emil. I thought it must have been him.'

'Or whoever Emil was shadowing? Could someone else have hit you, then you saw Emil when he checked on you a moment or two later?'

'That's silly,' said Julie. 'Why would Emil not raise the alarm then?'

'Because whoever he was following was up to something so suspicious that Emil wanted to keep close tabs on him. An alarm would stop that.'

'So Emil followed this person to lower engineering. Got jumped and left for dead,' said Charles. 'There was enough blood. He looked dead.'

'But managed to pull himself into the lift before he passed out, wedging the door. He should have come to us and told what he suspected. Except that he suspected us as well, of course. Those photos make us look as much a part of this as Sophie and Co. Maybe that's what he thought.'

241

'OK,' said Julie, her face almost bloodless. 'So what does this mean? What must we do now?'

'We must get the tow ropes aboard no matter what the risk,' said Richard decisively. 'We have to pull the ship on to Resolution Passage. At the same time, we must get as many people off as possible. We can come up with convincing excuses – particularly if it looks close run. If there were any risk of hitting the cliffs we'd have to get everyone off anyway. Then, when we're out in Resolution we can try to deal with Sophie, Antoine and Honore before they blow the whole lot up. Does that sound like a plan?'

'Sounds like a plan to me,' said Julie, but her words were almost lost as a fluke in the wind hurled over them; the roar of the surf against Kerguelen.

Sissy's messenger came aboard three frantic hours later. It came over on a rocket fired from the tug. The long line snaking behind the big firework whipped high above *Lady Mary*'s bridge house as the rocket itself thumped into the side of the funnel.

'That's bloody lucky,' said Richard to Julie. 'If you'd have had a top to that radio mast the line would have got all tangled up in it. That would have slowed things down.'

But nothing did slow things down. On the contrary, the work that Richard had overseen with the A-framed timber shorings, the preparation of the capstans and the windlass, meant that *Sissy*'s main tow rope was aboard and shackled within a quarter of an hour. Not only that, but it was ready – and able – to begin to take some of the strain almost at once. *Oscar Whisky* held a little back. She would add her bollard pull within the next hour or so. But she had an even more important function – without which *Sissy* herself may well have stood off and kept clear even now. This was to ensure that none of this activity was going to set light to the great puddle of oil-scum that the pumps were pouring out of *Lady Mary*'s bilges. For the plan that Richard assumed had been in Lucien's dying mind might still prove the most effective one of all. If the sea caught fire, then the tanker would still blow up long before she reached Kerguelen Island or Resolution Passage. And take the tugs with her likely as not. As *Sissy* began to take the strain, so *Oscar Whisky* laid down a carpet of foam through which the drifting tanker began to move. Foam that was even thicker and more retardant than the foam that had covered Lucien's fiery grave. It piled against the overhang of *Lady Mary*'s stern, giving the strange illusion that it might even be strong enough to buffer her safely against the rocks.

So the physics of combustion remained untapped for the time being. Instead the physics of mass and motion came into play; the force that *Sissy* could exert – the strain that her tow rope could stand. Set against the massive inertia that the drifting tanker represented, *Sissy* only had her power – she could never hope to balance *Lady Mary*'s size, weight or displacement. And her tow-line was not infinitely strong – any more than the deck furniture it was secured to, no matter how well supported. Turning the tanker's course was something to be done slowly and gently, over hours and sea-miles, therefore. Something that could never have been achieved without the fact that the hurricane had already set her drifting towards the passage in any case. The wind behind its coat-tails also remained a little north of west. It was lucky that the prevailing current ran westward beneath the prevailing wind – then turned strongly past the submarine foundations of the island into the wide mouth of the channel, pushing and pulling *Lady Mary* in the direction that *Sissy* wanted her to go. So at last the great hull began to swing. The sea remained safely swathed in foam. *Oscar Whisky*'s rocket thumped into the funnel as though the TAAF circle had been its target. The messenger fell safely beside the beheaded radio mast and within minutes the second tow-line was aboard. Richard looked properly at the cliffs then. They were less than ten miles distant and they looked terribly close. But it was not the fact that they were coming closer, when he already felt he could touch them if he reached out far enough, that held him breathless. It was the fact that they were beginning to slip away sideways, to his left.

'Richard,' said Charles DuFour, appearing silently at his

243

shoulder. 'We've lost Honore. One minute he was there, the next *pouf*! Gone.'

Richard looked at the sky. He did this at once and for two reasons. He knew immediately that there must be a plane or helicopter somewhere nearby, full of pressmen with their cameras. That would be the only signal he could imagine might send Honore off to get his final fiery spectacular under way. But the sky would also tell him how best to counteract the threat. What he saw told him what he wanted to know all at once. For there, indeed, came a helicopter, skimming low over Cape Challenger almost dead ahead, coming south out of Porte Aux Français. And, behind it, sat a patch of clear blue sky as calm and peaceful as a midsummer's morning.

'Contact Chung and Mr Song,' he said. 'Tell them to start getting our people into the lifeboats. Tell Julie to warn *Sissy* and *Oscar Whisky* we have boats out in the water. They'll pick them up if anything goes wrong.' He turned and looked at Charles with his most intense stare. 'Tell Julie I'll have the radio and I'll keep in touch. But we want everyone over the side as soon as they can be spared. Including Sophie and Antoine if you can manage it. Tell them we don't think *Lady Mary*'s going to make it round Cap George if they ask. It really doesn't look like we'll make Resolution Passage from here. I doubt whether either of them has the experience to see it's all an optical illusion and we should swing well clear.' He flung over his shoulder.

'Where are you going?' asked Charles.

'I'm going to get the Glock and then I'm going to get Honore. Before he gets to his bombs, if I can.'

Richard knew where Honore had gone first. He wasn't as sure where the engineer would head for next, but logic suggested a narrow enough range of places to give him a fighting chance. It was the poisoning that had been the vital clue. Perhaps because it was the only unconsidered and sloppy thing in the plan so far. It had the air of something improvised. And it gave so much away, therefore. It told Richard that Honore was a frequenter of the infirmary. That was where Mr Song had gone to look for the Ipecac – and found it all was missing. Why it should have been aboard heaven alone knew. But it was one of those interesting substances that had to be handled carefully. In careful doses it could cure the symptoms of dysentery. In large ones it caused them. Green shit and all. If Honore had used the Ipecac as Richard had suggested, then he had been in the infirmary. He might just possibly have been there stowing the corpses of poor Giscard and the rest from the generator room. Or even of Raoul. But on the other hand, that was also where Emil had photographed him in secret conclave with Antoine and Lucien. And a room full of dead people would make such an excellent hiding place for almost anything.

Unfortunately, Richard had to go up to Giscard's cabin to get the Glock, then down to the infirmary. Which, he reckoned, was probably why he missed Honore. Certainly, apart from dead people, the room was empty when he got there. But Honore had by no means been secretive about his visit. He may have hidden whatever had been in there carefully and tidily – but he had left everything open and piled on the floor when he had come to get it now. Richard paused, a corpse sprawled at his feet, looking into the depths of the drawer from which the corpse had been pulled. It was empty. There was no clue as to what it had contained. But Richard could guess. Incendiary bombs weren't the perfect things to blow up tankers – but they were all Honore and his cohorts had used so far. There would be room for a couple at the feet-end of the drawer with no one any the wiser. But two was the limit, he guessed. Still, in the right place, one bomb like the deathless beast that had destroyed poor Raoul would do. Richard was off on the hunt at once, his mind as ever racing through the possibilities as he ran.

There weren't many places that were guaranteed to bring success, though. Chucking one over the side would not do any longer – even if Honore reckoned on going down like Lucien had. *Oscar Whisky* would hose it down without even slipping her tow. She could generate eight thousand cubic metres of foam an hour if she needed to. No. He would have to use it somewhere aboard. And, as had been the case recently, Emil's input was a useful guide here. Even Emil's

245

final exit helped, in a brutal sort of way. There might be some temptation in going along the walkway between the tops of the tanks and the deck and slinging one down the drain that had gulped Emil himself. The bilge was awash with oil – demonstrated by the mess the pumps were churning out. But they were still full of inert gas as well. Honore would need a safer bet than that, thought Richard. And there was only one bet safer aboard that he could think of. A bet that also had the twin advantages of being accessible and very, very public. For it had been such a central part to the whole of this plane, Plan C, Honore's plan, that the 'spectacular' should have spectacle. Even eco-terrorist suicide bombers did not have such skewed motivations that they waited for their actions to be recorded on TV for the whole global audience to see then went skulking off to do their explosive deeds in anonymous secrecy. This was one of those 'Look at Me, Everybody' moments. This was 'Top of the World, Ma!' from the old movie classics.

Halfway down the deck, between the Sampson posts where the albatross still sat there was a raised walkway that stepped across the sheaf of pipes running between the bridge house and the forecastle. The walkway was there to allow access to the tops of the huge central tanks. Tops that only a madman would open during the voyage, for to do so would release a geyser of the most lethal inflammable gasses from the heated oil contained within them. But of course, Richard was dealing with a madman. A madman with an incendiary bomb.

Richard ran out on to the main deck, distantly aware of the gathering murmur of abandonment behind him – in the same way as he had been distantly aware of the approaching cliffs when discussing Emil's phone with Charles and Julie. He used the starboard side door because everyone aboard was assembling at the port side muster stations planning to abandon near the tugs. He saw at once that his quarry had also come this way – though he doubted Honore would have registered or understood the quiet bustle in the bridge house.

Whether he understood what was happening or not – whether he even realized that he was being pursued – Honore was certainly not hanging about. One behind the other, the two of them raced down the deck, under the uninterested albatross still sitting on top of the Sampson post, and up the rickety steps of the walkway. Richard reached the bottom when Honore was already well away from the top and in spite of the urgency of his mission he was forced to slow a little. The damage done by the storm surge was very apparent here. The walkway was simply falling apart. The great sheaf of pipes was bent slightly out of line. The whole deck beneath was slightly buckled. No wonder water had been pouring down on Emil and himself immediately below here. No wonder the pipes and tank tops nearby were leaking God knows how much into the bilge. Automatically, even in the still-stiff breeze, Richard started being careful to take only shallow breaths.

He came up on to the rickety walkway and began to creep up on the preoccupied saboteur. Honore was kneeling with his back to Richard, hunched over the tank top and wrestling with the opening mechanism. Richard took careful note of the way the air seemed to be wrinkling all around the man. Just as the fumes from the funnel had continued to make the wind waver like a heat-haze, long after the fire was out. Such was the sound all around them, the tumbling of the long seas, the roaring of the wind, the thundering of the surf against the island, that Richard was able to get quite close. Especially as he was all but holding his breath now. He flicked on the Glock's red dot sight and placed the bright point exactly on the back of Honore's skull. 'What I don't understand,' he said conversationally, 'is why you hit Jean-Luc on the head.'

Honore froze. Then he continued working just that bit more feverishly. Richard was reminded briefly of the way he had casually appropriated Emil's bag, cheerfully hoping that no one would notice anything. Wrong, no doubt. Like Honore was wrong if he hoped Richard wouldn't notice what he was doing now.

'I had to stop him damaging the radio, of course,' Honore answered, no doubt hoping the words would distract Richard from the feverish working of his hands. 'That silly bitch Julie DuFour didn't want you even to set it up. I heard them

247

discussing how dangerous it would be to broadcast a distress call. To bring in help and risk the publicity.'

'So it was as simple as that,' said Richard. 'You wanted to be sure of the publicity. Even then. You wanted your "spectacular" to match what had happened in the Amazon.'

'Of course.' Honore straightened and turned, clutching two incendiary bombs to his chest with his left forearm and holding a cellphone in his right hand. He looked straight into the red light of the Glock's red dot sight. 'That's what it's always all about, isn't it?' The top of the central tank hissed open, yawning to the same size as the drain that gulped down Emil.

Two things happened then so close together that Richard was never able to tell them apart. The albatross launched itself off the Sampson post and came battering across the deck immediately above his head. And the helicopter full of reporters settled out of nowhere apparently only inches above the bird. Honore looked upwards, stricken. 'If you push the button now,' said Richard, 'then the chopper goes up with the rest of us. All in one huge explosions. No reporters. No pictures. No "spectacular" after all.'

Honore hesitated. Richard should have shot him there and then, but he simply could not bring himself to do so. The man was a dead man standing, his lungs full of toxic fumes. There was a fair chance that his Heath Robinson bombs would not go off any more effectively this time than they had done last time. And, of course, it was all going out from the videocameras in the chopper. Live, on prime time. So Richard also hesitated. And another level of conflict entirely took over from the war on terrorism.

The mine was one of the mines Richard had thought of warning Julie about. It had been laid during the Second World War. It had remained chained in position for more than sixty years until the storm surge had done to the chain much the same as it had done to the middle of *Lady Mary*'s deck. In the hours that had followed, it had been washed out into the mouth of Resolution Passage past Cap George and Cape Challenger. Its magnetic sensors, its relays and its explosive charge, however, had lasted much better than its chain had, and had survived its last adventurous journey. So that when it made contact with the massive torpedo shape beneath *Lady Mary*'s cutwater, it exploded at once.

A column of white water as thick and as enormous as a tall oak tree erupted over the torn wreckage of the forecastle head. A wall of force and fire slammed through the huge ship's forward sections until it ran up hard against the water-filled solidity of the forward tank. The whole length of the tanker's deck gave such a convulsive lurch that Honore was simply flipped backwards into the hot oil in the central tank. He was dead before he hit the surface. And his incendiaries remained as dead as he was. Though, Richard thought, a good time later, that fact probably didn't make much difference. Mobile phones do not work as detonators from the hot depths of oil tanks any better than they work as communicators in the frozen depths of the Southern Ocean. So *Lady Mary* remained afloat and Julie was able to halt the abandonment after all. Richard, however, went over to *Sissy* at the first possible moment – with Sophie and Antoine under his guard.

And they got on the news after all. Richard and Robin listened that night, in fact, in *Sissy*'s radio room as the game little tug continued to pull the listing hulk of the helpless tanker out into Resolution Passage while the whole of the European Union got organized to rescue her:

Right up until the final moment the heroic members of *Lady Mary*'s crew were fighting to keep her alive. Two intrepid members of the crew, one of them tragically doomed, were seen on the damaged central walkway, fighting to ensure that the cargo was safe and secure right at the very moment that the accident occurred. A naval mine, laid during the Second World War, was torn loose by the power of the hurricane, and impacted with *Lady Mary*'s bows. One brave officer fell into the open tank top. The other ran forward to help his friend, but fell to his knees, overcome by fumes from the leaking tank.

The French President has echoed the words of the Prime Minster and the Foreign Minister this evening. All of them

249

have said that while officers of this dedication and quality crew the ships of the French Merchant Marine, the world may rest assured that the Terres Australes et Antarctique Français from Crozet to Kerguelen Islands and down to French Adelie Land on the Antarctic Continent itself remain in the safest possible hands . . .